The Cross Maker's Guardian

THE CROSS MAKER: BOOK 2

The Cross Maker's Guardian

JACK A. TAYLOR

THE CROSS MAKER'S GUARDIAN: BOOK 2
Copyright © 2019 by Jack A. Taylor

All rights reserved. Neither this publication nor any part of this publication may be reproduced or transmitted in any form or by any means, electronic or mechanical, including photocopying, recording or any information storage and retrieval system, without permission in writing from the author.

This is a work of fiction. Names, characters, places and incidents either are the product of the author's imagination or are used fictitiously, and any resemblance to actual persons, living or dead, businesses, companies, events, or locales is entirely coincidental.

Printed in Canada

Print ISBN: 978-1-4866-1858-3
eBook ISBN: 978-1-4866-1859-0

Word Alive Press
119 De Baets Street Winnipeg, MB R2J 3R9
www.wordalivepress.ca

Cataloguing in Publication information can be obtained from Library and Archives Canada.

This book is dedicated to the generation fighting to make a difference in our world, starting with Richard, Ericka, Michelle, Tyler, Laura, Marc, Tam, and Graham.

Acknowledgements	ix
Chapter One	1
Chapter Two	8
Chapter Three	15
Chapter Four	21
Chapter Five	31
Chapter Six	41
Chapter Seven	51
Chapter Eight	60
Chapter Nine	72
Chapter Ten	77
Chapter Eleven	88
Chapter Twelve	94
Chapter Thirteen	106
Chapter Fourteen	111
Chapter Fifteen	118
Chapter Sixteen	126
Chapter Seventeen	132
Chapter Eighteen	141
Chapter Nineteen	149
Chapter Twenty	155
Chapter Twenty-One	163
Chapter Twenty-Two	177
Chapter Twenty-Three	188
Chapter Twenty-Four	196
Chapter Twenty-Five	203
Chapter Twenty-Six	209
Chapter Twenty-Seven	216
Chapter Twenty-Eight	224

Chapter Twenty-Nine   232

Other Books In This Series   234

Other Books by Jack A. Taylor   236

Acknowledgements

There's no point in focusing on a cross maker if nothing significant happened on that cross. It's Easter weekend as I write this, and I cherish the Savior and Redeemer whose spent life on the cross brought life to so many who look to him and believe. I'm thankful the story didn't end at the cross.

Acknowledgement goes to my wife, Gayle, who patiently leaves me to my literary world while she holds together the real world around me.

My second acknowledgement goes to Evan Braun for his patient polishing of the story that fought to find its place on my pages.

Final acknowledgements go to the supportive staff at Word Alive Press and to the readers who will wrestle with their own inner realities as they follow the hopes and dreams of these characters who have become so real to me.

Chapter One

A gust of Mediterranean wind sliced through the Galilean hills like a legionnaire's dagger through the fire-kissed ribs of a wild boar. The twisting funnel of salt-soaked air whipped apart the olive branches that concealed Titius Marcus Julianus. The exposure lasted only a moment, but the three masked figures who'd been dancing around their fire, twirling like dervishes in a clearing of wildflowers, stopped as one and turned to stare directly at his hiding place. Titius's brown tunic, olive skin, and short black hair blended into the shadows of the tree in which he had perched, but a shiver ran down his back at the fear of being discovered.

The disembodied voice of Cleopas, a long-dead slave teacher from Titius's boyhood, arose like a phantom and goaded him: *"Tee–shuss, they've seen you…"*

If you're going to use my name, at least get it right, he thought back.

Cleopas's husky voice chuckled inside. *"Titius, wishes, sleeping with the fishes. You should have listened to me. You're a boy playing man games."*

Titius waved at the phantom like he was swatting a fly. *You wouldn't know a game if you saw one.*

But his stomach knotted and his neck and shoulder muscles tightened. Fear, the size of a mustard seed, had planted itself in his soul.

Dark-bellied clouds tumbled over ripening fields of barley toward distant hills. The sun's rays groped for the earth, just like they always had at the Roman estate Titius loved so well, the one where he had grown up. A single abandoned raindrop clung to the tip of a leaf and sparkled like a diamond in the sunlight. The faintest scent of roses drifted by.

He smiled as the particle of fear launched away on the breeze.

"I feel you smiling," Cleopas declared. *"Abee–gail's not here, you know."*

Neither are you.

Images of his family villa crystallized in his mind. Cleopas rubbing down a sword and holding it up to sparkle in the light. The raven-haired servant girls, Lydia and her sister Abigail, replenishing the incense, polishing the marble tables, plucking rose petals to float in the fountain. Looking longingly across the hills, speaking of a strange people in a strange land—a land where Titius now found himself on his own.

He sat ten feet from the top of the gnarled tree, his solid frame pressed hard against its trunk. The sentinel looked to have guarded the entrance to this grotto since the first days after Noah's flood. The grotto was a favored haunt of doves, pigeons, and ravens; nearby fields of barley, corn, millet, and wheat kept the birds well fed. As wind lashed the branches, hundreds of the birds sprang off their perches and sailed over the nearby city of Sepphoris.

A wild boar, clods of dirt clinging to his curved tusks, stopped his rooting for tubers and sprinted off, its tail raised high in the air like a flagpole. A small golden fox darted out of the boar's way and back into its den. A rabbit paused, sniffed, then hopped quickly into the underbrush.

The bitter tang of ash from the three masked men's ritual fire anchored itself in the back of his throat. He gurgled and spit to clear it.

Meanwhile, the trio of thespians turned away, their searching gazes having failed to discover Titius. The men abandoned their rituals, scooping up their black robes from the ground and fading into the forest.

Where are they going? Titius asked himself.

He scrambled down the tree, squirrel-like, and jumped to the ground from several branches up before rolling into the underbrush. The aroma of fresh dung was strong enough to overpower the fragrance of damp earth and flowers.

Moments later, one of the men returned to the clearing, his shadow interrupting the dappled sunlight falling through the leafy boughs. Then Titius spotted a second dark figure moving against the base of an olive and staring upward to where Titius had been hiding.

"They're close, Tee–shus," Cleopas hissed in his ghostly whisper once again. *"You waited too long. You always wait too long."*

I don't have to listen to you, Titius thought. *You're dead. Leave me alone.*

The shadowy figures blended into the trees and vanished again.

Titius took the opportunity to crawl out from behind the bush, his elbows and knees digging into the damp earth. He reached a rocky outcropping and kept crawling over the hard granite. He soon arrived at a boulder twice his height and scrambled around it.

From here, he had a good view of a sunlit meadow surrounded by dark forest. The treetops bent in the wind.

His neck and shoulder muscles tightened. Something felt wrong, but with the three masked men around he couldn't go back—and he didn't dare cross the meadow.

Titus spotted a patch of darkness at the base of a cliff face. A cave! He ran toward the cave and stopped just inside the opening, stubbing his toes hard against a rock hidden in the dust. He refused to even wince.

A lone figure stood an arm's length away, its glistening sword flashing and stopping just a finger's width from Titius's throat. He stepped back and the sword-carrier followed him into the light, where Titius finally recognized him.

It was a Roman centurion. The great Sestus Aurelius. A man he'd once accompanied for a leopard hunt in North Africa.

An ostrich feather had been mounted sideways above Sestus's glistening golden helmet, speaking of authority. The lion's head draped over his right shoulder spoke of courage. His silver breastplate, made of overlapping metal strips, featured five prominent war medals. It spoke of success.

"It seems you're mine again," Sestus said. He tucked an edge of his billowing scarlet cape into his waist belt to secure it. "Is it loyalty or fate that enslaves you to my whim?"

Titius took a step back. "Your whim would seek to enslave me?"

The centurion's piercing blue eyes measured Titius's every movement. His aquiline nose, set above a square, cleanshaven jaw, showed no emotion.

"You track the demons of death just as I helped you hunt the leopards in Tripoli," Sestus said, gripping in his right hand the vine staff he used for disciplining his men. "You put yourself at my mercy."

Titius knelt in the dust and bowed his head. "Of what service can I be to the great Sestus Aurelius?" He raised his head and spread his arms. "Surely, you have worthier dogs to pursue."

Sestus glared down at him. "You still wear your family ring. Since when did the lion become a dog? When my father marched with your grandfather into Rome after defeating the Gauls, you were there with your uncle. I saw you dressed like a miniature senator."

"That life is gone."

"Your own father perished at the hands of the Germans. You inherited his title, his estate, his honor."

"I have seen the illusion of it all," Titius said.

"You give up power so easily?"

"I am a shadow. A shadow has no power."

The centurion swung his sword tip hypnotically, like a pendulum, inches from Titius's nose. "Tell me. Why would a potential senator of Rome be stalking my thespian assassins?"

The rocks were hard on his knees and the dirt damp against his hands. Sestus's sword kept moving back and forth, now inches from his throat.

"I only wish to be one of your thespians," Titius said, finding his voice.

"Your life is on the line and all you want to do is take on the life of the theatre?"

"I've spent my days in the theatre. Now I want to serve you with my life, fighting for the honor of Rome."

Sestus stepped closer and steadied his weapon. "Help me understand. You want to leave a life of luxury so you can smash a hornet's nest of zealots in a forgotten corner of our empire? You want to live the rest of your life pretending to be someone you're not?"

Titius bowed lower and spread his palms in the rain-touched dust. "I want to live in a world where I feel like a man."

"Tired of slurping pigeon tongues and pig's feet with your uncles in the Senate, are you?" Sestus sneered and lowered the sword a fraction. "Willing to give up your villa and inheritance to curl up in the dust and beg for the trash of peasants? Ready to live invisibly, to kill quickly, to never truly be known?"

"Yes!" Titius ignored the fly buzzing around his ear.

"If anyone hears your story, there will be no more mystery and no more glory," Sestus warned.

"I seek no glory for myself."

"To join us would forever erase your story from existence." Sestus sheathed his sword. "But I fear your heritage and pride will never let this happen."

"Let it be as if I was never born." The fly landed in Titius's beard and he tried to blow it away.

"Look up!"

The three masked figures appeared behind Sestus, now dressed in vests of mail armor with black woolen tunics.

Sestus withdrew a dagger and held it at Titius's throat. "You are first and foremost a servant of the emperor, a legionnaire sworn to uphold Caesar's empire."

Titius raised an arm in oath. "I give my life again to Tiberius Caesar as my lord and protector. He above all is divine. He above all is my hope."

The fly disappeared.

Sestus grabbed Titius's raised hand and ripped off his family ring. "Without this ring, you are nothing. It is yours again if the emperor dies, or if I die before you."

The centurion opened a small pouch at his waist and dropped the ring inside.

Titius eyed the pouch carefully and weighed his choice. "The ring is yours until you die."

The Roman centurion brandished his dagger and held it tight against the side of the oathtaker's neck. Slowly and carefully, he drew the dagger from one side to the other. A thin line of crimson blood flowed from the cut, thickening quickly.

"You will need this mark in the work you do," Sestus said. "This is the mark of those who give their blood to Caesar. This blood will not be the last you shed."

Sestus nodded to one of the masked men beside him, who in turn flicked his wrist and produced a vial of clear amber liquid as if by magic. He uncapped it, drizzled some onto his fingers, and then traced the wound on Titius's neck.

Titius gasped at the intense sting even as he breathed in the fragrance of peaches, frankincense, and myrrh. The flow of blood staunched.

"I have a test," Sestus pronounced.

The three masked assassins stood like statues behind Sestus, and Titius knelt alone before them. The wind settled to a breeze, the trees stood straighter, and a deer bounded across the far side of the meadow.

"Whatever you wish," Titius said.

The centurion sheathed his dagger. "Good."

Sestus motioned to a second masked figure behind him. The man glided forward as if pulled by a string. With a flick of his wrist, a black hood appeared in his hand. Sestus took it and approached Titius.

"Starting tomorrow, you will become my cross maker's guardian. If he outlives his own foolishness, you, too, will live."

Sestus pulled the hood down over Titius's head and bound his wrists with thin rope. The hood smelled of smoke and incense.

"What now?" Titius asked.

"Stand and fight. The assassins are upon you."

Before Titius could shrug off the hood, a savage kick buckled his knees. Another cracked his ribs. His attackers made no sound as they came at him.

The assassins backed off, and then Titius sensed movement in front of him. A slight shadow blocked the sun. He set his feet and raised his arms to shield himself from the coming assault.

The attack materialized from behind and buckled his knees again. Titius fought through the mind-numbing pain before getting back to his feet. He spun, trying to sense the next point of attack, but he came up empty. One thing he knew for sure—the attack would come again. From in front, from behind, from the side, over and over.

Pain gripped his broken ribs in a vice. Thirst parched his throat. Oxygen escaped his lungs. Panic felt for his soul.

When terror had fully consumed him, he disjointed his shoulders and performed a back flip, distorting his body and skipping over his joined wrists so that the hands, once bound behind him, were now in front.

"Good!" he heard Sestus cry out.

The kicks soon became punches, targeting his arms, back, and chest. Titius clenched his bound hands together into a double fist and pretended to deliver a punch of his own. Instead of following through on the feigned punch, though, he brought up a knee, making solid contact and relishing the attacker's grunt.

He immediately regretted fighting back as a punch to the jaw staggered him and brought him to the edge of blackness.

Liquid splashed onto the side of his hood and down his arm. Olive oil. His senses heightened again, he heard the crackle of fire behind him.

"Stop!"

Titius spun to face Sestus's command. The hood was ripped off his head and sunlight poured into his eyes. He blinked, then closed his eyes for a moment. A line of oil dribbled down his cheek and lodged in his ear.

When Titius opened his eyes again, he saw an attacker douse his flaming torch in the dirt. He also saw a dark crimson stain grow on the thigh of his brown tunic. He blinked and felt a rough hand under his ear, where his neck wound dripped freely again.

"It's enough," Sestus said. "This test is done."

The centurion turned and waved his right hand above his head. A moment later, a majestic white stallion stepped out from a small break in the cliff. The centurion mounted and gave instructions to the leader of the three assassins.

"Jaennus, take this pitiful fighter to Sepphoris. Clean him. Heal him. Train him. I need him in Caesarea in one month. I need him to be a man who could be any man."

Chapter Two

The training never seemed to end. His ribs screamed for mercy after so many exercises with the three assassins.

Weeks into the soul-shriveling combat maneuvers, Titius finally faced off against Sestus. Titius had discarded the galea, a metal helmet, and the scutum, a rectangular shield of wood and leather. The vest of mail felt restrictive and heavy.

"Only a fool would discard his galea and scutum to escape the piercing of a javelin," Sestus snarled, poking at him with a javelin. "Do you think you have become invincible in a month?"

Titius parried with his short sword, known as a gladius, twisting and turning to avoid the centurion's jabs.

"My disguises will only allow me to conceal a gladius," Titius said. "I will never be able to depend on a shield or helmet. I'd be a fool now to depend on what can never be."

Sestus swung the javelin at Titius's knees. He then swung back at waist height, and Titius ducked under it, leaping out of reach.

A swiftly approaching shadow jumped across his peripheral vision. Titius dove to the ground and rolled away as one of the assassins struck at his back.

Two horses charged at Titius from opposite sides—the other two assassins. He could smell their lathered sweat in the breeze.

"Fool, you play with death," Cleopas screamed in his mind.

Before Titius could decide which warhorse to avoid, Sestus leveled him with a blow to the back of his knees. The slashing hooves pounded toward him and he instinctively curled into a fetal position.

Jaennus got down from one of the horses. He was the optio, the chief assistant to Sestus.

"Master, he hasn't yet been trained with the horses," Jaennus said.

"What kind of thespian assassin will he be if he can't defend himself?" Sestus demanded.

"We are first learning the secrets of living as a thespian. Then we will cover the secrets of being an assassin."

"I need him to survive," Sestus growled. He poked Titius with the butt end of his javelin. "Now get up, take your sword, and fight."

When Titius sprang to his feet, waving his sword in challenge, Sestus lowered his javelin and smiled.

He turned to Jaennus. "What is this? A dead man pretending to live?"

Jaennus held up his hand. "He acted the coward to draw you in so you could feel the point of his sword. Only my instructions kept him from severing your head."

"Jaennus, you have created a guardian worthy of my cross maker. Now show me the thespian. Will he be able to fool us all with his disguises?"

The masked warrior summoned his charge and disappeared into a small limestone hovel with a thatched roof. Another one of the dark-clad assassins stepped up beside Sestus.

"We have arranged a demonstration." The assassin pointed toward a crudely built platform near the building. "We will bring out five small groups. Each time, the initiate will be among them. His success will be in your inability to recognize him outright."

The first group featured four distinct individuals—a paunchy Pharisee in full regalia, a gaunt blind man little more than skin and bones, an elderly woman hunched and resting on a cane, and a legionnaire in full battle dress.

Sestus examined the quartet from ten strides away. "I would be a fool to choose any of these, but for this game I choose the woman."

"Titius, stand and be recognized," said the assassin.

The gaunt blind man rose and peeled off his goatskin hairpiece and soiled blanket. It was Titius.

"Well done!" Sestus declared. "One for you. Again."

The second group featured five options—a dark-skinned olive merchant, a veiled prophetess of Pan, a swarthy fisherman with his distinctive odor, a Roman of nobility, and a bushy-bearded zealot.

Sestus looked long and hard. "Surely it's not the prophetess or the olive merchant. I will choose the zealot."

"Titius, stand and be recognized," the assassin commanded.

The swarthy fisherman lowered his net filled with fish and pulled away his headpiece. It was Titius.

In the third group, Sestus chose the legionnaire, but Titius was the elderly woman. In the fourth group, Sestus chose the Pharisee, but Titius was the prophetess. In the fifth group, Sestus chose the Roman noble, but Titius was the olive merchant.

Sestus raised his gladius high. "I salute you, Jaennus. A new hypocrite is born to save the empire, an actor who can wear any mask with success. A guardian for my cross maker." He turned away and called for his stallion. "Now work with him until even his own mother won't recognize him."

Jaennus took Titius on horseback for a quick ride to a deep pool in a Roman fortress near Caesarea. The dark cloud overhead covered the sun, adding a chill to the air. As the two men stood at the edge of the large reservoir, its surface rippling under a steady breeze, Titius's old nemesis taunted him.

"You're a dead man," whispered the voice of Cleopas. *"You know how you hate water."*

"Still your tongue," Titius said under his breath. "You're the one who tried to drown me."

"I was teaching you to swim. I know you were trying to impress that girl."

He breathed in and out, quickly feeling faint. "I was only twelve."

"She was only fourteen," the phantom chuckled. *"You always did have a weakness for women."*

"You are my weakness," Titius muttered.

Jaennus, half a hand taller than Titius, seemed to tower over him when wearing his horsehair-crested helmet. He picked up a large rock and dropped it into the reservoir.

"You are about to face what no human being should ever face," Jaennus said. "Some days you will want to die rather than keep your vow. Some days you will wish you had chosen the life of a gladiator. Most days you will long for your time as a senator's son in Rome."

"I only want to be a man."

"We shall see. We shall see what happens when you start remembering what it was like to lounge on your couch, sipping your silver flagon of wine, surrounded by voluptuous servant girls, sucking on choice meats."

"Rome is a seething, poisonous serpent," Titius said. "Neither my dreams nor my taste buds take me there."

The rigor started at dawn each day, with Jaennus physically holding Titius underwater for longer and longer periods of time. Titius was pushed to swim faster, too. Following quick breaks for recovery, he then lifted weights, pulled himself up to eye level on horizontal wooden rods, and ran sprints and long distances.

Cleopas lectured him many nights on his foolishness.

"*Tee-shus, you have the mind of a goose and the soul of a scorpion. These Romans will skewer you and leave you to rot in the sun.*"

After these bouts, sleeplessness left him unfit for the next day's challenges.

"Who are you?" Jaennus shouted after Titius stumbled in an obstacle course. "You are food for the ravens. You are slop for the swine, scraps for the dogs."

"*I told you so,*" Cleopas echoed.

On the fifth day, under a blazing noonday sun, the world started spinning around Titius. His knees buckled under the heavy weights he had been carrying and he crashed to the ground.

Jaennus prodded him in the ribs with his vine staff. "Rise, you fraud. You're more worthless than a stillborn pig, galley slave, and bucket of slops all combined. You'll never be a man. I'd rather train a woman than a splash of dung like you."

As Titius struggled to breathe, the weight lifted. Like a vision in the night, he watched himself being dumped into the cool waters of the fortress's pool. He sank like a stone and called out to Neptune to release him from his trials. His lungs screamed for air.

Just as quickly as he sank, he was raised again out of the water. His rescuer pounded his back and compressed his chest until he lay coughing, spluttering water and gasping for air. The spirit of death danced like a shadow at the edge of consciousness.

Finally, his merciful ally dragged him into the shadows of a nearby cedar tree and left him to rest.

"*That insane assassin did what I couldn't,*" Cleopas said. "*He killed you. And still you won't come to the other side.*"

There is no other side, Titius thought.

Gentle hands prodded him awake in the morning and fed him broth. Every muscle screamed for mercy. The hands massaged him, then left him to rest again. The faintest smell of roses kept him hanging on.

Thoughts filled his mind of the servant girl Abigail. She had been eighteen, and sixteen-year-old Titius had found himself making excuses to be with her. He had been furious when he came home one day and found that his mother had sold Abigail to another family. He had shut his heart toward every woman since that day, even if Cleopas didn't believe it.

Life had become like a dance without music since then, a rainbow without color, a kiss without passion. His heart was like an eagle chained to the ground.

Cleopas's voice reached him: *"You need to quit before they kill you for good."*

For the first time, Titius agreed with the former slave. *You're right. I have to quit before I end up like you.*

That night, someone nudged him.

"Leave me alone, you stupid phantom," Titius whispered.

"I'm no phantom," he heard Jaennus reply. "Enough rest. Move. Meet me at the pool at first light."

Titius shook off his sleep, slipped on his gear, and satiated his thirst from a gourd of water lying at the head of his bed. The air was crisp and cool.

Mars and Venus still faced off in the heavens. The moon was nowhere to be seen, but the sparkle of heavenly lights fought to hold their sway as the first touches of color marked the horizon.

A trio of master assassins was preparing an obstacle course as Titius hurried toward the pool. The pungent odor of frankincense hung in the air from a recent sacrificial offering.

Titius sheltered behind an oak tree to preview his challenge.

"Did you hear about Cretius?" one of the assassins said to the others.

Another threw a rope ladder over a wall. "Do you mean that despot of Herod Antipas?"

"Guard your tongue, Marcus. His spies are everywhere."

"Anyway," the first assassin continued. "I heard him bragging that he had stolen the estate of General Julianus."

Titius's neck hairs bristled, like a cat on high alert. General Julianus had been Titius's own father, killed in the German wars. What had happened to his mother, his sister, and the servants, especially Lydia? He tucked in harder behind the trunk of the tree.

"What concern is that of ours?" asked the one called Marcus. "Those Roman senators steal each other blind while we risk our lives to help them live in luxury. I hope they choke on their pigeon tongues."

"Marcus, it'll be your tongue they choke on," one of them warned. "The general's son has disappeared and Cretius has ordered me to watch for him."

"No doubt Cretius slipped you a sack of gold to watch his back," Marcus said. "What do you think, Octavian?"

"Emperor Tiberius will likely reform the senate and ensure that this general's son gets nowhere near power in Rome," said the assassin named Octavian. "He's probably escaped to hide in the backwoods of Britannia. We just need to keep Jaennus happy."

"They're talking about you," Cleopas hissed.

Titius instinctively covered his mouth lest the trio overhear the phantom voice in his mind, impossible though he knew it to be. Anger raced like fire through his veins.

Cretius had stolen his estate in Rome.

"You told that centurion you didn't want it anyway. And now you're quitting. You might as well stay at the bottom of that pool next time."

When the trio slipped into the brush on the far side of the field, Titius backed away onto the path and hurried toward the pool, where Jaennus was waiting. He was dressed in full optio regalia; his raised horsehair mane and white-knobbed stick spoke of his authority to record and report all that happened among the centurion's troops.

Jaennus raised his stick in greeting. "I knew you would come."

"You don't know how close I came to not coming," Titius said.

Jaennus opened his hand and held out Titius's ring. "A gift from the centurion," he said. He held it out over the water and dropped it into the pool.

Titius watched it sink.

"The pool is ten times your height," the optio said. "Only one man has reached the bottom. Untold treasures lie within your grasp."

"There goes your life," Cleopas mocked.

"This will be your final test under the water," Jaennus said. "You will endure it or return to Rome. You will prove you are a man worthy of being a thespian assassin or you will prove you are no different than anyone else. Today is your day."

Titius stood at the edge of the pool and stared into its depth. This dark pit would be either his birthplace or tomb. He would not go back to Rome.

Without fear, he stepped off the edge and plunged into the water's icy grip.

Chapter Three

Surviving the water sparked a confidence Titius had never known. He didn't reach the bottom that day, and he didn't retrieve his ring, but he remained submerged long enough to qualify for the brotherhood. Afterward he finished the obstacle course and completed his tests of strength. He slept with a deep peace that night.

The morning sun was still a faint glimmer on the horizon when Sestus brought the butt of his javelin down on Titius's mat. Instead of the dull thud of wood, the javelin's energy was swallowed up by cushions carefully concealed under a worn blanket. Sestus lifted his torchlight higher, yanked off the blanket, and reached for the rounded form of a head resting under a small mass of hair. He pulled off the hair and discovered a melon.

He smiled.

"Titius," he called. "Step out!"

A nearby mat, which had appeared to be flat on the floor, moved aside and Titius rolled out of a hollow he had formed in the earthen floor.

Sestus stepped to the hole and examined it. "Hmmmph," he said. "It looks like your training is finished."

Titius followed the centurion without a word as he exited the sleeping quarters. And when Sestus mounted his horse, Titius mounted the unclaimed one standing alongside. The horse's short military saddle had four horns to brace his legs and back but nowhere to put his feet.

The sky seemed especially active as they rode. Hawks, kites, and eagles danced in the thermals and a pair of cranes flapped leisurely above a forested hill. Pelicans and cormorants made their way toward the sea. Partridges, spooked by some hidden predator, vaulted from cover. Warblers, starlings, and swallows flitted and flapped. A woodpecker pounded its bill against a tree trunk in search of grub.

The sun was halfway to its zenith before Sestus stopped his horse beside a small pond fed by a stream. A small flock of Egyptian geese waddled into the water and paddled away. He dismounted and motioned for Titius to do the same.

"You didn't get the ring," Sestus said. "Why didn't you fight for it?"

"I know where it is."

"Only one man has ever reached the bottom of that pool. Your fate is now bound to us."

Titius nodded. "Yes, my fate is now bound to you."

Sestus picked up a rock and threw it dead center against a tree trunk on the other side of the pond. He nodded to himself and smiled.

As Titius sat and rested his back against an old cedar, Sestus walked to his mount and detached a gourd that had been tied to the saddle. He heaved it at Titius, who caught it one-handed. Sestus opened his own gourd, dumped the contents on the ground, and began to refill it in the stream. Titius did the same.

"You learn quickly," Sestus said. "Why a thespian?"

Titius guzzled the water quickly, then lowered the gourd to his side. "I think it was the mask of an actor that first caught my attention and pulled my heart toward the stage." He eyed his commander. "I was a boy, maybe ten years free of the womb. The performer moved and spoke in courageous ways before his audience. No general would dare mock Caesar with such impunity and live to boast of it, yet this strutting cock pulled laughter from even the senators who lay prone on their gilded couches."

Sestus took a step toward his horse and smiled as Titius mimicked the action precisely. "You enter theatre so you can mock the emperor? Did your father approve of your choice?"

Titius took another guzzle. "My father turned on me as if to cut out my tongue."

"What did he say?"

"He said, 'Theatre?'" Titius swung his arms wide and turned his shoulders to act out the scene. "He paced back and forth in our courtyard by the fountain of Neptune. His scarlet tunic matched the bright red battle scar across his cheek. When he stopped pacing, he drew his sword and slashed it inches from my heart." Titius staggered back as if under attack. "'Titius,' he said, 'you are the son of a Roman legate. The heir of a warrior who has humbled the Gauls. Spit this cursed idea from your throat.'"

Sestus picked up a small branch and broke it. "Your uncles in the Senate will curse the day of your birth when they see you next."

Titius stepped behind a tree and spoke in a deep voice, one inspired by Cleopas. "They will never see me again. I no longer exist. I am only your cross maker's guardian."

"Guarding the cross maker may be more challenging than you think. The man is bent on taking revenge against Barabbas, the zealot who killed his father." Sestus threw down the broken twigs and looked toward the north. "He needs to be broken until he serves me willingly, but first he must be protected."

"I will protect him as if I was a senator protecting Rome."

"Don't you ever wonder what happened to your estate when you left Rome?" Sestus asked as he pulled out his javelin and sword.

Titius caught the javelin that Sestus tossed to him. "Once my mother died, I didn't care."

Sestus circled and tested Titius's reflexes with the sword. "You probably don't know that she died giving birth to our brother."

Titius paused a moment too long and the javelin was knocked out of his hand. He scrambled for it, but before he could pick it up Sestus had pointed the sword at his throat.

"I was told my mother was raped," Titius said.

Sestus chuckled and stepped away. "A true thespian assassin learns not to believe everything he hears."

The centurion swung his sword again as Titius reached for the javelin. The recruit dove for the ground and rolled out of reach.

Sestus waited as Titius picked up his javelin. "Your uncles worked out an arrangement with my father so your mother would be taken care of. Their union was more of a business arrangement."

Titius nodded as he caught the verbal dance. "No self-respecting senator would tie nobility to the common ranks of the military," he said while fending off a series of sword thrusts with the shaft of his javelin.

Sestus persisted, pushing Titius back toward the tree. "My father was granted nobility for his great victories in Gaul. Your mother needed protection… my father needed an estate."

"You know I believe nothing of what you say."

"Your mother died giving birth to the son who would have made us family."

"What did your father really want from my mother?" Titius asked.

Sestus smiled. "What else? Her servant girls."

Anger surged within Titius and he slashed his javelin at Sestus. Sestus defended himself against every attack until Titius tired.

"Your passion will be your weakness," Sestus said. "It was Cretius who raped your mother and stole your estate. Focus your rage on him." Sestus sheathed his sword. "Hear beyond the words others drop for you like breadcrumbs. Someday, you must restore your honor. Cretius must die."

Sestus walked to the edge of the pond and stooped to pick up a stone. He threw it nonchalantly toward the geese. A few of them fluttered away.

"When you reap your revenge, I will return your ring." Sestus continued after a moment.

"How will you do that?" Titius asked, panting from the workout. "You said only one man has ever reached the bottom of that pool."

"And I am that man."

Titius crouched, plucked a wildflower, and cherished the pleasure of its scent. "Jaennus has planned more training for tomorrow."

"We cannot wait."

"I am ready. Take me to your cross maker."

Sestus lifted his head to scan the sky. Dark clouds were creeping over the hills. "He doesn't yet know he is mine. He is arriving by ship from Alexandria. You will woo him to me. Now, it's time to begin your duty."

Titius groaned when the cross maker walked into view. This carpenter was a disaster in the making. He was broad-shouldered, long-armed, and he bounced along like an overgrown child prone to mischief. His carpenter's headpiece dangled halfway off his shoulder, held in place only by the weight of a crossbeam. The thong of one sandal was undone and the ends dragged along in his wake.

"Sestus has bonded you to a Jewish carpenter?" Cleopas asked. *"Galilean, no doubt. This is trouble."*

Titius scratched at the goatskin skullcap nestled under his own head covering. *If he gives me trouble, I'll feed both him and you to Neptune, Cleopas. He doesn't look like much of a cross maker.*

The young carpenter strolled down a dirt path in the heart of Caesarea. Crumbling limestone huts with chipped red clay roofs huddled tight together, blocking out the blistering sunshine. The path had been packed rock hard by thousands of feet, generation after generation.

It was clear from the cross maker's Roman attire and reckless stride that he didn't belong here.

Sestus had told Titius that this young man's name was Caleb ben Samson. He was clutching a six-foot crossbeam across his bulging shoulders. His dark eyebrows were furrowed and his piercing eyes focused on a shadowed archway ahead; Titius had just seen a young daggerman slip into the shadows beyond that arch.

But this wasn't Titius's battle. Not yet.

Not one passerby had given a second look to Titius, who had disguised himself as a pitiful old beggar. He had molded the old goatskin tight to his shaved skull and wrapped a leather thong of long white hair under his chin. A discarded blanket from the refuse pile added to the look—and the odor.

After three hours of sitting along the side of the path, he'd gotten used to the smell of rotting fish and dung.

His random call for alms yielded nothing in this neighborhood, but it also made it unlikely that anyone would drive him away. His walking stick rested close by, in case any rambunctious youth tried to test his apparent blindness.

His one mistake was pulling out the coded papyrus scroll Sestus had given him. It contained the centurion's instructions.

The passing carpenter grunted at Titius and fixed his eyes for a second too long on that parchment. Titius could sense his question: what was an old blind man doing with a scroll?

Three youths stepped into the laneway following Caleb, each carrying crude daggers designed to gut fishes or slice throats. Zealots. The carpenter acted like he didn't notice them, but Titius saw him reach for the knife in his toolbelt, caressing it like a lover. Without a doubt, Caleb knew exactly who was behind him.

Caleb adjusted the step of his sandaled feet and pretended to stumble. He was a poor actor, but the ruse seemed to embolden the youth, who increased the length and speed of their strides. The three walked by Titius without even looking his way.

"Caleb, carpenter of Nazareth!" the lead youth called out to Caleb. "You betray us with your blood."

Caleb ignored the taunt and wrapped his strong fingers around the beam like it was a giant club. He reached the cobblestones near the archway and swung at the young man waiting in ambush. The zealot fell to the ground, dropping a dagger. Caleb then raised the beam and hit the fallen man a second time.

"*This one has a death wish,*" Cleopas gloated. "*You'll never keep him alive.*"

Titius knuckled hard against his own temples and then reached into the dust for the smallest of pebbles. All the while, he positioned himself facing straight ahead with his chin lowered toward his chest. He hurled the pebble at the back of the leading zealot and saw him flinch and turn as the stone struck.

Caleb was focusing his attention on the three youths brandishing daggers. Instead of running, he adjusted his grip as if to throw the beam with both hands and then charged the boys. The beam hit them in the knees and knocked them down. He then grabbed their hair and smashed their skulls into the cobblestones.

A bag of apricots had fallen from the coat of one of the young men. The carpenter picked it up and ate the fruit.

Sestus had informed Titius about Barabbas's craving for the dried fruit. If this bag had been meant for the zealot leader then the cross maker had just made a dangerous play. He might need more protection than he realized.

Chapter Four

Two candlewicks flickered in the breeze as the door to the dockside warehouse squeaked open. Titius hunched in the shadows near a stack of bags filled with wheat kernels. He had come, under orders from Sestus, to prevent the cross maker from releasing his slave.

A lone figure stepped into the warehouse and closed the door behind him. Titius didn't recognize him.

"Nabonidus!" the figure called into the warehouse.

A moment later, a bald-headed Persian man rolled slowly away from the reed mat he'd been lying on. He jumped to his feet, his dark-skinned body blending into the lightless alcoves. Lamplight reflected off the man's head and his belly hung generously over his loincloth, revealing bulging biceps and a massive frame.

The dull clink of chains followed the Persian man as he stepped forward. "Is that you, Alexander?"

Hazy smoke from the lamps wafted between the two men.

"The centurion is looking for your master."

"I knew coming to Caesarea would mean trouble. We should have stayed in Alexandria."

"Nabonidus, is it true that the cross maker wants to set you free?"

When Titius heard Alexander's voice, he suddenly recognized it. Alexander was the owner of the warehouse and a suspected smuggler. His name had been associated with the zealots by Sestus.

"What will I do without you?" Alexander continued, scratching his beard. "When will you go and where will you stay?"

The Persian grunted. "Been a slave since I was five. Don't know where to go. Maybe just start walking in the morning and see what it's like to be free."

"I overheard a legionnaire saying that Sestus Aurelius wanted you taken away to make sure the cross maker kept his promises. I can hide you."

"Don't want to hide."

"Have you seen anyone suspicious around here, anyone who might come looking for you?"

"Only that old blind beggar," Nabonidus said. "Heard he's a fraud, that he hired a cart to pick up the bodies of some young zealots the master killed. Beggar slithers in and out of the shadows like a snake."

Alexander backed up against the door and peered into the darkness. "And who is this blind man? You should come with me now."

Titius slipped through the darkness, approaching the two men from behind. He quietly secured the Persian's chain to an iron bolt fastened to the floor. Within moments, he was standing just over Alexander's shoulder. He stretched out his cane and tapped the warehouse owner's unguarded shin.

Alexander swung hard and grunted when Titius ducked out of the way. Titius then put him in an armlock and pressed his face into the nearest wall.

"Life or death," Titius hissed. "You choose. If you take this slave, Rome will have your head as a thief."

Alexander bent from the pressure until he fell to his knees. "Nabonidus, do something."

The Persian tried to step forward but couldn't move.

"That's not the choice I offered," Titius said. "May the goddess Belona and the god Mars spare you from me."

Nabonidus remained rooted to the spot. "Alexander, just listen to the man."

"I'm listening."

Titius released his hold and waited for Alexander to rise to his feet and turn. Before Alexander could get a good look at him, Titius stepped back into the shadows. Meanwhile, the warehouseman strained to see him.

"Relax and live," Titius said. "You must not tell any of this to the cross maker. What happens soon with this slave will be for his own protection."

"Who are you?" Alexander asked.

"All you need to know is that those zealots' bodies are gone and you are still alive. Things are not always as they appear to be. You need to leave now. This slave is not yours and never will be."

With that Titius, slipped away.

As he scurried out the back door, Titius noticed four legionnaires approaching the front of the building. Time was short for Alexander and Nabonidus. If the Romans did find the Persian and hope to move him, they would first have to get close enough to break his chains.

Titius grabbed a handful of dates from a nearby vendor and continued toward the stables where he knew Sestus was preparing for the next phase of their journey. On the way, he discarded his garb in one of the four stashes he had established around the city.

Thirty minutes later, Titius arrived without his disguise in the courtyard of Pontius Pilate, the Judean procurator. Six Roman sentries had been stationed across the entrance, their hands resting firmly on their swords, their shields resting against their legs.

"Titius Marcus Julianus," he said, announcing himself. "Reporting to the Centurion Sestus Aurelius."

The legionnaires might as well have been statues for their lack of response. As Titius waited, a flock of storks skimmed the rooftops and headed for the forests inland.

A boy stepped out of the shadows and looked up expectantly at Titius, like a young bird waiting to be fed. The lad was a special messenger assigned to the centurion during his stay in Caesarea. He gave the proper prearranged hand signals to prove his role.

"What's your name, boy?"

"Simeon."

Titius gave Simeon what he wanted. "Here's a message for the centurion: the man he seeks is in the home of the tanner among the Greek traders."

The lad nodded, turned, and walked through the sentries into the fountained gardens beyond.

An hour after leaving the chained Persian slave, Titius stepped back into the shadows of the warehouse. Alexander was gone and Nabonidus was struggling with three legionnaires. A fourth soldier had arrived with a flickering torch, flame valiantly holding on in the stiff breeze.

Nabonidus's forehead was beaded with sweat and his muscles bulged with effort. The Romans worked to buckle his knees, but the tower of strength fought to maintain his balance.

When the giant fell to his knees and finally submitted to the crippling shackles that bound ankles to wrists and neck, Titius turned to watch a rat scrabble across the floor toward a basket of apricots, the fruit of Barabbas.

Titius looked on as Nabonidus was dragged protesting from the room.

One of the legionnaires stayed behind to clean up the scene. He nodded to Titius as he wiped up a small pool of blood.

"Is your cross maker going to cooperate?" the legionnaire asked. "Will he return to making crosses with the centurion?"

Titius picked out an apricot from the basket. "Depends how good your centurion is at persuading him. He is still like a wild unbroken colt."

The legionnaire accepted the apricot when Titius tossed it to him. He bit off half the fruit and dug out the pit. "If he favors that slave as much as you say, he'll cooperate. If he does, the Persian might get off easy. If he resists, that slave's life will end in the Ephesian Colosseum, or perhaps the galleys of a warship."

Titius raised his hand as he moved toward the door. "You better catch up with the others. That Persian might be too much for them."

The next two days were busy for Titius in his role as Caleb's guardian. The first evening, as he watched over the cross maker sheltering in an inn, he noticed a young zealot in conference with a woman dressed like a Greek goddess. Her long blond tresses flowed over her shoulders and drew a man's eyes toward her revealing linen tunic. Money exchanged hands, along with a gourd of wine.

As the woman next prepared a tray of food for Caleb, Titius interrupted and told her that the young zealot she'd been talking to needed her at the door. While she was away, he switched the gourd of wine for another like it. A sniff and small taste confirmed that the first wine had been poisoned.

Caleb had been like a boy jabbing his javelin into a hornets' nest, forcing Titius to intervene to save the carpenter from threats he didn't see coming. Sleep was a luxury Titius couldn't afford, and meanwhile Sestus was lounging in the palace of Pontius Pilate. It filled Titius with bitterness.

"Wish you were back in Rome enjoying all those Senate luxuries, don't you?" Cleopas said.

I just wish it was you I could leave at the mercy of the zealots.

Halfway through the second morning, Titius garroted a zealot who had been about to ambush Caleb with a dagger. He then rode over another zealot with his horse.

In the evening, sitting with his back to a wall near a flickering fire, Titius stared at the sleeping cross maker. What would it take to break this man so he'd just cooperate with Sestus?

Earlier, he had disguised himself as the old blind man and met Caleb on the wharf. He had tapped his cane in different rhythms, trying to get Caleb's attention.

Caleb had ignored him.

"The Persian slave is fighting his new masters," Titius had finally called. "His time is almost up. The Grecian goddess you spurned was bribed to poison your wine. I switched the flasks before she entered your room. Otherwise you would never have woken from your sleep."

He tapped Caleb's ankle hard and got a faint reaction. The cross maker focused on a kingfisher as it dove into the water.

"She has returned to the Gates of Hades," Titius had continued. "The zealots know that you and the Roman avoided their ambush. They will try again. Ominous winds are blowing for your Jewish Messiah. Things are not as they appear."

His mission accomplished, Titius had slipped away.

In the morning, Titius followed Caleb as the cross maker stopped by a fig vendor to break his fast. Titius distracted two young zealots loitering in the shadows near the vendor's cart by dumping a pail of slops onto their feet as he passed. By the time they had cleaned up, Caleb was gone. It took a while to find him again.

Later, when Caleb walked along the docks, Titius tried to tap a warning to his charge when two centurions emerged from a tavern close by. Caleb may have heard the taps, but he ignored them and stepped into the shadowed archway of Alexander's warehouse. Caleb waited there for a few moments, then stepped out again just as Alexander happened to pass by. Caleb grabbed the man's arm and they spoke briefly. They hadn't been together more than a few seconds before Caleb shoved Alexander away, then snatched a woven basket of walnuts and heaved it off the edge of the dock in anger.

Perhaps a woman would calm him, Titius thought.

With that in mind, he strolled through the slave market and noticed a young Grecian woman chained apart from the rest. He mused to himself that she looked similar to the woman who had attempted to poison Caleb with the gourd of wine. Her youthful face also reminded him of his first love, Abigail.

"Why is that Greek woman on her own?" Titius asked the seller, who held a long whip.

The owner's lusty eyes matched his twisted grin. "I have to break her. She looks like a goddess and she has the attitude of one, too. She acts like a queen!"

Titius examined the woman, his gaze travelling from her long, golden tresses to her strong legs and arms. She had the form of an athlete, a perfect model for the sorts of sculptures that filled the gardens in Rome.

He called to her, but the woman refused to look. Finally, Titius reached up and took hold of her chin, forcing her to look his way.

"I can take a goddess like you to heaven," he said, "or I can take you down to hades. The other men who want you won't give you that choice."

Uncertainty furrowed her brow and she blushed. Titius realized that her hard attitude was her only cover to maintain a sense of modesty.

"I'll take her," he said. "Thirty shekels."

The slave owner ran his hand through his long, greasy beard. "Thirty might get you another look. Offer me something reasonable. I know a few zealots who would pay twice your price."

Titius saw the hope drain from the girl's expression.

"I'll pay you forty shekels now so you don't have to wait on the empty promises of zealots," Titius said.

The slave owner snapped his whip near the woman's feet and chuckled when she jumped. "Perhaps I need to mark her up a little. For forty, it's clear you only want her to scrub your floors and cook your meals. Believe me, this one is good for something more than floors—and the zealots know it."

"This woman is hard-hearted and defiant," Titius said, stepping back. "Name your final price or I'll look elsewhere and leave you to your burden."

The slave owner looked around to see if any other man in the vicinity was interested in paying more. They each shook their heads.

Finally, the owner nodded. "Forty-five and not a shekel less."

The price was higher than anything Titius had ever paid for a slave, but he handed over the coins and waited while the owner counted them twice. When the payment was confirmed, he held the coins up in victory. The audience applauded.

Titius left the woman with the former owner for a time and stopped at the market to purchase a simple brown tunic and leather sandals. He returned, draped her in the garment, and removed the shackles from her ankles.

Titius walked away quickly and she shuffled along behind, her head down, as if she were still bound by the chains. At first, Titius ignored the crude and suggestive calls of the men watching them leave, but their impact on the woman was clear.

Titius slowed to let her keep up. "What is your name?"

"I am Taphina," she said softly. "From Sparta. This is my first time as a slave. Thank you for the tunic."

"Why are you being sold?"

"My father died of the fever and my mother couldn't pay his debts. My brother sold me to Hedicles so the family could survive."

"Are you afraid of me?"

She looked into his eyes. "Should I be?"

Titius examined the face that reminded him so much of Abigail. "I bought you to be a comfort for another man, to tame his spirit."

"I know little about comforting men," she said. "I assume you will train me with what is necessary."

As the first drops of rain sprinkled down, Titius took Taphina aside to a tavern and arranged for a meal of chicken, egg, dates, and bread. The young Greek slave stuffed the food into her mouth with both hands and hardly paused to swallow. Watching her, his insides twisted in a mix of compassion and anger.

It took three glasses of wine before she turned toward him again. "I am ready," she said. "Please be gentle while I learn."

Titius took her arm and they walked outside. He continued in the drizzling rain down to the docks, where he stopped by several vendors purchasing blankets, tunics, and food. She carried his purchases without question.

As Taphina stood in the shelter of a warehouse later that day to escape the rain, Titius negotiated with a sea captain. After exchanging money, he motioned for her to come to him, which she did—slowly, in obedience. Once by his side, Titius reached out and held both her wrists.

"I have bought your freedom. You will not learn how to comfort a man from me. This ship will take you home to your mother."

Taphina stood, her mouth open.

"The captain has some money he will give you when the trip is finished," Titius said. "Do not compromise yourself for any man."

The last Titius saw of the Grecian goddess was her wave from the deck of the merchant vessel, loaded with sugar and spices. For the first time in years, his heart felt warm. Caleb would have to get along without a woman—at least without this woman.

"Another woman, same weakness," Cleopas said, interrupting his moment of satisfaction. *"You know she doesn't stand a chance with that brother of hers. You should have kept her."*

"Sending her home to her mother was the noble thing to do," Titius said aloud. "I already know which woman I'm looking for."

"You'll never find her," Cleopas mocked.

"Hush yourself. I have work to do."

With the woman gone, and Caleb safe, Titius revisited the vendors. His favorite method of intelligence-gathering was to loiter in the vicinity of the vendors as they engaged in discussions with their customers.

Toward evening, when his strategy yielded no new information, he decided to be more proactive.

Taking on the role of a drunken sailor, Titius staggered toward an alley of small fires. The people huddled around them dismissed him as no one of consequence. He listened in on their conspiracies—to short-load a grain boat, to slice the throat of a signal man who had wooed a girl they knew, and to mutiny against an Egyptian captain. None of it mattered to him.

At the sixth fire, he stumbled and fell next to a quartet of men whispering to each other. The men noticed him but paid him no more mind than any other drunk.

"I tell ya, the centurion and procurator are plotting to silence the zealots," a voice urged. "And now they have a cross maker. We need to bury the lot."

"What are you thinking, Alexander?" someone asked. "You had your chance to stop this whole thing in your warehouse."

"We'll never get Pilate, but the centurion and cross maker are heading to Sepphoris tomorrow," Alexander said, standing up. "We have marked horses and an ambush set up along the way. We need to settle for what we can get."

As the conspirators kicked apart their fire, Titius moved slowly out of sight and dashed toward Pilate's courtyard. On the way, he visited one of his secret stashes. There, he picked up a pack filled with fresh clothing, figs, dates, and bits of cheese.

At the fortress, a new contingent of statue-like legionnaires guarded the entrance. Torches cast soft light on their fluttering scarlet capes and feather-bristled helmets. Their glistening shields formed a formidable wall against intruders.

"Titius Marcus Julianus," he declared. "Reporting to Centurion Sestus Aurelius. I have news of a conspiracy. Send a messenger to wake the centurion."

Titius walked confidently to a rain barrel and wiped the soot and dirt off his face. Meanwhile, the sentries remained anchored in place.

"He won't want to see you," Cleopas rumbled in the back of his head. *"You aren't as important as you think."*

I'm not trying to be important, Titius thought. *I was important... once upon a time.*

"You could have been off enjoying that woman. Instead you're standing out in the cold like a forgotten slave. In case you forget, I know what that feels like.

I choose to be here. I am not forgotten. Every moment is an opportunity to learn something.

Cleopas hissed. *"I'm the one who taught you that."*

An hour passed, and the sentries still hadn't moved.

"It's your disguise," Cleopas said. *"You've become so good at your disguises you're even fooling those you want to help. The sentries aren't going to disturb the sleep of a centurion for an old rag man."*

No one seemed to have noticed him from inside the fortress. Growing frustrated, he exchanged his rags for the robes of a holy man.

When a new watch of legionnaires stepped into place in front of the entrance, a familiar-looking boy stumbled out through the gateway.

"Simeon!" Titius called out. "For the love of Jupiter, hear me, boy."

Simeon wiped his eyes and stepped tentatively between the line of sentries.

"Wake Sestus, son," Titius called again. "His life depends on it."

Ten minutes later, the centurion, in full battle gear, stepped forward and breached the line of warriors.

"Speak," Sestus commanded.

Titius stepped forward. "Master, it is I." Sestus nodded. "Plans have been made to ambush you and the cross maker on your way to Sepphoris."

Sestus reached out and turned Titius away from the line of guardians. "How?"

Titius walked another ten steps as Sestus followed. "The plan is to kill the men on your particular horses—a bay and a black. One of the stable hands is to make sure the two of you get those horses. The zealots seem to have infiltrated everywhere."

Sestus glanced back toward the stables. "Find a horse, dress as you must, and go to the home of Barabbas. Find out all you can. The first scouts you meet may show you a burned-out farm, but wait until they take you elsewhere." He gave Titius's shoulder a squeeze and backed away. "When you're done, meet us in Sepphoris. I need you to train the cross maker to protect himself, and to fight for me."

"I am your servant," Titius declared. "If you command it, I will make it happen."

"Today, you are my servant. But one day soon, you will have your revenge on Cretius and restore your honor."

"You alone know this," Titius said.

Sestus held out his hands to Titius, fingers splayed. "Our art is tenfold," he said, raising his left hand and counting off. "The five abilities are distraction, disguise, sleight of hand, silence, and quick kills." And then he moved to his right hand. "The five qualities are power, endurance, healing, knowledge, and loyalty." He raised his hands to shoulder height. "Left is distraction, disguise, magic, silence, and death. Right is power, endurance, healing, knowledge, and loyalty." He clasped his hands together. "When the two become one, the assassin is unbeatable."

Titius raised his own hands and quietly repeated the tenfold art. Once he had the truth firmly in mind, he nodded.

"Now go," Sestus commanded.

Titius turned to leave, but Sestus called to him one more time. "Titius, you leave your soul unguarded with me. But guard your throat with Barabbas. Get close, but live to return."

Chapter Five

Half a day into the journey from Caesarea toward the Jordan, Titius luxuriated in the magic of silence and stillness. He chose to walk, avoiding the main roads and instead taking winding pathways. The blue sky held no hint of cloud and the breeze felt like a lover's caress. Flocks of sheep and goats grazed together in the open countryside, the shepherds' tents huddled near a small pond. Wildflowers dotted the hilly landscape as far as the eye could see.

The rise and fall of the landscape seemed endless and he began to doubt his direction.

"You're lost, aren't you?" Cleopas said. *"You never were very good at knowing where you were."*

"I know where I am," Titius argued. "It's just that I'm not sure how far I still have to go. With all these trees, there are no real landmarks…"

He looked for higher elevation, declining the limbs of a juniper and choosing instead to scale the tallest of a tightly knit cluster of oaks.

As Titius rested on the highest limbs, he caught his first glimpse of Megiddo in the distance. The Kishon River snaked its way just beyond it, toward Mount Tabor, which rose north and west. To the south, Mount Gerizim reached into the sky.

He opened his pack, searched for some food, and sucked on fresh dates as he looked back toward the vast expanse of the Great Sea. A fleet of Roman warships escorted a flotilla of trading vessels on their way to Alexandria, or points beyond.

Below him waved ripening fields of barley. Terraced fields of wheat showed the first sprouts of green, already knee-high, in fields divided by short walls of stone. Three large groves of pine trees, and another of pistachios, looked like hopeful places to take shelter if necessary. A river of white-winged butterflies flowed over him and disappeared into a gulley.

On a plain toward the south grazed a small herd of antelope. The buck held his head high, alert, and the females became skittish and moved in behind him. Two fawns folded themselves down into the grass as a pair of does leapt in zigzagging patterns. The buck lowered his long horns and waggled his head.

The flash of color was almost invisible as it slashed out of the tall grasses at the perimeter of the field—a cheetah, slender, sleek, spotted, and swifter than most predators, dug in its claws and positioned itself to chase down one of the females. In seconds, the cat was closing in on the does. The two bounced sideways and split in opposite directions. The cheetah hesitated, then spun right. The prey sprang higher and wider, back and forth, trying to dodge its assassin.

Within a minute, the predator had closed tight enough to swipe at the antelope's back legs. It tumbled and rolled, legs thrashing but not contacting the ground. The cheetah stiffened its front legs and skidded to a halt. Before the doe could dash away again, the cat was at her throat.

The buck whistled and the surviving doe and fawns hustled away from the scene.

"It's just like Rome and everywhere else," Cleopas said. "It's only a matter of time until it's your turn to die."

Titius looked toward the Jordan. "Speak for yourself, slave. You've already had your turn."

It took another two hours to reach the furthest grove of pines. He easily avoided the shepherds along the way, although he almost walked into the path of two young boys out hunting rabbits with slingshots. They already had two tied to their belts by the neck.

The way was spotted with the scat of lion, bears, and wild donkeys. Deer were numerous. At one point, he perched in a tree and caught a glimpse of an ostrich running mindlessly with its black plumage spread out as if trying to fly.

If Cleopas is right and there's a creator of this world besides Jupiter, then surely this one bird is evidence of a huge mistake.

He crossed the Jordan River at nightfall, praying in desperation.

"Oh Jupiter, Neptune, or whatever other gods will hear me, spare me from the crocodiles who live in these waters. Grant me safe passage and spare my life."

The prayer had no conclusion, just a statement of petition. He was used to the ritualistic prayers offered to the Roman gods, but this time he had prayed spontaneously, his desire to live infusing it with energy.

He stripped down, stuffing his traveling clothes into his pack, and scouted out the best passage across the river. He waded in from the sheltered bank and swam under the surface as far as he could, holding his pack above the water. He surfaced twice on his way across before arriving on the far bank without incident.

Despite his efforts, his pack had gotten wet and he wrung out his clothing before donning the simple robe of a village priest. This made the proceeding climb into the branches of an olive tree a little more challenging, but he secured himself in the crook of his sanctuary and nibbled on figs, cheese, and dried fruit from the deep folds of his pack.

Sestus had assigned him to infiltrate the zealot camp—in his words, to "get close." He knew he would soon encounter the rebels. The only way to survive would be to pass himself off as a zealot. Barabbas wouldn't be easily fooled; the man would be restless and eager to prove himself when his life was on the line.

At dawn, Titius changed into the garb of a zealot. It fit him loosely, so he ripped off the bottom of the robe and wore the top half underneath his disguise. It made him look bulkier.

He squared his shoulders for the final three-hour journey and trekked toward the farm of Barabbas, not far from the Yarmuk River. Jaennus had forced him to review the map over and over until he could reproduce it from memory. Others had found Barrabas's family farm, and the Romans had already tried an unsuccessful raid on it, leaving it burned and empty.

"Only a great thespian can do this," Jaennus had warned him.

"That's not you," Cleopas said.

Titius hid his pack in a cluster of pistachios as he made final preparations, dirtying his face and clothing with dust. He then pulled a knife from his pack and surveyed the farm spread out before him, trying to determine the best route forward. Smoke arose from behind a small shed at the edge of the property, perhaps a cooking fire—

Searing pain from his right shoulder alerted him to an arrow stuck in a tree next to him, still quivering. He ducked behind the tree as another arrow thudded into wood. He squirmed out of his zealot outfit until all he had left were the remains of his priest's robe.

The wound was significant. He staunched the flow of blood by wrapping his shoulder with a strip of cloth ripped from his tunic.

Shouts surrounded him until he raised an arm and shouted his surrender.

He stood and waited as blood trickled down his arm, dripping onto his wrist and off his fingertips.

Two young warriors, their tunics tucked into their belts, stepped out of the brush. Another came into view next to the smoke-filled shed. They looked ready for action.

"On your knees," shouted the man standing near the shed.

Titius hesitated. One of the men had a bow and the other two brandished knives. He watched their approach, watched how they handled their weapons.

"You could kill them easily," Cleopas coached.

I need them to lead me to Barabbas.

He anticipated the beating ahead. At least Jaennus had trained him well in pain management.

"This time they'll knock out all your teeth," Cleopas sneered.

At least I have some.

He held his arms up to protect his head as the young men punched and kicked him into submission. To manage the pain, Titius pictured his grandfather's return from Gaul. He had forced his prisoner, an enemy general, to kneel before the angry mobs of Roman citizens. Kicks and punches had drained the life out of this once-proud leader, yet the people weren't satiated even by his death. They turned on each other and only the harsh intrusion of legionnaires had returned the streets to peace and celebration.

Titius remembered his father's vice grip on his shoulder, ensuring that his son remained impassive despite his churning anger and horror.

When the young zealots had spent all their energy and the force of their blows stalled, Titius disciplined himself enough to focus on their words.

"Roman dog!"

"Galilean pig!"

"African snake!"

They didn't seem to know who or what he was.

"You forgot 'friend of Barabbas,'" Titius added.

Their kicks stopped immediately. "You know Barabbas?" one asked.

Titius uncoiled himself and got stiffly to his knees. "I have been imprisoned by the Romans in Sepphoris. I escaped from a work crew only three days ago. I'm so hungry…" He managed a sly smile. "…for the taste of apricots."

Two of the youth grabbed him by the elbows and helped him to his feet. "You haven't given the secret words."

Titius reviewed Jaennus's careful instruction: "The last zealot we tortured gave us the words 'the apricots are ripe,'" Jaennus had said. "There are probably new words now, but you can use them to show at least some connection."

Titius bowed his head before his captors. "When I was last active, we used 'the apricots are ripe.' I'm sure there are new words by now, but I've been kept isolated by the Romans. I need protection."

The realization that they'd beaten a friend of Barabbas seemed to energize their compassion.

"Let me check that wound for you," one said as he cut off the hem of his own tunic and tied it tightly in place.

The shortest of the three ran to the shed and returned a moment later with a gift. "Here's a handful of apricots to help you get some strength," he said.

"I'm Philip," said another. "I'll lead you to the camp so you can get the help you need. They'll make sure you're safe."

Titius nodded and followed. They passed the remnants of burned fields and empty buildings.

The shrub forest they travelled through was high enough to block any visible landmarks except the steep climb up to a tableland beyond. In a forested ravine, Titius followed his guide into a clearing where they approached three small mud shelters. The hills rose like protective parents around a sleeping child.

Titius scanned the setting, picking up important details from his training. Two men knelt sharpening swords while eight women weaved baskets. Two other women breastfed babes and shouted instructions to a trio of toddlers picking flowers at the edge of the clearing. Dozens of chickens pecked at the ground and ignored the newcomers. Songbirds fluttered and sang as though they were inhabiting Eden itself. Green grass grew knee-high in the shade.

Four young women stood up to meet Titius at the perimeter of the settlement. A tall brunette with almond-shaped eyes took the lead.

"Philip, who have you brought us?" asked the woman.

"A friend of Barabbas heading for the southern camp," Philip answered. "He yearns for apricots, but he needs healing."

She nodded toward a stump illuminated by a patch of sunlight. "Sit there. I'm Cassandra."

Titius followed. "I'm David. Thank you for your help."

Cassandra tended to his wounds with a simple herbal ointment and a strip of torn cloth. She didn't say a word before handing him over to two others for the night.

By nightfall, Titius was asleep on a mat in the corner of a zealot shelter.

The sound of a pigeon's clicking feet against stone alerted him to the arrival of a new day. Its call was loud in the still morning air. The first trickles of daylight crept through a blanket that had been hung over the hut's window, the light competing with a single lamp that flickered dimly. A tiny spiral of smoke twisted up into the darkness.

Titius watched as two women rose from across the room.

"Miriam," said one to the other. Her long braided hair reached almost to her waist. "The bird is here… it is a message from Barabbas."

"Yes, Sarah."

The woman with the braided hair secured her outer wrap and slipped out the door. The other woman, Miriam, sat down again, propping herself up on an elbow and looking in his direction. Satisfied that he wasn't going anywhere, she eventually lowered her head to her mat.

The room was generously equipped with weapons—spears, swords, and clubs. Sets of grappling hooks rested on pegs driven into a wall lined with stacks of crates. The smell of strong goat cheese and apricots arose from the stash. Faint perfume, like the wild roses in his mother's garden in Rome, drifted by.

"Come here, pigeon," a soft voice coaxed from outside the window. "Now hold still."

The woman with the braids, Sarah, apparently succeeded in her task of relieving the bird of its message.

Once back inside, Sarah walked straight toward Titius and nudged him with her foot. Titius feigned awakening.

Miriam sat upright. "Sarah, what are you doing?"

"Show me your neck," Sarah demanded to Titius.

Titius slowly rose to a kneeling position, shirtless apart from the wrapping around his wound. Sarah ran her hands needlessly across his muscular back and shoulder before tracing her finger along the faint scar made by Sestus.

"Barabbas says we should check his neck." Sarah bent closer than she needed to. "You definitely have a scar."

"You should wait until Benomi returns," Miriam urged her.

Sarah cupped Titius's chin in her hand and tilted his head up. She ran her fingers through his beard and under his chin. "Look at me! Are you truly a friend of Barabbas or just another spy? If you're a spy, we'll butcher you and feed you to the dogs."

Titius stared calmly into her eyes.

She finally released him with a laugh. "Miriam, he has the eyes of a child."

Sarah backed away toward a small table just as a third woman entered and began to lay out food. Sarah twisted her braid up onto her head and fastened it with a headband.

"Who is the woman in your life?" Sarah asked as Titius rose.

Titius watched Sarah tie off her shawl at the shoulder. "I have no woman. My loyalty is to one man."

Sarah scooped up a wooden bowl and filled it with pistachio nuts, apricots, and cheese.

"You are a man," she cooed. "Surely you have known love. Do you look on me then as someone who can feed your stomach… or as someone who can feed your passions?"

She handed him the bowl.

Titius glanced at Miriam and saw the scowl in response to Sarah's flirtation.

"You are no doubt the favored wife of someone very close to Barabbas," Titius remarked. "I would be a fool to mistake your actions for an invitation."

Sarah smiled coyly and stepped away. "I see you know Barabbas well. Even now we are being watched. If you laid a hand on me, we'd have removed that scar on your neck along with the rest of your head."

From behind a crate, two men rose into view. One of them Titius recognized from the night before; he had been sharpening his sword. This time he held a dagger. He moved toward Titius and grabbed an apricot from the dish which Titius still held.

"Eat quickly," said the man. "We will be travelling soon."

Miriam held out a long robe and a shepherd's staff. "Put these on," she said. "You will travel with the shepherds to our southern farm in the Decapolis."

"Is there a head covering?" Titius asked.

"You should have brought your own," Miriam replied. "Do you really expect us to believe you came here without the proper clothing? Certus and Mathias will certainly find out who you are."

Titius shrugged. "I have nothing to hide."

"It's obvious you have nothing to hide." Miriam threw the robe at his feet. "You had Sarah drooling all over you. Now, cover up. She's promised to a cousin of Barabbas."

The whole group walked outside the hut and approached a pair of horses that had been harnessed together, with a large box laid across their backs. A group of shepherds were buzzing around the horses, hoisting a young boy up so he could sit on the box and help guide the animals.

"Did someone die?" Titius whispered to Miriam. "It looks like a coffin."

"Just make sure it isn't yours," Miriam said. "The shepherds' dogs will want to test your scent. I hope you're not afraid of dogs."

When the shepherds were ready to leave, Titius followed behind them with their large flock of sheep.

Along the way, they passed a herd of oryx foraging at a small oasis, and Titius became fascinated by them. Their white bodies and black leggings set them apart, but their incredible features had to be the pair of long horns rising like spears from their skulls. When the animals stood sideways, they resembled the mythical one-horned flying horses which Cleopas had told him about as a child.

"Those animals are sacred to us," one of the elderly shepherd guides explained, his weathered old hands gripping his staff. He had introduced himself as Hosea. "Look over there, by those acacia trees. See those desert deer eating the fruit? And right behind them? Those are addax. They look like large cows with long, twisted horns. They're sacred, too."

Titius examined the animals. "It all seems so peaceful and quiet here."

Hosea released a belly laugh, a rumble of joy. "The zealot who cuts throats for a living never finds peace anywhere. "Of course, you would know that. Tell me of your sacrifices for the cause."

Titius watched a wolf skulking along the edge of a bluff as it hunted passing sheep. The shepherds' dogs barked their warnings and rushed to stand between the predator and the flock.

The shepherds ignored the sideshow and kept plodding.

Titius used the moment to change the subject. "Hosea, do you have to face down many predators out here?"

"It is not the animal predator you need to worry about in this area."

"What do you mean?"

A gust of wind caught Hosea's salt-and-pepper beard, causing it to billow off his chest. "Bedouin raiders may be ahead. You will fight for us."

"What will I fight with?" Titius asked.

"That is none of my concern," the shepherd replied, quickening his pace. His sandaled feet stepped with confidence around each rock, over each dip, and up each incline. "Now, tell me a story of your conquest."

Titius worked to keep up. "My stories are the same sort which your grandchildren will tell to their great-grandchildren."

Hosea stopped, and Titius almost crashed into him. "Tell me what you know about the new Messiah. We hear that he has come to take our land from the Romans and finish our peace."

Titius stared at him hard. What had the man heard? Where was Cleopas when he was needed? As a Hebrew, Cleopas knew all their ancient stories.

"By his hand or ours, we need deliverance," Titius said. "Many Messiahs have arisen without success. Time will tell us whether his claims are true."

Hosea began to walk again. "So, you have met him? You have heard the words of Yeshua ben Yuseph? You have seen his magic?"

"I have only heard of him. The Romans spoke of him while I was imprisoned."

Hosea nodded. "Yes. Now, you are stalling. Tell me these stories of yours, the ones my grandchildren will tell my great-grandchildren."

Titius racked his mind for every story he had heard from Jaennus, every tidbit that had been stripped from the souls of tortured zealots.

"Most of my feats were accomplished in Alexandria and Libya," Titius said, grasping for a story to appease the old man. "Perhaps you have heard of the desert fox."

Hosea cleared a branch off the path with his staff. "Yes, he is well known. Barabbas says he may be the true father of the Sicarii, those of us who cut the necks of these Jews who dare to cooperate with Rome. How do you know this desert fox?"

Titius sensed the intensity of the question and called off his plan to pass himself off as the desert fox. The old shepherd might even know this man personally.

"The fox was my teacher," Titus said after lifting his gourd to swallow the last of his water. The noonday sun seemed hotter today. "There were four of us he trusted in his inner circle. He often sent us in his place to carry out attacks, to make it appear that he was everywhere at once."

Hosea pointed at an outcropping of rocks near some scrub trees. "There, see? That is the true fox."

Titius squinted to see what the shepherd was pointing at. A moment later, he spotted a fennec fox hiding in the scrub.

"He has ears like a bat, absorbing every word you say," Hosea said. "His golden brown fur blends in with the shadows of the stones." The shepherd used his cane to point a little farther away. "Near him are the rock hyrax. You can hear them chattering, warning the other life around us."

The voice of Cleopas chose that moment to reappear: *"You arrogant fool. He knows you're lying. For all you know, Hosea himself is this desert fox. They're leading you into a trap."*

Chapter Six

When the sun reached its apex, the shepherds turned and scaled a small hill.
"Have you been up here before?" Hosea asked.
"No."
"Toward the Great Sea, across the Jordan, is Beth-Shean." He pointed north. "Damascus is there, and Canatha as well." Next, he pointed east. "On this side of the Jordan, there's Gerasa, Gadara, Pella, Philadelphia, Capitolias, Raphana… every king in his own empire despising and embracing all things Greek, Roman, and Hebrew. We live as chameleons among them."

Hosea confidently led the way down the other side of the hill as the dogs rallied the sheep. The sounds of bleating, barking, and shouting blended together.

Hosea untied another gourd of water from his pack and handed it to Titius. "Drink a little," he said.

Titius took a sip and handed it back.

"How long have you been with Barabbas?" Titius asked.

"If you know Barabbas, as you claim, then you know: don't ask questions."

Titius slowed his pace.

A shepherd boy soon fell into step with him. The lad came to Titius's shoulder and wore a striped cap. His stride was as steady as Hosea's.

"I heard you question the master," the boy said. "No one does that. The only way to learn is to listen to their stories around the fire."

"What's your name?" Titius asked.

"You still ask questions?" The boy smiled. "I'm Jonathan."

"And I'm David," Titius said. "The Hebrews have a story, you know. A king's son named Jonathan once befriended a future king named David. Perhaps that story is an omen for you and me."

"I don't believe in omens." Jonathan pointed across the Jordan, which had just come into view. "See the vultures circling near Beth-Shean? Some would call those omens. More likely, it's merely a sign that a wolf has killed a sheep. Or a Sicarii has cut someone's throat… someone who was caught helping a Roman."

The dogs started barking furiously, causing the shepherds to cluster around the pair of horses carrying the box. Two shepherds ripped off the box's lid and began to produce spears, swords, and daggers. As they handed them out, Hosea grabbed a bow with arrows.

"Choose your weapon," Hosea said to Titius. "In fact, you'll lead us. If you fought with Barabbas, this will be your chance to prove it."

Titius chose two long-bladed spears.

They continued on, warily, closing on the Jordan. When they arrived at the riverbed, six Bedouin horsemen charged out from a copse of low trees, carrying curved Arab swords.

Titius rushed forward.

"On your stomachs, side by side!" he yelled. "Plant your spear butts and point them toward the horses' hearts! Form a wedge beside me!"

Several of the young shepherds threw themselves on their bellies next to him and raised their spears.

"Secure those spears in the ground," Titius said. "Like this!" He showed them how to brace a spear in a divot of earth.

Hosea began to shoot arrows, and suddenly the leading Bedouin fell from his horse. The others spread out to form a wall.

Cleopas's voice shrilled in terror. *"You fool, they'll trample us!"*

From his right hand, Titius hurled a spear into the chest of the closest horse. It reared and threw its rider to the ground. It thrashed, driving the spear in further. As it rolled, one of its hooves caught its rider across the knee and he let out a scream.

The next Bedouins veered to avoid the shepherds' spears as another man fell prey to Hosea's arrows.

The first fallen rider got to his feet and charged at Jonathan. Titius lunged with his second spear and left the attacker writhing. Jonathan finished him off with a dagger to the throat.

Another shepherd felled the Bedouin who'd been shot with an arrow. Several dogs then rushed in to ensure his demise.

The surviving Bedouins retreated, unwilling to lose any more of their numbers. They fled, chasing after the riderless horses now running off along the riverside.

The shepherds closed ranks.

"What do we do with the bodies?" Titius asked.

Hosea kicked the three dead Bedouins. "Leave them. Once we're gone, the others will come back, otherwise the wolves or hyenas will get them—"

The sound of a sheep's terrified bleating caught their attention and Titius spun. With one hand, he grabbed the bow from Hosea. He planted himself, nocked an arrow, and shot toward the brush.

"What are you doing?" Jonathan demanded, scanning the bushes. "Are they back?"

Titius returned the bow to Hosea and started walking toward the spot where he'd aimed. "Look."

At the edge of the brush, a wolf lay sprawled on the ground, a lamb held in its jaws. The lamb squirmed, but the wolf was still, an arrow having pierced its heart.

Jonathan raced over and freed the bloodied lamb.

"Barabbas will be pleased you're back with us," Hosea remarked.

Over the course of the afternoon, they traversed short stretches of desert and then rested in oases where sheep and shepherd alike could drink.

At the third oasis, Jonathan sat down next to Titius.

"You asked Hosea how long he'd known Barabbas and he told you not to ask questions. He will not answer you, but I will," Jonathan said. "Hosea has known Barabbas since before he was called Barabbas. He got that name because his father was honored among our people. You remember the farm where we met you?"

While Jonathan spoke, Titius kept his eye on Hosea bantering with two other shepherds. "I saw the remains of a farm. It was burned, and the orchard cut down."

Jonathan scooped up water with his gourd. "I used to eat apricots there when I was small. It's where my father died, you know. Fighting Romans. The legate sent spies disguised as harvesters to infiltrate us."

"Did you eliminate them with your dagger?"

"No." Jonathan shuddered, shaking his head. "I wasn't even born yet. The Romans came in with a legion and destroyed our families. Barabbas was just a youth, and he was out with the sheep when he saw the smoke rising. He found them all with their throats cut. Now he cuts the throats of all who help Rome. Rome showed no mercy, so we show Rome no mercy."

Delayed by the Bedouin attack, they didn't get far before the sun dipped below the horizon. The quarter-moon cast its dim light over the camp as they corralled their sheep and lit small fires. A dog and a shepherd rested by each fire.

Hosea motioned for Titius to join him on a slow walk away from the camp. The occasional sounds of animals crashing through the bush on either side sent shivers up Titius's spine, but Hosea pressed on as if he didn't notice the noises. Hours passed as the moon slid to its zenith.

An owl's screech stopped Hosea in his tracks.

"We're not alone," he said.

He cupped his hands around his mouth, repeated the screech, and waited. Within moments, two sentries stepped onto the path holding small clay lamps. After speaking with Hosea, they lit torches for Hosea and Titius before returning to their hidden posts.

"This camp survives by silence," Hosea said. "When we reach the gate, don't say a word. Sleep where they tell you. We'll speak further in the morning."

Titius followed Hosea past the sentry, through the gate, and into the sleeping enclosure.

The walls around the small village were a foot higher than he. The moonlight showed an orchard of trees surrounding dozens of small plastered homes covered in thatched roofing. Before they got too far, a pair of burly men thrust torches into Titius's face. Someone else grabbed him from behind and tied his arms.

"Roman pig!" one of the zealots muttered. "You look like one and you smell like one."

"I just came for the apricots," Titius said.

The punch to his jaw made him wish he'd heeded Hosea and stayed silent.

The two sentries escorted Titius across a small courtyard to a shed with its door open. They threw him inside, still tied up, and he stumbled. The smell of goat dung was strong; the ground seemed thick with it. He maneuvered himself into a sitting position against a wall.

Hours later, the door was flung open and Jonathan stepped inside, holding up a torch.

"David, the people here don't seem to know who you are. I told them how you rescued us, so they say I can release you as long as you stay with me until morning." He backed away, covering his nose. "Why did they put you in the dung shed?"

Titius braced himself against the wall and struggled to his feet. "I need to wash," he said.

Jonathan led him to a small barrel of water where he cut Titius's hands free and handed him a rag and a fresh tunic. "The women will be arriving soon. Wash and I'll meet you here later."

When the sun rose, Hosea met Titius outside the dung shed. Despite the wash and the new tunic, Titius still smelled.

"I see you survived the night," Hosea remarked. "You should find a better place to sleep."

Titius gritted his teeth. "I'm hungry."

"The women will be here soon," Hosea replied. "I'm going back for the sheep. They don't trust you, but Jonathan has agreed to take responsibility for you."

After a breakfast of flatbread, goat cheese, almonds, and dates, Jonathan led Titius past the gate and up a nearby hill where they had a good view of the surrounding countryside. Desert stretched to the southeast, the Jordan Valley lay west, and low-lying scrubland led the way south toward the sea.

Titius and Jonathan sat and watched the clouds play overhead. At one point, Titius marveled as they formed the unmistakable shape of a dragon. His father had once told him a story about meeting a dragon.

"During my campaign in Gaul," his father had whispered to Titius as the boy got into his bed. "It was twice as tall as my tallest warrior. My men outflanked the dragon and hurled their javelins. The weapons bounced off its hide."

"Did it eat you, Father?" Titius had asked.

His father had crouched low. "Only the optio and I dared track it. When we found it sleeping in a cave, I hurled my javelin into its belly and its whipping tail almost took off my head. I dropped my lamp and there was nothing but darkness. It took us all day to find our way out of that cave."

The memory made Titius smile.

"What makes you smile?" Jonathan asked.

Titius glanced back up at the clouds. "Memories of home," he said as the dragon cloud floated past.

Jonathan pointed to the hilltop where Herod had built the Machaerus prison. "Many zealots die in that prison."

"Where is Barabbas?"

"He comes here often when he's home." Jonathan sighed. "He carries a heavy burden. At the end of this, he'll either die in prison or rule in Jerusalem."

"I've proven myself. Let me talk with him."

"Barabbas and the Sicarii leaders are with the Parthians right now, trying to open a route for more weapons. No one here knows what to do with you."

Titius gazed down and tried to memorize the layout of the zealot settlement. He counted twenty-one homes nestled near the wall. Six buildings formed a line down the middle of the settlement. Apricot trees and apple trees grew along the northern and southern walls. A large pen for the sheep stood next to the gate. A well was central to everything.

"The Romans send new reinforcements every month," Titius said. "Why does Barabbas keep going?"

Jonathan frowned. "If you know Barabbas, you know that his grandfather fought in the battle for Sepphoris, where they stole the Roman armory. Caused great losses. It took years, but the Romans learned the identity of the leaders and sent spies after them." Jonathan heaved a stone over the edge of the hill. "Barabbas's father cared for his people with the money he earned from his apricot orchard. Most people on this side of the Jordan have worked for him. He kept them alive during the drought. When the Romans invaded Galilee, he helped many refugees and opened trade routes with the Parthians to supply everything they needed."

Titius pulled at a piece of grass and chewed on it. "So Barabbas's father died fighting for his people?"

Jonathan picked up a rock and threw it, aiming at a chicken down the hill. He missed. "No. He taught people how to dry apricots during times of hunger. He was a man of peace."

"Then why did the Romans kill him?"

"A Roman legion looking for Parthians stopped at his farm. They took bushels of apricots, more than they needed, and some people protested. So the Romans killed them. They then killed the witnesses, burned the buildings, and chopped down the orchard. Barabbas's father was on his knees pleading when they speared him with a javelin."

"But why does Barabbas cut Galilean throats?"

"Because the Galileans helped the Romans."

Titius nodded. "What can I do to help until Barabbas returns?"

Jonathan paused. "Do you see the smoke rising near the well? The elders are calling us to come back."

Jonathan started down the hill without answering Titius's question.

When they got back to the village, four old men sat at the gate. The bowl of ripe apricots in front of them contrasted with their emaciated frames.

Their spokesman looked hardly strong enough to lift the sword he held, but he spoke in a commanding voice: "Kneel and bare your neck."

Titius complied.

The old man ran his finger along Titius's scar. "It is neither recent nor old," he said. "We do not believe you are who you claim to be."

He laid the edge of the sword on Titius's neck, and Titius didn't move. The cool blade angled against his throat. One quick movement would finish it all. His hands trembled until he clenched them into stillness. No prayer arose.

"No god can save you now," Cleopas whispered. *"Let them finish it quickly."*

Titius focused on the steel under his chin, knowing that he could only make one decision: wait.

"We don't know who you are, but you've shown yourself willing to protect us and our flocks," the elder said. He removed the sword and Titius inhaled. "Most of the men will be gone for a time. We're charging you with protecting our women and children until Barabbas returns. Your betrayal will mean your death."

The next morning, Titius sat by the well watching a heron fly overhead. He had gotten dressed for action now, wearing a chiton that he'd hitched up to his knees. His belt held a razor-sharp dagger, and a javelin and sword rested against the base of the well.

A young woman stepped out of the small shelter next to him. Her uncovered hair glistened like flax in the morning sun. Her long chiton gleamed white, draped with a thick blue cloak, a himation. She could have passed for a Roman noblewoman.

She marched toward him, eyeing him up and down. "So you're my new guardian," she said. "I'm Phoebe, Barabbas's sister. Your life is now in my hands and mine in yours." She pointed at the bucket next to the well. "My mother needs water. Bring it and we'll talk."

"I'm David," Titius said.

"It doesn't matter who you say you are. Bring the water." Phoebe spun on her heel and walked back through the door she'd come from.

Titius drew the water and then knocked firmly on her door. An elderly woman, frowning at the sun, opened the door and stood aside. She wore her himation pulled over her head and across her neck.

"I'm Elizabeth, mother of Barabbas, Phoebe, and two others who are no more."

"And I'm David," Titius said. "Without father, without mother, without anyone to call family."

Elizabeth motioned him inside. "Leave the water by the door. We have porridge, bread, and fruit. There are no servants here." She pointed to a basin inside the door. "Pour your own water. Wash your own feet."

Titius set down the bucket of water. Elizabeth waited a moment, then picked it up, poured a little into the basin, and moved it to an inner room. Titius doffed his sandals, stepped into the basin, and scrubbed off the dirt.

Phoebe appeared without her blue himation, her hair secured by a crimson band. Titius found himself staring. His pulse quickened and he fought to control his breathing.

She motioned for him to sit on a stool near a small table.

When Elizabeth returned with flaxseed porridge, Phoebe retrieved a platter of dried fruits and cheese.

"Eat quickly," Phoebe said. "Today, the shepherds are away and we must go to the pool and bathe. You'll learn to guard us without looking, or your eyes will be a delicacy for our dogs."

Not a skill he'd been taught, but clearly this was another test. Would they never finish testing him?

Titius tested a spoonful of the porridge. It had an unfamiliar flavor. "If I'm to guard you, I must guard my own life," he said. "Until I'm sure this is safe, I cannot eat it."

"How dare you malign my mother's hospitality? Eat what you're given."

Titius stood. "If your brother himself offered me this porridge, I couldn't eat it without knowing it was safe."

"Suit yourself," Phoebe said. "Don't complain of hunger. Now come. We must bathe quickly."

The pool was the result of a large spring at the base of the hill, surrounded by trees. Titius checked a cavern near the spring and assured the women that all was clear. Titius stood with his back to the seven women, several hundred paces from the pool, and tried to ignore their laughter and splashing. He especially tried to ignore the crude comments Phoebe threw in his direction. Even now she dared him to turn and die.

He occupied his mind remembering the Roman baths near his villa back home. Naked men and women had strutted freely as they dipped in the frigidarium, tepidarium, and hot springs before enjoying a massage. This land's preoccupation with modesty didn't make sense, but testing it wasn't worth his life.

"You can look now," came Phoebe's voice. "We're decent."

Fearing another test, Titius refused to turn. "Follow me home."

Several hundred paces on, Phoebe grabbed his arm. "Wait! My mother can't walk this fast."

Her touch sent fire racing through him, but he didn't react. He simply waited for her to walk in front of him. She wore a clingy white chiton. Her hair hung loose and dripping.

Titius looked away.

"You've saved your eyes," she said. "Now keep us safe. It isn't just shepherds, Bedouins, and Romans we fear. Its snakes, lions, and wolves. If you can't look *at* me, at least look *out* for me."

Titius kept his eyes on the trail, glancing back every few minutes to track the women's progress.

"I was told to guard the women and children," he said. "I see women, but no children."

"They'll be brought out once we know you're safe," she said. "Nothing is more valuable than our children."

"Too bad that wasn't the case in Rome," Cleopas taunted.

A knot twisted in Titius's stomach. Back home, the few beggar children he'd seen by the market were routinely beaten. There had been boys and girls living at the temples whose purpose was only to pleasure worshippers. No children had laughed and played in the gardens.

They returned without incident, and Titius wandered around the compound's perimeter while the women ground grain, made bread, washed clothes, swept their homes, hauled water, and chatted and laughed together.

At noon, harvesters arrived with baskets of apricots. Titius guarded the women; none of the workers gave them trouble. One behemoth who got close to Phoebe backed off quickly when Titius raised a dagger to his throat.

The women fed the crew, sent them back on their way, and processed the harvest. Some fruit was set aside for eating, some to trade, and the rest for drying.

Phoebe stood in the courtyard, her hair braided back as she gave instructions to the women. Not once did she stop pitting apricots.

"Dorcas, put these in those baskets. Eleah, crush these apricots for supper. Lydia, bring me another load and take away these pits."

When a young woman, barely out of childhood, made a point of brushing against Titius and making eyes at him, Phoebe chastened her quickly. "Tamaris, mind yourself. The elders will choose you a man who isn't so dangerous."

Toward late afternoon, she passed Titius along his patrol route.

"I think I could use another trip to the pool," she said with a smile.

"I thought you said I was dangerous."

"Are you?"

Heat ran up his neck, but Titius extinguished the image rising in his mind.

"Oh, you're such a man," she said. "You see a woman and can think of only one thing. How did you survive guarding us at the pool the first time?"

"I'm just a man," he said.

"You're a wise man to remain alive. For now. Next, you'll teach our young men to fight. They'll be here tomorrow." She looked over her shoulder at him as she continued on. "And you were right: the porridge was poisoned. And there was an archer hiding to pierce you with an arrow if you turned your head toward us bathing."

Chapter Seven

Three weeks into combat training, Titius had taught his recruits those skills he was willing to share. However, Sestus and Titius's fellow assassins might soon be facing these zealots on the other side of the battlefield—and Titius would be expected in Sepphoris soon.

Even more than the training, he enjoyed engaging in philosophical and religious debates with the young men. They often gathered round the fires to argue until they dropped off to sleep.

Jeremiah was the tallest, with tight dark braids and an early beard. Amnon was short, muscular, and went barefoot every chance he got. Simon was the swiftest, but Issachar the smartest; he could quote the Torah verbatim, recall every detail of any place he'd ever been, and was often the first to find a solution to military problems. Timna was the best archer, Magdiel the shepherd could knock an apricot off a tree with a slingshot, Iram could track and hunt almost anything, Shaul could anticipate the weather, and Ethan could outdo anyone in storytelling. All loved to debate.

One day, while they all sat around a fire, Issachar pointed in the direction of the town of Gadara. "These pagans copy Rome and Greece. They claim we're barbarians because we're circumcised. Before we cut Roman throats, I think we should cut pagan ones."

Titius shifted uncomfortably. "We're guests in their land. When you have power, you can consider your options. But these pagans merely live as their gods demand."

"Are you saying that Jupiter is the same as Yahveh? That Baal is the same as Molech?" Timna asked, trying to spark an argument.

"Romans are descended from pigs," Shaul declared. "Their leaders are cowards and they hide behind their legions. The generals rape, steal, and destroy everything they touch. Isn't it true, David?"

"David, is it true?" Ethan asked.

Titius adjusted the scarf round his neck. "I can only tell you what I've heard. Romans train their legionnaires harder than we've ever trained—"

"Not true," Magdiel interrupted. "I can hardly feel my body at the end of the day."

Titius waited for the laughter to finish. "A legionnaire can carry almost half his own weight in his pack—tools, weapons, food, and trowel. Every day they march twenty miles, then build a new camp before nightfall. The rule of decimation means they'll never back away from death."

"What's 'decimation'?" Issachar asked.

Titius stirred the embers of the fire. "At the end of each battle, legions are judged. If any legion hasn't done its best, the men are divided into groups of ten." He gathered sticks, then moved around the circle, letting each recruit choose one. He sat. "Each member of the group draws sticks. The one who loses is clubbed to death by the others: decimation. Every tenth man is killed. They'd rather be killed by an enemy than by their own."

"How can we fight against beasts like that?" Amnon asked.

"In a new way," said Titius.

Iram raised the bow he'd been stringing. "They'll always need archers."

"Maybe so," replied Titius. "Let's clean up and secure for the night. Set your guards."

The young men spread their blankets around the fire and secured their weapons near their beds. A jackal barked and crickets chirped off in the darkness. Clouds obscured the moon. The flames died down to embers.

"David, tell us about the senators," Ethan said. "To help us sleep."

"By the will of the gods, Rome may destroy herself before her enemies do," Titius said as he laid a log on the embers. "Generals strive for their own glory and power, but the senators conspire and plot against each other. Emperors survive by being suspicious of those closest to them."

"It sounds," Shaul mused, "like the best way to defeat the Romans is to let them destroy themselves."

They all cheered at that.

"But there's great discipline among the troops," Titius went on. "Four thousand eight hundred troops in a legion, ten cohorts of four hundred eighty. Six centurions, each overseeing eighty soldiers, ten groups of eight."

"How do you know these things?" Magdiel asked.

"It's my job to know," Titius said. "Now get some sleep. We'll talk tomorrow."

"Tell us about the chariot races," Ethan called. "And gladiators. Who's the greatest warrior?"

"Tomorrow I'll tell you about the glory of Rome," Titius said. "To face your enemy, you must know your enemy better than he knows you. Until then, embrace glory in your dreams."

The next day's march passed without incident, although the men kept begging him for details about life in Rome. Two days passed before he settled in back at the camp. His stomach rumbled as he sat with his back against the wall at Phoebe's house.

"David," she called from within. "Who impressed you the most from this group of recruits?"

"Each has his own strength," Titius responded.

Phoebe emerged holding a bowl of steaming stew. "It's goat and it isn't poisoned. I'll taste it if you want."

"You trust me, so I trust you."

"Barabbas will be pleased with you, David."

"One day you'll slip up," Cleopas whispered. *"They'll find out who you are."*

As Titius fulfilled his duties, it seemed to him that Phoebe went out of her way to show up, needing his help, wherever he was working. Although she was self-sufficient and independent, Phoebe had even insisted he go with her on her morning walk from time to time. She would prolong their time away by identifying songbirds, mesmerizing him with her knowledge of kingfishers, bee-eaters, flycatchers, and warblers.

One morning, on just such a walk, a pair of swans flew onto a pond nearby. Phoebe grabbed Titius by the arm. "This is the best day of my life," she declared.

"The day is as lovely as you are," Titius responded.

"Whether you're David or someone else, I almost don't care anymore."

"What do I still need to prove?"

"Tell me truthfully about who your parents were," she said.

"My father was a Roman soldier and a businessman. My mother was Jewish."

"Why are you here?"

"Right now, I'm here because of you."

Phoebe twirled in circles, her arms spread like wings. "This is the best day of my life," she said again.

"She knows something," Cleopas growled. *"Watch out."*

His fear of discovery grew the next evening by the fire. Ethan began telling a story about a crazy relative of his who had lived among the tombs nearby.

"This man is not normal," he said. "He lives among the pig farmers. He cuts himself and screams. My cousins have chained him and he breaks free as if the chains were string. It's rumored he's possessed by a thousand demons. We should get *him* to lead us against the Romans. He could defeat them all by himself."

Issachar and Amnon stood.

"David, take us to this man," Issachar pleaded. "Persuade him to fight the Romans."

Cleopas screamed, *"Don't! I won't be able to control the others."*

What others? Titius thought.

"David?" Shaul said. "Did you hear us? Will you take us to see the demoniac?"

"Taking you on this mission will have to be cleared by Barabbas," Titius said. "Tonight, we must learn to navigate by the stars."

They were silent as Titius pointed out the star markers and marched his charges home. Back at camp, the young men went back to their jobs as harvesters and shepherds. Titius was left to guard the women and listen to old men's stories.

Phoebe's young cousin Tamaris talked to him a little more each day. "Tell me, David," she asked one morning. "Which woman are you most likely to wed?"

Titius smiled. "Perhaps Barabbas will decide."

"I see how Phoebe looks at you," said Tamaris. "Always trying to be near you. Surely you notice."

That afternoon, Titius guarded the women by the pool. He stood in his usual spot and listened to the laughter behind him. He tried to think of Abigail back in Rome, but her face was fading from memory. Phoebe's face often surfaced in her place these days.

Once again, on the way back to camp, Phoebe walked beside him.

The next day, Titius found Tamaris beside the gate, sobbing.

"What's the trouble?" he asked.

She kept sobbing until Phoebe arrived and shooed him away.

"She's become a woman and doesn't understand her body," Phoebe said. "She needs to be alone."

Titius remembered an incident from his years as a young man. He had once ordered a slave girl to get him some water, and the girl had knelt and whimpered. Titius had moved to strike her, but Abigail had stepped in, explaining that the girl had become a woman and that he should let her be. Only years later had Titius understood the monthly suffering all women endure.

"David, she will find her peace," Phoebe said, calling him back to the present. "We all survive this ordeal. Come, walk with me."

Titius followed Phoebe into the orchard.

"You see this fruit?" Phoebe asked. "We grow it for Barabbas. He eats it every day in memory of his father." She picked a ripe fruit and handed it to Titius. "We're all the family he has. Providing this fruit is our part in freeing our land."

"A leader like Barabbas only survives because of your loyalty."

Phoebe smiled her golden smile, the sunshine illuminating her hair like a halo. "Some of our best are already serving in places like Sepphoris, Caesarea, and Jerusalem. The weaver and his daughter in Sepphoris are especially good at infiltrating the Romans and opening the silk trade."

"What more can I do?" Titius asked.

Am I being asked to be a spy for Barabbas? he wondered. *Is Phoebe trying to set up another test for me?*

Phoebe backed up against a tree. Looking shyly at Titius, she said, "Barabbas is the man in my family who will arrange my marriage, but he's away too often. I need a man. I want you to talk with him."

Was she asking him to contact Barabbas so that a marriage could be arranged? There hadn't been any other men around.

"What do you want me to say?" he asked.

Phoebe searched his face. "David, tell him you want to be that man."

Titius's jaw dropped open. "Me?" He crushed the apricot; juice ran onto his closed fist. "How will I speak with him? You hardly know me."

"David, you took a Roman knife to your throat. You fought the Bedouins. You saved our sheep from the wolf. You guard us while we bathe. You train our new fighters." She reached for his hand. "I don't need to know any more than that."

"What have you done?" Cleopas accused.

Titius knelt, looking up at Phoebe. "You honor me more than I deserve. Where will I find your brother?"

"You don't have to find him. He'll find you."

Titius didn't sleep that night, and not just because Cleopas hounded him. What was he to do about Phoebe? What would the Romans do if their thespian assassin married a zealot, and Barabbas's sister? What would it mean to have children related to Barabbas?

If he married Phoebe and moved up in the zealots' hierarchy, he could send messages to Jaennus and limit Barabbas's effectiveness. If he married and stayed, he could bring in others to set up the network. People would trust him.

On the other hand, he'd be under Barabbas's scrutiny, and his disguise might not hold up to serious questioning.

His death wouldn't help Sestus. It wouldn't help get his estate back. It definitely wouldn't help him stay unknown.

Worst, it would mean giving up on Abigail.

He cherished the admiration that David had earned in this community. Mentoring young warriors affirmed his sense of manhood. Phoebe's trust and companionship had strengthened that sense even more. He loved the family atmosphere all around him.

Knowing his mission would lead to the deaths of passionate zealots made him regret being the cross maker's guardian.

After his walk in the apricot orchard, he entered through the gate and came face to face with Phoebe's mother. It was clear she'd been waiting for his return. She motioned for him to sit on the edge of the well.

"I don't understand why your mother called you David," Elizabeth said. "The men tell me you're not Jewish, that you don't keep the Sabbath or the dietary laws. You aren't Roman, and you don't burn incense to Caesar. You aren't

Greek. You don't worship Astarte. Are you Parthian? Armenian?" Titius remained silent. "Perhaps you're pretending to be no one. But be the man who makes my daughter happy."

Titius stared into Elizabeth's stern eyes. "I will never make a promise to your daughter I can't keep."

After another sleepless night, but before first light, he knew what he had to do: run. But had he trained the young warriors so well that he wouldn't be able to escape?

He decided to test the camp's security before dawn. He stepped into the crisp morning air and scanned the courtyard. Seven of his trainees rested outside. Two more stood fully alert with daggers, swords, and javelins. Both pulled their daggers as Titius approached.

"Good," he said to them. "I was hoping you'd be ready. Today we cross the Jordan and prove ourselves. Today you become warriors. Now, go get your supplies."

They did so, and assembled some time later by the central well.

"You know the sentries at the gates and they know you," Titius said once everyone had gathered around him. "Their replacements come before the rooster's third crow, and they've been told to watch for you. The first part of your mission will be to sneak out of the compound without anyone seeing you. If anyone sees you, make an excuse and come back." He pointed toward the far wall, away from the gate. "The second step is to find hiding places over the wall where no one will notice you. Avoid pathways, though, as you will encounter more sentries until you reach the first oasis." He picked up his wineskin and filled it from the well. "Don't draw attention to yourself. Meet at the second oasis, north of here, before the sun hits its zenith. If you don't make it, you'll be left behind. If that happens, return home and say nothing about the mission."

Jeremiah examined the wall behind them, his dark braids bobbing. Amnon flexed his fingers, anxious to begin. Timna gripped his bow tighter. Magdiel swung his slingshot in nervous circles. Shaul examined the weather. Ethan stood quietly.

"We're ready," Issachar said.

Titius paced around the well as the young men dispersed. The sentries watched him, and he waved to them. In his peripheral vision, he saw most of the recruits successfully scale the back wall before any women emerged to prepare the morning meal. Only Shaul failed to slip away unnoticed. When he was caught, Titius heard him tell a sentry that he had wanted to go out for an extra training run. The sentry refused the request and Shaul returned home, but two others managed to use the distraction as an opportunity to escape.

Once everyone else had gone, Titius tossed his pack over the wall and scaled an overhanging apricot tree where the sentries rarely patrolled. He looked back toward Phoebe's house one last time before vaulting down and scampering into the brush.

The compound dogs were silent. Even the song birds were quiet.

Several hundred paces from the wall, he withdrew from his pack a chicken whose neck he'd twisted the night before. He cut it open and drizzled its blood on a robe he often wore. He cut slashes into the robe, then tore up branches and scuffled the dirt to feign evidence of a struggle. He left the robe in a bush where it would be easily found.

Titius reached the Jabbok River by noon and decided to ford it north, where it met the Jordan. By the fork in the river, a doe and her fawn stepped out of the tall grasses to take a drink. The usual hippos and crocodiles were out of sight, and swallows darted up and down the banks. A plover stepped casually, probing the sand with its beak.

More importantly, a group of women washed their clothing on the opposite riverbank. They plunged to their necks in the water when they noticed him.

Titius stayed dressed for the crossing. Wading as far as he could stand, he then swam as slowly as he dared until his feet found the other side. The women watched him until he emerged and hid himself among the trees. He wrung out his robe as best he could and belted it knee-high.

He skirted up into the Samaritan hills and by evening managed to reach Mount Gilboa, overlooking the town of Scythopolis. His stomach growled but he refused to approach anyone to ask for food. Just one poor choice could lead to discovery.

He drank from a creek and took shelter for the night in an oak tree. In the dark, Cleopas plagued him: *"Don't go back to those Romans. Octavian and Marcus will be watching for you. By now they must know you're the heir of the estate Cretius stole. They'll kill you and say they mistook you for a deserter."*

"I suppose you think I should go back and marry Phoebe," he said aloud.

"How did you learn anything at all from me?"

Titius pressed both sides of his head, trying to shut the voice out. "I didn't. Not from you anyway."

"Don't tell me it was Abee–gail."
"Why do you think I came to this cursed land in the first place?"
"You'll never find her."
Titius broke off a small branch and threw it as far as he could.

Chapter Eight

When the sun crested the Galilean hills, Titius was rushing toward Sepphoris, having changed into one of his best disguises—that of a blind man. The time away from Jaennus had softened him; he was panting when he rounded the last corner and saw the city on the hilltop.

Sepphoris was racing to become a Roman jewel in Galilee. The year after Titius had been born, rebels had seized the armory of the hill fortress and the Syrian legate had ordered his legions to crush the town. It had been burned to the ground, the inhabitants sold into slavery. Herod Antipas, fresh from his education in Rome, had arrived as its new king and focused his energies on building a Roman masterpiece upon the ashes. Every carpenter in the area had been recruited for the work.

Herod had secured vineyards and tracts of wheat and barley to feed his population. Soldiers, artisans, slaves, traders, and many visitors had needed to be satisfied day after day to ensure happiness and peace.

On this day, when Titius got to the city gates, the legionnaires on duty were playing knucklebones, having placed wagers of salt on the outcome. They didn't question him when he passed, so he walked through and headed straight for the newly built soldiers' quarters and left a message for Jaennus: "The apricots are ripe for picking."

Titius then slipped away and wandered among the market vendors, examining goods and weighing their use for new disguises. He filled his belly with the freshest breads and the finest leeks, onions, and olives.

Near the back of the market, he noticed a bright canopy fluttering in the breeze. Under it, piles of orange fruit had been arranged into pyramids. A dozen men stood around them in animated discussion. One of them, a baker, gave him a look of recognition.

He sauntered up to the orange vendor and picked up one of the fruit. He bit into it and found its juice sweet and tangy. A flavor he'd never tasted. He washed it down with a small gourd of wine. The cost of a small coin was worth it.

Then he curled up in a quiet corner of the market, behind crates of pistachios, and fell asleep. In a dream, he and Abigail plucked petals from his villa's rose garden. Her laughter bubbled like a brook as she threw petals into the breeze. Her tightly fit chiton allowed her to blend in perfectly with the garden's marble statues. She was every goddess—Diana, huntress; Pomona, gardens and fruit trees; Aurora, the dawn; Venus, love; Ceres, mother love; and Vesta, home and family. She was the divine essence in all living things, what Romans called numina.

Nearing wakefulness, he remembered once seeing his father in the garden stroking Abigail's hair. Jealousy and anger churned inside. He had also seen his mother crouching behind a hedge, watching. How could his mother have allowed this?

He'd determined to woo Abigail, but she'd disappeared before his father returned from his next campaign. When Titius had asked Abigail's sister, Lydia, where Abigail had gone, she'd replied, "Ask your mother. Abigail needed to go home." Home for Abigail was somewhere in Galilee.

His determination hadn't wavered. He would still find her, but two things stood in his way: getting his estate back from Cretius and finishing his term as the cross maker's guardian.

He fully woke up when he overheard two of Sestus's assassins talking nearby.

"Marcus, I've heard from the guards at the city gate that Titius is back," Octavian said. "We have to find him before Jaennus does. Cretius is getting impatient."

"Not my problem," Marcus shot back. "You're the one he paid."

"I can't believe that cross maker didn't die when his throat was slashed. We should send someone else down to Nazareth to finish the job. These Sicarii are incompetent."

Titius remained huddled under his blanket, out of sight of the conspirators.

"Ah, some of Rome's finest here for some of the homeland's best fruits and nuts," said a nearby merchant to the assassins. "I'm back now, here to serve you. It seems you know what you like."

"We've eaten what we want," Octavian said to the merchant as he dropped a dozen almonds back onto the pile of nuts. "If you wanted to sell this trash, you should've stayed on your watch. You never know what kinds of thieves and no-goods are likely to take it."

Marcus laughed as the pair wandered away.

When they were gone, Titius rolled out from under his blanket.

"You stupid beggar," cried the merchant. "What are you doing here?" He kicked at Titius's ribs, but Titius blocked the kick with his shoulder.

"Alms for the blind, kind sir?" Titius chanted. "Alms for the blind?"

"I'm sorry, old man. I didn't know you were blind. Are you hungry?"

After eating his fill, Titius tapped with his cane back toward the secret passage he knew that led to the assassins' den. He took off the goatskin cap and white beard while he walked and discarded the dirty, smelly rags. Instead he wore his assassin's mask.

The entrance to the passage was hidden behind a blanket near the bakery and was just wide enough for a man to enter if he stepped sideways. Titius inhaled the heavenly scent of fresh loaves before entering the tight space.

The tunnel twisted and turned. After several sharp curves, all light disappeared. The stone walls dripped with moisture and mud mucked up Titius's sandals. He counted two hundred paces, then felt for the blanket that marked the way into the assassins' den.

He stepped through and slid into the shadows, where he immediately noted a young woman lighting a fire. The wood crackled loudly and the room filled with a dim light from the fire as she turned and began to dust a bust of Tiberius Caesar.

Titius emerged from the shadows and put out a calming hand. "Peace. Do not fear."

She bowed, the feather duster quivering in her hand. She raised a shawl to cover her mouth and nose.

"You're new," Titius said softly. "I haven't seen you before. Don't let this mask be a cause for alarm. I'm a messenger with news for the centurion."

She shook her head.

He tried again in Latin, thinking she might not have understood. "A message for the centurion. The guardian has come back to finish his duty."

She bowed, still trembling.

"Repeat the message back to me," Titius said.

She mangled the words, and it became clear she still didn't understand. He repeated it in Aramaic, Hebrew, and Greek. At last, she replied in Greek: "The guardian will do his duty."

Nazareth was less than an hour's walk by road, but Titius slipped through the forest to ensure he wouldn't be seen. He changed into a carpenter's garb before approaching the village's main gate. He set up a stash with his bigger pack in the hollow of a tall oak tree and covered it over with branches and leaves.

As he approached Nazareth, he came upon two young men dragging a large branch out of an olive grove.

"Let me help you," Titius called. "My name is Bartholomew."

The taller lad nodded. "I'm Simon, and this is Judas. We're sons of Yuseph and Miriam from Nazareth. Many thanks for the help."

"Is this Caleb ben Samson's house?" Titius asked.

Judas pointed toward the gate, a hundred paces away. "He lives with our family near the synagogue. My brother Yeshi was here yesterday helping him with his wound."

"The Sicarii cut his neck and beat him badly," Simon added.

"Then wild dogs attacked him," said Judas. "It's a miracle he made it home."

"We're going to be carpenters in Sepphoris with our father," Simon said. "He's making special sticks to help Caleb walk. We need to get him this wood."

Titius walked the length of the branch and nodded sagely. "He'll be pleased with your choice."

The two young men lifted one end of the branch and Titius hoisted the other onto his shoulder. The weight threatened to buckle his knees, so within a dozen steps Judas called for rest. They concluded it would be best if all three of them dragged their treasure.

At the gate, they stopped.

"Wait here with Samuel, the gatekeeper," Simon said to Titius. "We need to find out where to put this."

The two young men wandered off into the village.

Titius couldn't wait, though, and the gatekeeper was preoccupied with a pair of children and a goat. Titius slipped by him and made his way into the heart of the village. Near the synagogue, he found a rabbi perched on a rock, bowing over an opened Torah scroll.

Titius stepped up and waited until he was acknowledged.

"Yes, my son?" the rabbi finally said.

"Rabbi, I wish to know where Caleb ben Samson is resting. I'm a friend and want to pray for his recovery."

The rabbi stared at him with dark, piercing eyes. "If you're his friend, you should know where he lives." But he pointed toward a home not far away. "Your friend is there, at the house of Yuseph and Miriam. A miracle has happened. Perhaps he will tell you how he was healed."

Instead of walking straight up to the house, Titius hid behind a thorn hedge so he could spy into the yard. Caleb was indeed there, sitting on a bench and eating some bread. A young woman was wiping his brow. His beard had been shaved, and he had a scar on his neck that ran up to his right ear.

"He could have been killed while you were off with that zealot woman," Cleopas said. *"Your weakness for women will get you killed—and it will kill those you're responsible for."*

A middle-aged woman was sweeping the yard as chickens raced around her feet, but she soon set down her broom and went indoors.

Titius listened as Caleb and the young woman began to speak with each other.

"Why did you have to come back now?" the woman asked.

"Rebekah, I know you're betrothed," Caleb said. "I really was coming to see Yeshi."

"Those men almost killed you."

Caleb ran his hand over his scar. "I can't thank you enough for your care."

"What else am I supposed to do?" Rebekah dipped the cloth into a bucket and wrung it out. "You're like a brother to me. Maybe more."

"When will Yeshi return?"

"He's gone back to Capernaum," she said. "We hardly see him anymore, not since the rabbi and the others tried to throw him off the cliff."

"I wish I'd been here. I still can't imagine them doing that. Yeshi grew up in this synagogue."

Rebekah sat down and rested her forehead on her fists. "He's always been good, but things have changed since the Baptizer immersed him."

Caleb rested a hand on her shoulder. "He's been doing amazing things, like that wine he brought out at your sister's wedding."

"I still don't know what to believe." Rebekah stood again, brushing off his hand. "The servants say one thing, the master of the feast another."

Caleb stretched and looked around the yard. Titius ducked down to avoid being spotted.

"Your cousin says Yeshua used deep magic to stop a crisis," Caleb said.

Rebekah glared at him. "Stop a crisis? After that, he went to Jerusalem and threw the moneychangers out of the Court of the Gentiles." She picked up the broom and swept up a dust cloud. "People have started talking like he's the Messiah."

"Rebekah, we know him. These are crazy times. People want our land back. They want peace in Jerusalem."

"It's not just Jerusalem," she said. "I heard that the Samaritans think he's the Messiah, too, because of something he said to a woman there."

Caleb took the broom from her and leaned it up against the house. "Things will settle down. Give it time."

"Time? The rabbi tried to *kill* him. He doesn't have time."

"What will you do?"

"We're leaving," Rebekah said. "I'm going to Cana, and Dad will go to work in Sepphoris. The rest of the family? Capernaum. Someone has to talk sense into Yeshi."

With that, the two went into the house and shut the door.

As Titius stepped back from his hiding place, he saw the rabbi crane his neck and walk in his direction. Titius ducked behind a hedge and scooted, keeping his head down. He could imagine the rabbi trying to figure out how he had disappeared.

A child looked at him quizzically and he took off one of his sandals and played with the straps. After fumbling with it for a while, he walked around the hedge as if going into a nearby house.

Titius wanted to stay in Nazareth longer, to check in with Caleb, but Sestus needed to hear the information Titius had just learned. Yeshi had healed the cross maker from his wounds. Rumors of the Messiah were creating disturbances even in his own village.

As he slipped out of the village, Titius looked back: the frowning rabbi was watching him.

Once Titius had jogged away from the village and reached the forest, he looked for the tall oak under which he'd left his pack. Finding it, he forged through the bush, retrieved his supplies, slipped out of his carpenter's disguise, and rolled the items into a brown woolen wrap. He hid them in the hollow of the tree roots, covering them with dirt and leaves.

Titius then donned a disguise new to him: that of a farmer, barefoot and covered with a short, dirt-stained tunic. He began to walk east.

As he walked toward Sepphoris, some villagers on their way to Nazareth rushed by him. One of them, a short, stocky man in a blood-spattered apron, huffed to a stop. He smelled of blood and carried a large knife. His free hand tugged at his beard.

"Did you see a carpenter running this way?" the butcher asked between gasps. "Someone about your height and build?"

"No."

With that, the butcher left him behind.

Ten minutes later, he heard wings overhead and looked up to see a flock of quail. Several of the birds dropped around him, stunned. Titius didn't know what had caused it, but he gratefully took a few, wrung their necks, and put them in his pack.

"It's a wonder these stupid birds survive," he muttered.

He arrived before nightfall and headed toward the secret passage that led to the assassins' den. Titius paused at the blanket door and stopped short of entering when he heard Octavian's voice in the room beyond.

"Marcus and I followed him to the edge of the Jordan," Octavian was saying. "Our spies have confirmed that he's training young zealots to attack us. He'll expose us and destroy our operations."

"What does Jaennus think?" Sestus asked.

"Jaennus suggests we wait. But I think perhaps Titius is a better actor than we thought."

Sestus sounded impatient. "Are you questioning my judgment in choosing him?"

"Not at all. Perhaps the zealots have turned him. They may have told him the story of how we treated Barabbas's father."

"Send Jaennus to me," Sestus said. "Go back to Capernaum and see if Titius is hiding with the new Messiah. I hear there are zealots joining the man's ranks. Perhaps you and Marcus will become disciples of Yeshua ben Yuseph."

Titius heard footsteps, and then the distinctive sound of a door shutting.

He stepped into the room and once again found himself facing the centurion's sword. But when Sestus realized who he was, he lowered it immediately.

"For the love of Jupiter, where have you been?" Sestus demanded.

Titius knelt on one knee and offered up his dagger. "Octavian has given you his report. My neck is yours."

Sestus walked to the door and checked the hallway to see if anyone was listening in. He then looked through the curtain into the passageway. Satisfied that they were alone, he turned to Titius, still kneeling.

"Rise," the centurion said. "If you survived two months with Barabbas and his ilk, who am I to sever your neck? Especially before you've given your report. Now, sit."

Titius sat and reported everything he'd heard about Caleb and his miraculous recovery.

Sestus began to pace, rubbing his chin. "Impossible," he muttered. "I saw him after they cut his neck. He cannot be healed already. What kind of magic does this Messiah have?"

They heard a gentle banging on the door. Sestus opened it slowly and welcomed Jaennus into the chamber. The optio took off his helmet, nodded to Titius, and took his position guarding the door.

Next, Sestus asked for a report on the zealots. As Titius recounted his mission, Jaennus took notes. He said nothing about Sarah's flirtation, his sentry duty at the washing pool, or Phoebe's proposal. But he did describe his time with the shepherds, his role in fighting the Bedouins, the incident with the wolf, training the young zealots, and his eventual escape.

"Did they tell you of Barabbas's father?" Sestus asked. "How we slashed his throat and burned his precious trees?"

"The evidence I saw supports that story," Titius answered. "True or not, they believe it. And they use it to motivate their fighters."

Sestus grabbed the report Jaennus was writing and looked it over. "Go over the story again, from the beginning," he said after a moment. "When you're done, we will go over it one more time—and ask questions. I want to hear every word."

The night was half done when Sestus finally dismissed himself.

Sestus returned hours later with a servant carrying a tray of food and a flagon of wine. Jaennus followed behind, holding up the report, but Sestus waved it off and went back to pacing.

"The Sicarii killed five Nazarene carpenters last night," Sestus said. "Throats slit like pigs. This changes everything."

"Do we *know* it was the Sicarii?" Titius asked from his seat on the floor. "Jaennus says the Sicarii cut Caleb's neck a month or more ago, but he looked fine to me."

"Thanks to that Messiah healing him. I saw myself what they did to him."

"Maybe these carpenters defied their Roman masters."

Sestus stopped and stared at him. "Only the Sicarii would butcher innocent people like this. Perhaps they found out who you were and sought revenge.

Perhaps they heard about the cross maker being healed and wanted to send a stronger message."

The centurion grabbed the report from Jaennus, tore it to pieces, and threw the pieces into the fire.

"Sir?" Titius said.

"The city leaders say they are now ready for thirty thousand people to move into this city and we won't put their necks at risk because of a few zealots!" Sestus shouted. "No more compromises. I want that cross maker to cover this land with his work. We will bring peace through the power of the cross."

"This is the monster you've given your life to?" whispered Cleopas. *"You risk your soul and he pronounces your own work worthy of the flames?"*

Titius ignored the jab and watched the pacing centurion, remembering that he alone could retrieve Titius's ring from the pool of death.

Sestus chewed on a handful of almonds as he turned to Jaennus. "I don't trust Marcus and Octavian to give me an accurate report on that Messiah. Something is up with those two." He reached for more almonds, but Titius raised his hand. Sestus glared at him.

"I may know something about Marcus and Octavian," Titius said. "But I've taken the assassin's code, and we may not speak against a fellow member."

"That code is meant to protect conversation between the troops. But if you speak falsehood about another assassin, I myself will club you to death. Quickly, speak the truth."

Over the course of the next few minutes, Titius told the centurion about the conversation he'd overhead between Marcus and Octavian regarding the theft of his father's estate. He also mentioned overhearing the pair implicate themselves in the attack on Caleb outside Nazareth.

"Are you sure it was Marcus and Octavian?" Sestus asked. "Did they mention Cretius by name? Are you saying that your fellow assassins are responsible for trying to kill the cross maker I assigned you to protect?"

"Yes to all of those questions. But I was on assignment across the river in the zealot camp when the attack on Caleb occurred. I couldn't have saved him from it."

Sestus pondered this for a moment, then changed the subject. "What does it matter to you that Cretius has taken your family estate? Didn't you give that up when you chose to serve me?"

"It's a matter of family honor and justice."

The centurion threw another log on the fire. "I'll send someone to recall Marcus and Octavian. In the meantime, I want you to take over Caleb's training for a time. He's going to come back motivated for revenge and he needs to learn to be a thespian assassin like you."

With that, Sestus marched toward the door, only turning back at the last minute.

"Good report, Titius. What you've given us is too valuable for others to know. The flames and our minds will guard the truth."

"*You might as well jump into the flames,*" Cleopas urged. "*Now he sends you to waste your time training a useless soldier. After that he'll send you chasing that pseudo-Messiah. He's finished with you. Go back to Rome.*"

Titus fumed. He wouldn't run like a dog, his tail between his legs. If Cretius was nearby, thinking he was safe, Titius would do whatever it took to win back his family's estate.

It took a month before Caleb came back. Titius had grown out his beard and colored his hair black. He adjusted his accent and took on the role of Latin instructor so that Caleb could understand the conspiracies being planned by legionnaires who wouldn't suspect Jewish carpenters of knowing their language. He watched the cross maker improving his skill on horseback through the afternoons.

Marching and running with the new recruits came next. Sestus had been inspiring the seventy recruits with speeches, but he was also ruthless in his training tactics, applying whips where needed. Twenty-two men were eliminated for failing his tests of endurance.

Two months into the drills, Sestus and six other centurions gathered a cohort of five hundred fifty legionnaires. Titius, his beard cut short, joined the coordinated thud of military sandals pounding on the ground with a fearsome sound. Each legionnaire was given a sword, javelin, and shield. A hundred cavalry and hundreds of archers moved in around them like a warm blanket on a warm night. It was almost suffocating.

This was no drill. Titius tucked in tight behind Caleb, who didn't even notice those around him. His role as the cross maker's guardian was about to be put to the test. The ill-equipped villagers opposing them hardly stood a chance. Titius kept his shield up but only had to deflect one arrow falling toward Caleb. The troops continued to step over the fallen until there were no more rebels left.

Titius stood back to watch Caleb combing the battlefield for the javelin he had hurled during the charge. The cross maker found it in the body of a small boy whose neck had been severed by the killing squad. Caleb knelt to vomit until another soldier walked past and jabbed him with the butt end of a javelin.

The commander called Caleb over and chastised him before calling for Sestus.

"I expected more by now, carpenter," Sestus announced when he arrived. Titus watched quietly. "You will never be a match for Barabbas. We'll have to train you differently."

When Caleb had walked away, feeling like a dejected failure, Sestus motioned for Titius to approach. The centurion dismounted and Titius knew he was displeased even after such a clear victory.

Sestus whacked him three times hard with a rod across his arms and legs. "The failure of the student is the failure of the teacher. I will do what I need to do."

"What do you desire of me?" Titius asked, his head bowed. Welts had already risen where the rod had struck.

"Titius, you'll go to Capernaum and stay with this Messiah for a fortnight. Bring me a report of everything you see. After that, you'll go back to guarding the cross maker. By that time, he should be back with me."

Titius gathered a generous pack of supplies and slipped out of the city. Once on the road, he basked under the cloudless sky spread over mountains and valleys. Thousands of slaves were busy tending the vines in Herod Antipas's vineyards. The blistering sun had ensured a perfect crop.

Cleopas kept taunting him. *"Not only have you betrayed the zealots and the assassins, now you're also betraying the Messiah so this Roman can crucify him."*

"How can I betray someone I don't even know?" Titius growled.

"You'll find a way. Have you learned nothing from what happened with your family?"

"I've learned everything from what happened with my family. From you, I've learned nothing."

"Your whole family—your grandfather, your father, and now you—are betrayers."

His great-grandfather had been present when the Romans had crucified the six thousand slaves of Spartacus's revolt along the Appian Way. His grandfather had then turned on his own son, Titius's father, by naming him a rebel.

But that had nothing to do with Titius himself.

"When they brought the Gauls into Rome and crucified them, you pointed to me as their secret informant," Cleopas said. *"Weren't there enough crosses? You had me crucified for no reason!"*

Titius removed his pack and tossed it away as if it were a burning coal. "Not for no reason!"

"*Then for what?*"

Titius pounded his temples. "You hounded me to forget about Abigail. You mocked me over and over, telling me that a child like me could know nothing about love. You wouldn't stop."

"*You had me crucified to shut me up?*" Cleopas laughed faintly. "*Now you get to listen to me forever. At least until you join me on this side.*"

Titius kicked a boulder and cried out in pain.

After retrieving his pack, he marched through high bushes until he found a stream where he lowered his aching toes into the water. He took a long drink, curled up under a mulberry tree, and took a nap. Thankfully, Cleopas was silent.

Some time later, he awoke refreshed, his toes aching less. He heard birdsong and a fox bark nearby.

He nibbled on dates and figs, then laid out his disguises, trying to decide who to become next.

"I don't think I'll meet the Messiah until I'm sure Marcus and Octavian are back in Sepphoris," he mused aloud, holding up the wig for his blind man's costume. "There's no use risking my neck unnecessarily."

He completed his change and continued his journey.

By mid-afternoon, Titius came to a point overlooking the new town of Tiberias. He sat and watched fishing boats along the edge of the Sea of Kinnereth in Galilee. The arid basalt tableland across the lake reminded him of the land around the zealot encampment.

What had the zealots done when they'd realized he was gone? Who'd found his bloodied robe? Had Phoebe grieved for him? Did they still believe David was someone they could trust? Would he ever meet Barabbas's forces again?

By nightfall, a breathtaking sunset touched the skies with slashes of pink, orange, red, yellow, and purple. A young woman on the lakeshore raised her arms toward the heavens and Titius remembered Abigail doing the same. She'd danced and sung one of her favorite Hebrew songs. She hadn't seen him watching her from his upper balcony. She'd seemed as free as the hawk with whom she longed to fly.

Abigail had grown up in Bethsaida, near Capernaum, where the Messiah was building his following. He could make a stop there without changing his plans…

His stomach churned at the thought that he might actually see her again.

Chapter Nine

From his perch, Titius felt the vibrations of two Roman legions thundering by on their march toward Tiberias. Twenty cohorts and twelve centurions pounded their studded sandals in unison. They beat their shields with their swords in time to the march. The legionnaires wore full battle gear, tunics covered with metal breastplates. Brass helmets. Full packs. The standard-bearers' helmets were covered with open-mouthed bear heads and they wore grotesque metal masks.

He watched as flocks of birds flew out of the oak trees toward the lake. A rabbit raced by.

Titius suddenly understood young Amnon's question when he'd asked, "How can we fight against beasts like the Romans?" Indeed, how could poorly equipped followers of Barabbas accomplish anything at all under Rome's thundering feet?

Two hours after the soldiers had settled into their quarters, Titius skirted the town and continued on his way, jogging by Magdala, Gennesaret, Chorazin, and finally Capernaum. By sunset he was descending into Bethsaida, where the last of the fishermen were storing their nets for the night. Many boats were moored at the river mouth as it opened into the sea.

Titius, dressed as a Greek tradesman, sat on a log near the water where three fishermen bantered animatedly with their partners about the Messiah's actions in their town. As they said their farewells, Titius rose and walked in their direction.

"Peace to you," he said.

"Peace to you," one of the fishermen responded. "You're new here. What's your name? Where are you from?"

"I'm Alexander, and I've come from Sparta."

"You don't sound Spartan," the tallest of the three declared.

"I've spent a long time in Rome," Titius answered without hesitation.

"I'm Philip," the first fisherman said. "And this is Simon ben Jonas and Andrew, his brother."

"Did you have a big catch this evening?" Titius asked.

"Someone should give you a torch," Simon said. His broad shoulders and dark skin told of many hours pulling up nets under the sun. "There's not a fish in the boat. If you overheard us talking, it wasn't about fish. We were talking about what the Messiah did." He pointed to a house up the beach. "Galilean hospitality won't let us abandon a stranger. Come and eat with us. If you have nowhere else to stay, we have room."

"I would be grateful," Titius said. "I've only just arrived."

Cool water lapped against their sandals as they walked. The fires in the nearby village guided them home.

"The Messiah is Yeshua ben Yuseph of Nazareth," Simon continued. "He's preached all over Galilee, the Decapolis, the Jordan, even Jerusalem. We can't count the numbers who are following his every word."

"Leave these men," Cleopas hissed. *"They're deceived."*

Titius felt his spine tingle, like ants were running up and down his back. He shuddered.

"Today in Capernaum, he healed a leper with a touch," Andrew said. "He also healed a centurion's servant, with a word from a distance. He even cured Simon's mother-in-law of her fever! That's why we're so amazed."

Philip laughed and raised his hands. "He's like no other man. He casts out demons, raises the paralyzed, and calls us to leave all to follow him."

"Run!" Cleopas sounded anxious.

"Do the Romans know about this healer?" Titius asked. "Do they understand the magic he uses, the power he has over the people?"

Simon doubled over with a belly laugh. "You think Yeshua is a magician?"

"Yeshua is a prophet from God," Andrew declared. "He works under God's power."

Philip nodded. "Yeshua has spoken to all the people about God's kingdom. He's called us to be peacemakers, to forgive, to live pure lives."

"But what do the Romans think of him?" Titius asked.

Andrew grunted. "You should have seen them earlier, marching into Tiberias like they owned the world. When Yeshua heals the servant of the region's leading centurion, what can they say?"

"He tells us that when the Romans demand we carry their pack for one mile, we should carry it for two, so what can *we* say?" added Philip. "He preaches peace and love to all."

They finally reached the house and Andrew explained that it was his family's home. Philip lived up the hill, and Simon stayed with his wife's family in Capernaum down the coast.

"We can see that you're a trader," Philip said, "but where are you going from here?"

Titius looked east. "I've heard the Parthians are opening up the road for Chinese silk. I'm sure some of our delicacies and sculptures will fetch a worthwhile price."

Philip pointed out the road where several traders were pulling into an inn for the night. Their torches flickered in the breeze. "This is a crossroads of trading routes. If those traders will buy our fish, I suppose they may buy your delicacies as well. For now, come in and rest."

"I've been on the western roads a long time," Titius said, sighing as Andrew threw a log onto the fire. "Perhaps I'll rest a while and see what Galilee has to offer."

The fish-and-lentil soup and bread satisfied Titius. After dinner, the family sat around the fire and talked on and on about the Messiah.

"We saw him produce wine out of water and heal a nobleman's son in Cana," Simon exclaimed. "He's been casting demons out of people and making fevers, leprosy, and disabilities disappear."

"His teaching makes the religious leaders angry," Andrew said. "That makes the people happy. He's a defender of the weak. He fears nothing."

"Should the Romans fear him?" Titius asked.

Simon laughed. "Fear someone who preaches love and peace? Who heals and teaches people to be good followers of God and the authorities? Why?"

A week later, Titius sensed the strong presence of the man next to him, but he dared not look. It was the so-called Messiah, Yeshua ben Yuseph. He squeezed his eyelids tight, held out his rag-clad arms, and called out, "Alms for the poor."

The man's gentle laughter reached his ears. "My friend, pretending to be poor and blind doesn't mean you're not *really* poor and blind. You're more than you seem. So am I."

A torrent of human voices rolled over Titius as the crowd moved, many calling for the Messiah's mercy.

Three nights ago, Titius had given his farewells to the fishermen and slipped into Capernaum in his blind man's disguise. Ever since he'd moved unnoticed among the houses.

Titius recognized Simon, Andrew, and Philip among those who lingered close to Yeshua, and they passed an arm's length from Titius without recognizing him.

Yeshua was like a benevolent king spreading riches to the masses, and in another way he resembled a confident, conquering general. But this man also had time for children, women, and beggars.

Titius remembered his grandfather. The great general, after routing a tribe in Britannia, had ridden his golden chariot through Rome, sunlight glistening off his golden armor. The crowds had cheered for him more loudly then they did for winning gladiators.

Titius had been six years of age, standing on a dais beside his mother, lost in the pageantry. When his grandfather's chariot had stopped in front of him, he'd walked over to where Titius stood in his little toga. Grandfather had lifted him up high, causing another tsunami of shouts. For years, that's all Titius had longed for, to be like his grandfather, to hear the people's cheers.

Titius shook his head and squinted as the crowd moved on in Yeshua's wake. A few shekels lay at his feet.

"*He knows who you are,*" Cleopas murmured.

Titius moved toward an alley behind the synagogue, where he'd hidden his pack in a bush. Within moments he had changed from a blind man to a Roman noble in a purple-edged toga. Changing clothes took only minutes, but it took longer to don the new persona inside.

"*Do you really think you'll be mistaken for someone important in that toga? Maybe in Rome, but not here, not with him.*"

He ignored Cleopas and instead pondered Yeshua's words: "Pretending to be poor and blind doesn't mean you're not *really* poor and blind." What did that mean?

As Titius walked, he noticed a tax collector counting money. The man was middle-aged with thick, curly hair, and he wore an opulent striped robe. He counted, recorded, and locked money in a box.

Titius sauntered to the booth and threw two shekels on the table.

The man looked up and examined him. "Peace to the nobleman from Rome. I'm Levi, at your service. What do you declare for taxation?"

"I am Portius Festus, from Alexandria," he said. A few tradesmen were getting close, so Titius spoke quickly. "No declaration. I seek only information."

"No declaration, then no taxation," Levi said. "I take only what's required."

Titius had never met a tax collector who didn't take any money he could get. "I see. Does that mean you won't give me information?"

"What do you want to know?"

Titius leaned closer to Levi. "The Messiah. What do you know of him?"

Levi chuckled. "Surely you just saw him pass. He brings me good business. He pays his taxes. He comes for a week, leaves for a month, then returns for a week. What else do you need to know?"

"Where is he from?" Titius asked. "Who is he, really?"

"I've never heard anyone accuse him of deception. Anyone like him deserves a following."

Titius nodded politely and backed away.

Over the next five days, he used seven disguises to gain as much information as possible from different sources. Every time he got close to the Messiah, he attracted a look, smile, and nod from the man. It unnerved him. Was this the only man who could see through his charade?

Disguised as a Roman nobleman, he asked an innkeeper if he'd heard of a slave named Abigail who'd worked in Rome. As a Greek trader, he asked a local fig merchant about Abigail. As a fisherman, he asked a rabbi the same question. The answer was always, "No."

At this rate, he wasn't going to have much to report to Sestus about the Messiah, either.

Yeshua ben Yuseph's message was always the same: "Repent, for the kingdom of heaven is near." He told parables and stories that seemed little more than entertainment for the crowd. Sometimes he stood in a boat and spoke, other times on a small hill. He never seemed to be too rushed for anyone who needed him, especially children.

Nothing Rome needed to worry about.

Cleopas remained strangely silent during these reconnaissance missions, but he spoke relentlessly at night, urging Titius to leave the area as soon as possible.

On the sixth day, Titius determined to confront Yeshua with what he meant by his words and his looks. He got up at the second rooster crow, ate, and went out.

But Yeshua was gone—and so were the crowds.

Chapter Ten

On his hike back to Sepphoris, Titius passed a caravan of youth singing and dancing at the side of the road. The harvest was underway and celebrations like this were frequent away from the city. He envied the energetic carefreeness of these who didn't yet worry about lost love, stolen estates, or the brutal demands of a centurion pushing his cross maker to work against his own conscience.

As Titius absorbed the scene, one of the young women waved him over to join in. He shuddered. The girl danced and smiled exactly as he'd seen Abigail dance among the roses on his Roman estate. He moved quickly to her and then paused mid-stride. A horrifying thought grew in him: *I've forgotten what Abigail looks like.*

Three of the young men grabbed hold of his arm and pulled him into the circle. His feet stumbled to find the rhythm and his eyes drank in the face and form of the girl who danced on the far side of the crowd. She continued to invite his gaze with her own.

The dance ended and one of the young men handed him a gourd of wine. "Drink up, my friend," he urged. "If you're going to take on Dina, you need to fortify yourself."

Titius held the gourd and watched as the girl sidled up to him.

"What's a good-looking man like you doing out on the road by yourself?" the girl named Dina asked. "Looking for something fresh and alive?"

"Now's your chance," Cleopas whispered. *"She's just like Abigail. One girl is as good as another."*

Her dark eyes drew him in. Longing eyes. Eyes with a depth and light different than Abigail's.

And that's when a clear memory captured him—Abigail standing on a bench, looking east toward her homeland. She had watched a hawk circling above. Then she'd looked down at him…

He shook his head and dropped the gourd of wine.

"No," he stammered. "Just wanted to make sure your father knows you are safe."

The surge of anger in her eyes surprised him. She spat out her response. "You know my father?" She backed away and pointed a finger at him. "You tell that God-forsaken rabbi in Nazareth that I can take care of myself. If he wants me safe at home, he can come and get me himself."

With that, she marched off into the forest with several of her friends chasing after her.

"You better leave," one of the young men advised.

Titius nodded. "I'm on my way."

When he arrived back in Sepphoris, he disguised himself and then scoured the streets for signs of Caleb. Most of the Hebrew carpenters were away for the Sabbath, but there was plenty of activity in the market. He paused near a fountain where one of those carpenters had once given his life smashing a statue of a Greek goddess.

"I wonder how these people would react to a tour of all the human beauty on display in my garden in Rome," Titius mumbled to himself.

"They'd smash you right along with the rest of your god-forsaken images," Cleopas replied.

As he looked up, he noticed a familiar figure moving through the market—the cross maker dawdling from vendor to vendor. Titius scrambled toward the bakery and slipped into place at a corner table there. Within a few moments, Caleb arrived. He stood before the purni oven and watched the fresh loaves of Roman bread bake inside.

When the baker directed him toward Titius, Titius kept his head low and pushed three loaves across the table toward Caleb.

"I only purchased two," Caleb said.

"Perhaps the Almighty is providing for you," Titius replied in an altered voice.

Caleb's eyes bored through his disguise. "I won't take what isn't mine."

"A worthy man, no doubt." Titius withdrew a small parchment and held it out. "The Sicarii are closer than you think. One day you will need this. Hide it well until that time. This is not Caesarea."

His message had been cryptic, in case it fell into the wrong hands:

Beware the spider and the fly.
Test all before you taste.
The rebel heart beats deeply under the most beautiful faces.

As time went on, Caleb met him there each Sabbath, and sometimes Caleb left a scroll behind as he picked up his bread.

Titius saw Deborah before Caleb did. The cross maker was sitting with his feet in a fountain when the woman moved deliberately toward him, touching his shoulder, stepping into the fountain, and luring him to ogle her braided hair and long-sleeved crimson tunic. She flirted without shame and Caleb became drawn into her game.

The pair chatted freely while Titius wormed his way through the market toward them.

When Caleb finally stepped out of the fountain and put out his hand, Deborah waded to the edge and stepped out to be with him. They put on their sandals and stood face to face. As they spoke, she released her hairpin and let the waves of her hair flow down over her shoulders.

"This is what I warned you about," Titius muttered.

The two ignored him and began to walk, she chasing after him. Deborah was clearly trying to coach Caleb in how to behave around her, and he was slow in responding.

After reporting back to Sestus, Titius was sent on the road again to observe developments in Capernaum. Nothing much had changed in the intervening weeks. The Messiah was away, so Titius spent his time exploring the surrounding communities, searching for Abigail without much success.

On the morning he intended to leave Capernaum, Titius awoke refreshed. Something had changed. The fishermen returning with their catch were jovial, the birdsong was clearer, and the flowers at the market seemed brighter. His lentil soup and bread tasted better, too. The time away from Caleb had allowed him to relax.

He packed his gear and headed for the hills where he knew Sestus would be waiting. He smiled as he took a shortcut between oak trees, wondering what assignment the centurion would send him on next.

The undergrowth was thicker than he remembered, so he headed for the main road. As he emerged from the forest, he noticed five fishermen cresting the hill on their way to Sepphoris. He was about to hail them when he noticed Caleb walking among them.

What was Caleb doing with the Messiah's followers in Capernaum? Titius slipped back into the forest and shadowed the group.

Titius sorted through his disguises, noting to himself that Caleb was too familiar with the usual ones. He couldn't dress as the Greek trader, the Roman nobleman, the blind beggar, or the legionnaire.

"Curse that son of Hades," muttered Titius.

"You can't even be yourself anymore! Do you even know who you are?"

"I've never had the chance, thanks to you."

He belted on a rougher, thicker tunic and rubbed dark red powder mixed with dust and cream into his face and neck. At last, he slipped on a long grey beard and silvery wig. A shepherd's prayer shawl completed the outfit.

As he jogged through the forest to catch up with Caleb and the fishermen, his full pack caught on some low branches and he fell.

"Curse that carpenter," he growled when he got up and examined his scraped shin. He set his wig and shawl back in place.

Hearing shouts ahead, he ducked behind a mulberry tree. He abandoned his pack and crept through the shrubbery. The beard kept snagging on undergrowth and a swarm of bees hovered over him.

More shouts reverberated through the trees. Latin.

He scooted behind a pistachio tree's spreading roots and saw the fishermen cowering on the other side of the road. A Roman cavalry scout, his javelin drawn, had trapped them. Other scouts on horseback soon joined him, surrounded the men, and forced them down. They fell to the ground, begging for mercy.

Five scouts with javelins! The cross maker had put himself at risk again. Perhaps if he created a diversion…

"Will you take out the whole Roman army for one man?" Cleopas asked. *"Sestus will understand. There are others who can make crosses."*

Titius shushed him, climbed an oak, and made his way along a large overhanging branch. He would knock off a scout, steal his horse, and lead the others away.

He moved slowly. The shepherd's garb was a nuisance now.

The scout leader's shouted questions were quickly drowned out by hundreds of hobnailed boots pounding. As Titius watched, a legion of soldiers paraded by, drumming their shields. He hung on the branch, hoping no one would look up and spot him. He almost choked on the dust.

After the cohort passed, the scouts moved their horses away from the fishermen and galloped off through the dust raised by the soldiers.

They're obviously afraid of a good fight, Titius thought. *Run along, little horses.* "Someday your luck is going to run out."

Not until I kill Cretius or Caleb.

Titius waited long enough to make sure the fishermen were safe, then scurried down the tree and rushed back for his pack.

He cut through the grove of oaks and crossed the road ahead of the travelers, his costume snagging over and over. Finally, he took off the headpiece, tucked the tunic into his belt, and changed his sandals.

After another hour, he stopped to rest by a stream, cooling his face and neck in the rushing water. A small sip was all he permitted himself before heading off again at a brisk walk.

He kept going until he reached the city's familiar aqueducts. Neither Octavian nor Marcus were on duty at the gate, so he managed to slip by undetected. He found a secluded perch on the wall near the market entrance. Goats bleated; cattle lowed. Vendors and customers haggled. Two doves settled under the bakery awning. Still Titius watched to see if Caleb might arrive there with the fishermen.

His stomach grumbled at the smell of bread, but he remained at his post. The sun slid toward the Great Sea and he watched the golden glow of red-bellied clouds.

As the last of the day's returning merchants came through the gates, one of the sentries began to beat a beggar. In the falling shadows, Titius almost missed Caleb hiding behind an ox cart as its owner protested against a legionnaire who had struck his donkey.

Titius slipped down off the wall and began to follow.

The cross maker wove his way past the agora and stepped around a pile of slops under a window. The rains had been poor and the sewage ditches running down each street had gotten clogged.

Caleb stopped at a weaver's house and knocked on the door. It was obviously a code, and nothing happened for several minutes. Then the door opened a few inches.

"The stench of death is great," a female voice said from inside.

"The hope of life is greater still," Caleb replied.

Deborah peeked her head outside and let him in.

Titius had warned Caleb about this weaver's daughter and her ways with men. "Beware the spider and the fly," he had said. "Test all before you taste. The rebel heart can beat under the most beautiful face."

She was the spider, and men the flies. Well, the fly was on his own now.

Titius walked away, fearing for Caleb. The man was a cross maker for the Romans. What other excuse would the zealots need to assassinate him? Deborah, her father Eustace, and unknown zealots often met secretly around the city. He knew they had to be planning something.

Deborah's cruelty would spew like lava one day, but men seemed helpless around her and Caleb was like a fallen leaf before the wind. Titius needed to report this to Jaennus.

Titius scrambled back into the assassins' den, where Jaennus was offering incense. Titius waited a few moments, then announced himself and told Jaennus about the cross maker's newfound relationship.

"It's foolish," Jaennus confirmed. "I'll alert Sestus. Your charge needs a lesson he won't soon forget. Perhaps in our dungeon. Leave it to us."

"One more thing," Titius said. "I can't help wondering about the new Messiah. I wouldn't be surprised if Herod Antipas plans to kill him."

"I'm not sure how much political capital Herod Antipas has to work with. His list of betrayals is long."

"What do you mean?" Titius asked.

"Do you remember what happened after the last Herod died? The zealots captured the city, ransacked the armory, and took control. Who helped the Romans regain the city and burn it to the ground?"

"The Arabs under King Aretas."

Jaennus picked up an orange and threw it to Titius. "And what political arrangement did they make afterward?"

"Antipas married the king's daughter and secured a treaty between his kingdom and the Arabs at Petra. He built a new palace for her on the spot where her father had claimed his victory for Rome."

"Yes!" Jaennus peeled his orange. "Antipas planned to eliminate his Arab princess so he could marry his brother's wife. He meant it to happen while he was in Rome, but she found out and snuck away before he could do it." He broke the orange in half. "The treaty is broken. Aretas is out for revenge."

Titius finished his fruit. "So Antipas betrayed his wife, his brother, and the Arabs all at once by taking his brother's wife. But the Arabs control the trade routes and they're proud warriors. Why would Antipas risk an uprising by betraying them?"

"It's Herodias, his wife," Jaennus said. "She manipulated events so he had no choice. Antipas wants this new Messiah out of the way. After all, he needs to keep the emperor happy."

"I remember how upset the emperor was the last time there was trouble here."

Jaennus looked hard at Titius. "Antipas wants someone else to take care of things so he doesn't have to get his hands dirty. His forces are searching for a way to take the Messiah quietly."

"What must I do?" Titius asked.

"Go back to Capernaum and track the Messiah. And keep your eye open for Antipas's spies, and zealot infiltrators." Jaennus knelt before the altar and added a pinch of incense to the flame. "Don't betray me, and don't betray your gods."

"I need to make a few stops along the way," Titius said. He took the ensuing silence as permission.

Caleb spent four days in the dungeon, and when he emerged back into public life afterward he was a wreck of a man. Titius watched him walk through the city, carrying his carpenter's axe, swinging it heavily like a man twice his age. Caleb took frequent rests and tended to retire to his quarters by mid-afternoon.

While Caleb was recovering, Titius spent time writing reports for Sestus. He also scoured the city, following Deborah around until he was satisfied, for the time being, that nothing was amiss.

He and Caleb continued to pass messages to each other at the bakery. Titius gave him a message urging him to be cautious with Deborah. Something about that woman rubbed him the wrong way.

One morning, Titius slipped out of the assassins' den, having learned that Caleb had gone away from Sepphoris. He changed into his shepherd's disguise, all the while trying to ignore Cleopas's taunts. He emerged from the passageway, murmuring to Cleopas under his breath, and exchanged his sandals for a clean pair.

"Who were you talking to?" the baker asked.

Titius waved him back into silence, then bought a loaf flavored with orange juice. Without another word, he bowed his head and disappeared into the crowded agora.

He descended the acropolis on the western side of the city, away from the road to Nazareth, where the last grapes were being gleaned and made into wine. He took a hidden trail that circled westward toward the Great Sea, and which would take him back to Nazareth, which is where he suspected Caleb had gone.

He caught up with a small trading caravan travelling toward the Via Maris. He walked close behind it to protect himself from bandits.

As he neared Nazareth, he remembered the rabbi who had been suspicious of him. He took out the goatskin cap and white beard to return to his blind man identity. When would he ever be able to go about in the world without a disguise? Would he ever again feel normal human freedom?

He tapped with his cane and moved along the road toward the main gate, where the gatekeeper was on duty. As Titius got closer, however, he saw that the old man was asleep under an olive tree. Titius moved quietly around him and made his way to Yuseph and Miriam's house.

He walked first by a butcher shop, tapping his cane. A skinned goat hung from a hook while a living one nibbled grass beside the shop.

"That's you," Cleopas said. *"Nibbling away by death's door."*

Titius could smell bread as he passed the bakery. The baker sat at a table inside with his head on his arm. Next door, a colorfully dressed woman was fanning herself under the awning of a shop that sold cloth, spices, and fruit.

"I smell something good," Titius said as he approached her shop.

The woman stood. "Watch out, old man. There's a post three steps in front of you. Go right. Come toward my voice. Come! Come!"

When he had avoided the post, she took his hand and rested it on her chair.

"Sit," she said. "I'm Hannah and this is Nazareth."

"Ah, Hannah, may the Almighty bless you with all you can dream."

She smiled and touched his shoulder. "Be careful, old man. I can dream a lot."

"I am Benjamin ben Jonas, born blind in Bethlehem."

"So far from home. You've really lost your way."

Titius lowered himself into the chair. "My feet... some days it's a blessing not to see them."

"I'll bring you water and bread. Stay. The bakery and well are close by."

As she left, he noticed two children playing with a puppy in their small home's doorway, oblivious to the heat and dust. An old woman waddled toward the synagogue down the road. So far, the rabbi was nowhere to be seen.

The woman returned with a flask of well water and a barely warm loaf. She set them down on a table by Titius, then gave him a few dates and figs from her own stock.

"May the Almighty bless all that he's given through his servant," Titius said. "May the land's bounty be hers as long as she lives."

"Now Benjamin ben Jonas, eat and tell me how you came to Nazareth. Almost everyone here is chasing after that Messiah because he was throwing things around in the Jerusalem temple." She swatted at a cloud of flies and rotated some overripe apricots. "You know, we almost killed him here."

She went on to explain that she thought the next generation was losing its way. The Sicarii were terrorizing the villages! They'd murdered five carpenters, Caleb almost being the sixth. And the theatre being built at Sepphoris would, she swore, warp the workers' values.

By mid-afternoon, Titius had taken in as much as he could. And he'd thought listening to Cleopas's prattle was bad.

"I actually came to see Caleb ben Samson," he said when Hannah had paused to take a sip of water.

Hannah stood, wiped her sweaty hands on her chiton, and grabbed another tray of dates. He pretended not to notice.

"There are more dates by your left hand," she said. "Eat! It's a mercy you were born without sight." She wagged her finger. "As for Caleb, such scandal! Not that this isn't known outside heaven, but Miriam and Yuseph had their first child before their betrothal ended. The child was never schooled by anyone with a name, and now he's abandoned his carpenter's trade. He passes himself off as a rabbi."

"Is the family at home, then?" Titius asked. He groped for his cane and made as if to rise.

Hannah stood. "Praise the Almighty, it seems Miriam and Yuseph will be moving soon. He's not really from around here—."

"Is Caleb ben Samson still in Nazareth?"

Hannah took Titius's hand. "Benjamin ben Jonas, let me take you. The man you want left for Cana yesterday to see his sister. She's newly married, you know." She tugged at his arm. "It's a good thing Yuseph took that daughter of his. Who know what she's up to."

Titius feigned difficulty getting to his feet. "These young people do have a mind of their own."

"People claim Yeshua turned water into wine, that he healed lepers, made blind men see… even that he healed Caleb after his throat was slashed. Our rabbi told us to use our minds, not our eyes. We know there's darkness in this land."

It was a short walk to Yuseph and Miriam's house, where Titius made a show of settling down on a stool. The home was simple, plastered with limestone floors and immaculate furniture. Through an open door, light fell on a row of nearly arranged carpenter's tools: squares, chisels, plumb lines, levels, saws, mallets, planes, adzes, bow drills, and dowels. Two axes leaned against the wall. Under an overhang lay untouched lengths of walnut, cedar, olive, cypress, pine, and oak.

Hannah picked up a small carved flute. "Caleb made these. Can't imagine how, but the Almighty has blessed him that way."

Titius stood up and deliberately tapped in the wrong direction toward a wall.

"Whoa," Hannah said, grabbing his arm. "Wrong way! There's no one here and nothing to see even if you could, so let's go. Where to next?"

"What did they make here?" Titius said. "I smell wood."

Hannah looked around. "Nothing special. They're carpenters, just like a dozen other families hereabouts."

"May I touch something they made?" Titius asked.

Hannah led him to a table and laid his hand upon it. "This table is oak, very heavy. Yuseph carves and makes chairs and stools on his lathe. He also makes lamps, beds, bowls, ploughs, yokes, carts, wagons, threshing boards, houses… I guess we wouldn't do too well without him and his wife."

Titius took her arm as she led him out the door into the street.

"It's too bad they had to leave," he said. "I guess I'll see if I can find Caleb in Cana."

"You can't walk blind all the way to Cana, old man. I think the rabbi is taking his cart over that way tomorrow. Let me see if he can give you a ride. You can stay in my shop tonight."

"Hannah, I've walked here from Sepphoris. Cana isn't much farther. I can travel at night. I won't be troubling the rabbi on this trip, thank you."

Hannah shrugged and led him to the front gate. "Go in peace," she said as she walked back to her shop.

At the gate, the old gatekeeper sat carving a small whistle. He was never very alert.

"Hello, Samuel," Titius said to him. "I see you're on duty again."

The old man blew his new whistle, but no sound came out.

"Nothing gets by me," he said. "Have I seen you before?"

Titius tapped his cane against the ground. "Nothing gets past you? Then of course you've seen me before. Peace to you and yours."

"Watch out for wild dogs," Samuel said. "You'd be easy prey for them. Go in peace."

Titius walked toward the bluff overlooking Sepphoris, a cliff three hundred paces high. According to Hannah, this was where Nazareth's people had tried to kill the Messiah. Yeshua had grown up in a tough neighborhood.

The shadows were growing long, though the sun hadn't quite descended into the hills yet. Titius lowered his head to go, and turned—just as three broad-shouldered, full-bearded, scowling young men appeared five paces away from him.

Their leader rushed at Titius, who stumbled and brought his cane up under the attacker's jaw. The young man crumpled to the ground, motionless.

"Hello, is someone there?" Titius called. He pretended to stumble over the prone figure and crawled back to it. "Hello? Hello, are you well?"

"Get your hands off him, you beggar!" a second man shouted.

Titius brought his cane down hard on the second man's knees, and he staggered. A moment later, Titius hit him again, this time on the back of the neck.

Two bodies now lay on the bluff. The third man stood staring at the supposedly blind man, open-mouthed.

"Hello?" Titius said. "What's happening? Is all well?"

"You ask too many questions," the man snarled. "The rabbi sent us to bring you back."

"Who are you? Where am I?"

The man pulled a dagger. When he lunged, Titius sidestepped the attack, grabbing his wrist and snapping it across his knee. The knife fell to the ground and Titius flicked it over the cliff with his cane. The young man grabbed his broken arm, screaming, and charged again. Titius swung his cane against his head and left him, unmoving, with the other two.

Chapter Eleven

Titius approached Sepphoris dressed as a carpenter, tunic hitched to the knee, apron belted firmly, and shawl tossed over his head. He kept his eye on the legionnaires posted along the city wall. To hide his approach, he walked beside an oxcart pulling a single massive limestone ashlar from the nearby quarry. It glistened white under the mid-afternoon sun. Titius walked with one hand on the stone as if steadying it. The craftsman on the other side never even lifted his eyes.

"The guards will be waiting for you," Cleopas whispered. *"They know you have to report back to Sestus. They've seen all your disguises."*

The moment Titius prepared to step away from the cart's protective cover, he heard the voice of Octavian shouting at one of the workmen swarming the area. A burly foreman keeping watch over every slave and passerby. A large oaken crane was preparing to lift another load of heavy stones over the walls. A man stood on the load and used his own weight to balance the stones as they rose into the air. In fact, a different man seemed to be accompanying each load on its journey up overtop the wall.

Titius stepped into the line of men waiting their turn, and when the next ashlar was secured to the crane, Titius jumped atop it, as had the craftsman before him. He swung up over the wall just as Octavian came into view behind him, examining the cart he'd been hiding behind.

After ensuring his stone's safe landing, Titius melted into the general population. By evening, he'd filled his belly, quenched his thirst, and changed into his assassin's attire. He approached the blanket-covered entrance to the assassins' den; the baker who'd been assigned to cover the entrance slipped him a fresh loaf.

No one was inside the den, and the fireplace was cold. He left an apricot pit on the table by the door and stepped back into the dark and cramped passageway.

As he waited for Jaennus, Sestus, or one of the cleaning girls to come by, he dozed.

Between snatches of sleep, Cleopas baited him. *"How do you know Octavian and Marcus haven't turned Sestus against you? You know this game. Your uncles played it to get into the Senate."*

"My uncles were worthy men."

"Ha! The emperor has eroded most of the Senate's power. You're no different from them, prancing around in purple so the poor can slander you behind your back."

"My grandfather earned his way with Julius Caesar, and my father survived Augustus's reforms. Under Tiberius, I could have qualified to be quaestor. I still could, if I wanted to. After all, the treasurer's role is the lowest and easiest to qualify for."

"Except Cretius took your estate. Without it, you could never qualify."

He tried to shush the slave's voice.

"Or what? You can't kill me again."

After supper, when still no one had come by, Titius left the assassins' den to watch the more traditional thespians flaunt their skills in the theatre. The seats were cushioned and inviting and spectators babbled in Latin, Greek, Aramaic, Persian, Egyptian, and Hebrew.

Unlike in Rome, the actors in Sepphoris used makeup instead of masks. They could portray emotion and thought with just a change of expression. Titius loved how the play could mock people of importance, empower lowly citizens, and give voice to reality. Perhaps there was still time to evade his oath with Sestus and take up a simple actor's life.

Life could be confusing. Ultimately, he wanted nothing but to pursue his mission to find Abigail, but there was no point in finding her if he had nothing to offer. That meant dealing with Cretius and reclaiming his estate. His commitment to Sestus and the cross maker was complicated. Everything seemed to pull him further and further away from what he really wanted.

The next morning, Titius returned to the assassins' den, where Jaennus was offering incense to a bust of Caesar. Without turning, Jaennus sensed his arrival.

"I hope you wanted me to find that apricot pit," Jaennus said.

Titius warmed his hands at the fireplace. "I leave my fate in the gods' hands."

Jaennus rose to his feet. "As do I."

Titius accepted the tray of dates and figs Jaennus offered. "I need wisdom."

"Wisdom is experience's reward."

"I'll have to depend on your experience then." Putting himself in the role of student, Titius sat on a nearby stool. "I'm listening, master."

Jaennus tossed a log into the dwindling fire, then returned to his own stool. "You're pulled by fear, doubt, or love. Which is it?"

"Perhaps all three." Titius clutched his temples between his hands. "I fear my mind. I doubt the loyalty of the brotherhood. I want to love."

Jaennus picked up a date, chewed it, and spit the pit into the fire. "Wanting to love, you must control. Doubting the brotherhood's loyalty will preserve your life. Fearing your mind, though... that will take more discipline."

"Speak plainly, if you will."

Jaennus rose and stared into the flames. "When a man is pulled apart by the things that give him a reason to live and love, he can be lost."

"Before I submitted to Sestus, I was preparing to be a senator in Rome. But Cretius, an assistant to Herod Antipas, has stolen my estate. I fear for my family. The woman I cherished is somewhere in Galilee."

Jaennus stroked his clean-shaven chin. "What is your desire?"

"I want to abandon my vow to Sestus, or take time away from it to reclaim my estate, to restore my family's honor."

"You've given all to Caesar and Sestus," Jaennus said. "To the emperor and to your centurion. To the brotherhood of thespian assassins."

"So I'm bound then?"

"Until death—yours, the emperor's, or the centurion's."

Titius rose and bowed. "I know my duty. The cross maker waits for me in Cana."

"You may sleep here until morning," Jaennus said. "I'll send you some food and wine."

Once down the road toward Cana, Titius stepped into the forest and walked through the brush to find the pack he had hidden near Nazareth. Along the way, he came upon a group of carpenters from Nazareth in the forest clearing brush and chopping cedar trees. The men greeted him as he approached and seemed glad for a break to chat with a stranger.

The tall oak tree he was looking for was easy to spot and he was relieved to see that the branches covering his stash hadn't yet been moved. After a short conversation with the woodsmen, he took a circular route away from them, where he waited for several hours until the men had abandoned their task and returned to their homes.

The sun was already touching the horizon by the time he'd finished changing into more comfortable traveling gear. He kept a few belongings in a small pack and returned the larger pack to its hiding place.

The city gates in Cana would be closed by now, meaning that he'd need to spend another night in a tree—but better a night in a tree than another moment listening to Hannah in Nazareth. As the sun gave its last light, he found a sturdy cedar to sleep in.

During the night, he heard the baying of wild dogs moving quickly toward him. Before he could settle himself, the dogs arrived at the base of his tree, barking and growling. Fighting a pack of wild dogs would mean certain death.

Long ago, Cleopas had told Titius stories about wild dogs, about how intelligent and ruthless they were.

"One pack was so smart, they used the shepherd's own dogs against them," Cleopas had said. "They used their females to lure away the domestic males. The shepherds set fires, traps, and guards around the flock, but in the morning there would always be one sheep missing."

Titius remembered his teacher crouching in the gardens as he spoke.

"The shepherds figured out how to keep their trained dogs near them, but each night a sheep would still be taken." Cleopas had acted out the scene. "They tried poisoning the wild dogs with meat, but the dogs wouldn't touch it. Never underestimate a wild dog."

Some time before dawn, though, one of the dogs below Titius's tree picked up the scent of easier prey and they left, still baying.

He prepared to descend, but the hair on the back of his neck was standing straight. Normally he would wait until a rabbit, deer, or similar animal passed the base of the tree to show there were no predators nearby. But this day, no animal passed by.

The sun rose above the hills and still things didn't look safe. Near a tree stump, he noticed some bushes that looked different than they had the day before. He heaved his pack into those bushes, and three dogs sprang upon it, shredding the pack with their fangs. Then they gathered at the base of the cedar and glared up, their heads cocked at him.

Titius waited, and eventually the trio got too hungry and raced off after the rest of their pack.

"Cleopas, I am in your debt," Titius whispered. "I did learn something from you."

When Titius got nearer to Cana, he passed an olive orchard along the road. He stopped for a while, since he loved the cool air and fresh scents of earth and foliage. To his surprise, as he was about to leave, he saw Caleb amongst the trees, walking alongside a raven-haired beauty.

Titius felt a spike of jealousy coursing through his veins but calmed himself with two thoughts. When he'd last seen Deborah, she had definitely been rubbing her abdomen, as if she was with child. Titius knew Deborah and Caleb had had an opportunity to couple. What was Caleb doing here?

To Titius, it appeared to be a chance meeting. As he watched the cross maker, Caleb applied his charm and walked with the woman to Cana. Along the way, Titius passed close enough to learn that this woman's name was also Hannah, a common name among the Hebrews.

In Cana, Caleb and Hannah paid a visit to the rabbi, who happened to be Hannah's father. Titius remained outside, waiting for whatever would happen next.

"Another good man falls for a woman," Cleopas said. *"You two have the same weakness. You've taught him much."*

Hours later, Caleb left the home, his brow furrowed. He walked slowly and Titius got the impression that the visit had gone badly.

Titius was about to follow Caleb into the bush outside the village when a horseman charged down the road. Instead he ducked into the shadows and watched as two strangers emerged from the nearby bush to converse. Suddenly, their conversation ended and one of them followed Caleb into the bush, javelin at the ready.

Remaining in the shadow, Titius went into the bush and looked for Caleb, desperate to warn him. When he spotted Caleb, crouched behind a tree, it was only just in time to see that the man with the javelin had seen him as well.

Titius resolved not to lose his charge today, not after all this time. It was impossible to approach Caleb without being seen. Besides, by the time he maneuvered his way to Caleb's side, it would be too late anyway.

That's when Titius realized the man with the javelin hadn't spotted Caleb after all. He walked right by the hiding cross maker, still searching the dark forest. Caleb was proving to be a worthy student after all.

Caleb didn't emerge from his hiding place until just before dawn, which Titius was glad for. Eventually, however, the cross maker escaped out toward the road. It would be a long run back to Sepphoris.

Chapter Twelve

Through his network of tradesmen, Titius confirmed the rumor that Deborah was part of a conspiracy to open a new route for Chinese silk. One day Titius followed her to Tiberias and got his first actual look at Barabbas. It was clear that the two had a deeper relationship than mere co-conspirators against Rome.

When he returned to Sepphoris, Sestus ordered Titius to begin more intensive training with Caleb.

A week later, a legionnaire came to the bakery and reported that Caleb had been manipulated into crucifying Deborah, who had been pregnant with Barabbas's child. They had beheaded her father, too. In fact, Sestus had ordered many crucifixions around Sepphoris.

Caleb was no longer just a cross maker, Titius realized, and Barabbas and Phoebe wouldn't take these losses lightly.

Titius went for a long walk around the city. He dunked his head in a fountain and shook it like a dog. What had he done? He had helped turn a simple carpenter into a weapon of destruction for Rome.

Titius, playing the blind man, delivered three loaves and a scroll to Caleb's quarters, trying to contact him. The scroll read:

The spider has been squashed.
Your time for training has risen like an eagle on the wind.
The apricot feeder is within your grasp.

When he got back to the bakery, he left another note there for the cross maker: *"Gone to the baths."* He needed to draw Caleb out and talk this situation through. Things were changing too fast.

In the baths, Titius waited until Caleb arrived. Scanning the rooms, he made himself small among the towel boys near the entrance and remained unseen.

When Caleb showed up, he dipped into the tepidarium with its warm water, then dunked quickly in and out of the frigidarium. Titius remained where he was, for the time being.

Caleb must have tired of waiting for Titius to show himself, so he went for a massage. As the masseur's firm hands began their work, his strong fingers working down his spine, Titius saw Caleb relax.

This was his opportunity. He approached and nodded at the masseur, indicating for him to move away. Titius then set his hands into place against Caleb's skin.

"I could break your neck," Titius whispered into the man's ear.

Caleb swung hard with his elbow and Titius grabbed the cross maker's arm, wrenching it behind his back. Caleb's audible gasp caused many men to back away.

"Who are you?" Caleb demanded, trying to turn his head.

Titius increased the pressure. "I'm your trainer. Lesson one: never relax your awareness of who's around you."

With the message delivered, Titius slipped away to where a small boy was holding a towel out to him.

Two hours later, Titius, in the disguise of a gardener, followed Caleb toward some barracks. He tapped his cane several times, and this time Caleb moved toward the sound. Titius poured water on the plants in the garden and used his stick to squash locust invaders. A large headscarf hid his face.

"Titius, I'm here," Caleb said. "I'm ready."

Titius turned. "So we begin."

Titius became a Latin teacher and combat instructor, performing for Caleb the role that Jaennus had performed for him. Exposing another man to his weaknesses before he'd taken care of his own was brutal, but Titius knew his role and performed it well.

In the coming weeks, Caleb trained in self-protective maneuvers both with weapons and without. Titius continually pushed the carpenter to his limits, even teaching him the art of disguise. Soon the younger man's body filled out, as a result of running and fighting and building crosses. Caleb became an expert horseman and could soon hit a moving target with a javelin at full gallop. By paying attention to his breathing, Caleb became able to run to Nazareth and back without stopping, and even submerge himself in water for almost three minutes.

For the first week, Titius taught Caleb basic fighting skills. The carpenter was motivated by something deep inside him and he learned quickly.

As the pair went on longer and longer training runs, Titius thought often about how this time with Caleb was taking him away from exacting his intended revenge on Cretius, away from finding Abigail. He wasn't sure which he wanted more.

At the end of the second week of training, he decided that it was time for him to pursue Abigail. That had to be his first priority.

Titius tried to think of how he could gain some freedom from the training regimen to pursue his own causes, and as a result he found himself often distracted. Caleb almost pierced him on several occasions when he daydreamed during practice duels. Soon after, during an intense wrestling match, Caleb forced him to submit to a hold and refused to release him.

"The master has been mastered," Caleb shouted to all around.

Titius relaxed under Caleb's lock. "Why do you treat Sestus like you do?" He monitored his breath carefully. "You try so hard to please him. It seems like he's become a father to you."

Caleb relaxed just a fraction, and in a moment Titius had reversed the hold and had the cross maker on his face with his arms pinned behind his back.

"Never lose focus," Titius snarled. "You will never be the master if you do."

A few days later, Sestus watched Titius trying to teach Caleb how to disarm a warrior who was attacking with a dagger. Sestus marched up to the pair, furious.

"Titius, he's going to be fighting Barabbas, not a child."

Sestus then stepped in between the combatants and urged Titius to attack him. When Titius thrust the dagger toward Sestus's ribs, the centurion stepped in close, blocked the stabbing motion, and drove his forearm up into Titius's jaw.

Titius went down and passed out.

"Titius!"

Titius opened his eyes and found Caleb hovering over him as he lay on his mat. He had no memory of anything after Sestus's attack. His jaw ached and his head pounded.

Involuntarily, he groaned.

"Either I'm getting better than you or your mind is somewhere else," Caleb remarked.

Titius opened his eyes wider. "Where's Sestus?"

"Gone to Caesarea."

"There's something I need to do."

"Can I help?"

"Not this time. I need to get away for a while."

During his five-day reprieve, Titius returned to Bethsaida and inquired after Abigail. For the first three days, no one he spoke to knew a former slave of that name.

"But if she came back here, would she announce to others that she had been a Roman slave?" Cleopas asked. *"She probably wouldn't come back at all. Her parents were probably Parthian sympathizers in conflict with Rome."*

Titius tried to ignore him, and in the process he was nearly run down by a horse-drawn cart. He jumped aside with a hand width to spare.

"Watch it!" the tile merchant who'd been driving the cart yelled. "I could have killed you!"

"Too bad," Cleopas said.

"What did you say about Parthians?" Titius asked Cleopas once no one was around to overhear him. "I suppose it makes sense that Abigail's family were Parthian sympathizers. That could be why they ended up as slaves."

"Forget the girl," Cleopas said.

"But someone has to know something about her family."

For his next move, Titius dressed as an olive merchant and walked into a tavern. When he asked for the owner, a large-bellied man at a table waved at him.

"What are you selling?" the owner asked.

"Nothing," Titius said. "I'm looking for family who used to live here. Parthian sympathizers. They were taken away to Rome."

"No one I know," he said.

An old fisherman in the back piped up, though. "I might know them."

Titius walked toward him in three strides. "What do you know?"

"Sounds like old Judah ben Jonas," the fisherman said. "Used to put up Parthian scouts at his place. He had four little ones, two little girls and two boys. Romans took them all away in chains."

His heart beat quickly and he worked to control his breathing. "Would you show me where they lived?"

"The Romans burned it. Then piled rocks and dirt on it. No one's dared to build there since."

"You don't know if any of the little ones ever came back?" Titius asked.

"Can't see why they would. Might still be a relative over in Capernaum."

Titius thanked the old man and walked out into the brisk night air. This had been his first glimpse at hope—and on the day before he had to depart, sadly, back to Sepphoris.

Upon his return to Sepphoris, news of the Messiah was like fire on people's tongues. Yeshua ben Yuseph had brought back to life a young girl in Capernaum, calmed a storm with a single word, and given his twelve followers the same power he had to cast out demons and heal all who came to them.

As the weeks passed, Cleopas increased his chatter, reciting Titius's weaknesses. Meanwhile, Caleb chopped trees, made crosses, and took several covert trips to Cana. Titius kept training and watching the cross maker.

Sestus soon dispatched Titius to monitor the Messiah's mood in Capernaum, and on that trip Titius noticed only a small increase in the number of people who had been healed or exorcised. The Messiah was always expanding his efforts, sending his followers to lead while the master worked with those who came his way.

Disguised as an olive merchant one day, he listened to a group of Pharisees speaking about the Messiah. One of them clearly declared, "We have to kill him." Titius dismissed the threat, not believing it to be serious. He merely continued to busy himself gathering the rumblings and praises of Yeshua floating throughout the region.

At last he was able to nudge closer to Yeshua and his followers eating lunch together.

"The Almighty looks behind the mask to the actor's heart," Yeshua said to him, speaking gently and without judgment. "Nothing is hidden from his eyes. You don't have to pretend to be blind, to be blind."

In response, Titius looked into Yeshua's eyes. No matter what disguise he wore, the Messiah always seemed to recognize him. Could this man help him find Abigail?

Instead of asking, he bowed and backed away.

Like a shadow, he followed Yeshua around Capernaum, even mingling with his close disciples. Outside Andrew's house one day, the crowd pressed in on their teacher. The master massaged his temples, rotated his tense shoulders, bowed his head, and sighed. He shared a half-smile with Simon before turning to face the people behind him.

A blind man was pushing through the crowd, calling, "Make way, make way!"

"Yeshua, son of David, touch his eyes!" a woman called.

"Yeshua, make him see!" a young man pleaded.

As Titius watched, Yeshua rose and took the blind man's hand. The group parted like the Red Sea and the Messiah led them outside the town. Titius followed close behind, to see what would happen next.

To his surprise, Yeshua spit in the blind man's face, on his eyes, then rubbed the spit onto his eyelids. No one seemed offended by this vulgarity.

"Do you see anything?" the healer asked.

Suddenly, the blind man looked right at Titius and blinked. "I see people who look like trees…"

Yeshua rubbed the man's eyes again and stepped away. When the blind man opened his eyes a second time, he grinned broadly. His eyebrows lifted and he touched the Messiah's face. He then looked into one face after another and began to scream with joy.

"Don't go back into Bethsaida," Yeshua ordered.

But his family needs to see what's happened, Titius thought. What kind of Messiah was this? Spitting in people's faces, making them see, ordering them away from their families?

The crowd pressed in on the man as he walked back toward Capernaum, and Titius was caught up in the crush. He pushed hard against the press of bodies, but by the time he got clear Yeshua was nowhere to be seen.

"*Good riddance,*" Cleopas spoke up. "*You know he sees us, don't you?*"

Titius squeezed his skull between his hands. "Who is 'us'?"

"*Me, you, us… how do you think you play all those parts so well? I help you.*"

"I'm good at what I do because I'm trained," Titius said to himself as he walked toward the beach. "I've practiced the magical arts. I've learned the secrets of disguise. I've learned to speak without accents. Not *we*."

Titius shook his head and rubbed his ears hard. He couldn't stop the tremors that ran up and down his spine as he headed for the water's edge.

"I don't need your help to be who I am," he said in defiance.

Cleopas was quiet.

As Titius looked up and down the shore at the stream of humanity moving slowly toward Capernaum, he reflected on the fact that the lake appeared to be little more than rippling glass. Others stood along the shore, thinking about what they'd seen.

One such man, a Pharisee, joined him. He still wore his phylacteries, the long tassels hanging from his robe. His face was lifted toward the sun as if God's favor smiled on him, a son of the law. His deep-set eyes were confident under bushy grey brows.

"How blind people can be!" the Pharisee exclaimed.

"How much one sees if one only looks," Titius replied.

The Pharisee turned and nodded. "I am Zedekiah ben Saulus, from Jerusalem."

"I am Jonah ben Gad, of Sepphoris," Titius said.

"You seem perceptive," Zedekiah said. "What do you think about this charlatan of a Messiah?"

"I'm a follower of the theatre. He plays a hero to bring hope to his people."

Zedekiah grunted. "He plays with fire, like a child. He doesn't see, and soon the Romans will squeeze the life out of our land and temple."

"The Romans build roads, arrest bandits, and secure trade," Titius replied. "What life are they squeezing out?"

"This Messiah caters to tax collectors, harlots, and foreigners. Everything of value will be sent to Rome."

Titius picked up a smooth stone and skipped it onto the lake. "I see the forces of fear and love preparing to collide," he said.

"I know that no prophet comes out of Galilee."

"If you know about the Baptizer, then you know the authorities don't deal well with those who oppose them," Titius said. "They've killed almost every prophet who claims some judgment from God."

The Pharisee pointed up the hill toward Sepphoris. "You couldn't find two more different men. Herod Antipas, surrounded by opulent finery and sucking on pig's feet, and the Baptizer, living in the wilderness gnawing on locusts." He spread his arms like a great bird. "Rumor has it that now Herod is going after this new messianic pretender."

"It doesn't take a prophet to see. Any leader who is jealous for his people's adoration won't stay quiet long. Not when those people's love turns to another."

"Do you speak of Herod Antipas?" Zedekiah queried.

"Perhaps I speak of you."

Titius walked away, but the Pharisee called after him. "You should go back to Sepphoris before you're led astray. One day even the blind will see."

Why did everyone keep talking about the blind seeing? Yeshua's words echoed in his mind: "You don't have to pretend to be blind, to be blind."

As he walked, a deep conviction settled over him. *I'm not just playing the part of a blind man. I am a blind man.*

Titius looked in the direction of Bethsaida, where the blind man had been healed. Where Abigail had once lived.

"Cleopas, how did Yeshua know?"

"Know what?"

Titius rubbed his eyes. "How did Yeshua know I'm not really blind?"

"Ignore him."

But how could you ignore someone who saw through your disguise?

Titius spent a week in Sepphoris only to find that Sestus and Caleb had gone off on an adventure together. He headed back to Capernaum, and on the way he counted twenty-three different species of birds. He hurled small rocks at tree trunks and felt an inner satisfaction when each missile struck its target.

And he worked to fend off Cleopas.

"Which of your gods made that bird?" Cleopas mocked as a pelican flew past. *"Why are you aiming for big trees you can't possibly miss?"*

A few paces later, three bandits attacked him. He used his shepherd's staff to knock the closest two unconscious with whacks to the jaw. The third he rammed in the belly and then smacked on the back of the head. He dragged them into the bushes and left them.

"I should have slit their throats," he announced aloud. "Why didn't I?"

"Losing your thirst for blood?"

The smell of the pigsties he passed was unmistakable—pigs raised by Roman proxies for banquets and altars. Horses for Herod's cavalry grazed in an irrigated pasture. Legionnaires guarded a herd of imported cattle for some wealthy landowner. And as he left the main road, he noticed a caravan of camels carrying huge loads, their drivers plodding as if asleep.

When Titius felt the welcoming arms of the forest over the road, he breathed deeply. It seemed that all of creation was settling in for the coming rains. Dust scattered with each step along this road. Withered grasses lay stretched out on the hardened earth.

His mind returned to bird-watching. When he was young, Abigail had been the one to identify the birds in his family's garden. Here there were different birds, though; ducks, geese, herons, cranes, and spoonbills filled the waterways along the road. He saw bee-eaters, starlings, larks, swallows, and ravens. Occasionally a partridge raced across the road to distract him from a nest. A pair of storks flew through the cloudless sky.

In the afternoon, he took time to trap a rabbit, which he roasted over a fire for his supper. The meat, bread, almonds, and dried apricots filled him up nicely. He then stored the leftover meat between two pieces of flatbread and stuffed it into his pack.

His peace changed to weariness as he walked along. An ancient olive tree looked as though it would serve as the perfect bed, so he hung up his pack and tied himself into the crook of two branches. Settling in, he heard a snarl.

He forced himself to lie still. Below, the bushes rustled as a leopard's silky hide slunk toward him. It circled he tree, waiting.

"It smells the rabbit meat," said Cleopas.

"It also smells me."

Once before, he'd encountered a wild leopard, while hunting in Libya with Sestus. A small contingent of Roman noblemen and soldiers had been capturing the black cats for the empire's zoos, circuses, and arenas. Sestus hadn't yet been a centurion and Titius had hardly been grown. But his father had sent him out to have an adventure. The group had captured six beasts in netted traps and secured them in cages.

On the hunt's final evening, they had lit the torches. Five of the cats had been fed and tore into the meat. The sixth lay sleeping in its cage, seemingly uninterested in the food Titius offered. He had moved closer, swinging the meat, calling, insulting, wooing. He'd wondered if the cat were dead, but he'd seen it pacing and snarling earlier in the day.

It had proved unresponsive to his javelin pokes, so he moved in closer. The laughter and drunken talk of everyone else covered up the noise.

With one hand, Titius had unlatched the cage door and stretched out his arm to put down the meat. Just then, the cat had launched itself at the door, knocking Titius onto his back. When the door had swung open again, the black leopard sprang at him. He'd planted the butt of the javelin in the ground and swung the point into the animal's throat. One claw had raked across his arm and he still bore the scars to this day.

Sestus had been the first to come to his aid and had speared the beast before it could recover its footing.

When his father had heard of the encounter, he'd only said, "Waste of a good cat."

Today, though, he looked down his tree at the even larger leopard stalking him. He readied his javelin and dagger and waited as the cat paced below.

"*Throw down the meat,*" Cleopas urged as time dragged by.

"I've got other ideas," Titius said. "It wants me to show fear. Any sudden moves and it'll stop waiting."

Hours passed, and the leopard made several feigned charges up the tree. Titius never moved.

At last, the cat sprang onto a lower limb and started climbing toward him. The devious creature snarled as it slithered up the trunk to reach Titius's branch. It had scouted well.

But Titius had also scouted well. While the cat had been pacing, Titius had draped ropes from one branch to another, webbing himself in. So when the cat began to climb, the ropes blocked its approach.

The moon finally crested the hills and its light penetrated the forest. The leopard's glistening eyes and flashing fangs sent a shiver down his spine.

At first, Titius hoped the black demon would just give up and leave. When it didn't, he set his javelin and thrust for its heart.

Suddenly, a high-pitched scream pierced the night. Titius froze. Had that sound come from the leopard? The impaled beast lost its footing and fell to the ground, thrashing and whimpering as it died.

In the morning, he skinned the carcass, wrapped the pelt in his shepherd's cape, and kept on toward Capernaum. All sense of peace was gone, though. Every tree became an enemy's hiding place. He walked quickly and purposefully.

"I don't think that was just a leopard last night," said Cleopas.

"I skinned it," Titius said. "It was a leopard."

"I've heard that scream before," Cleopas continued. "It comes from something you could never handle."

"I handled it just fine."

"You're fortunate there was only one."

When Titius reached the hill above Tiberias, he looked down on the palace where Herod Antipas lived with his wife Herodias and daughter Salome. Carpenters were scurrying over the palace roof like ants. Oxcarts were lined up as craftsmen unloaded Persian carpets, Grecian tiles, Roman statues, Cretian pottery, and basket after basket of fruits, nuts, and local delicacies. There seemed no luxury this king of the Jews would deny himself or his queen.

He kept walking and soon reached Capernaum, where he moved easily through the streets. He left the leopard's hide with a tanner who displayed dozens of skillfully cured sheepskins. The man had seemed eager to prove his craft with the leopard's black fur.

Dressed as the nobleman, Titius stopped near one of the gates to look for Levi, the tax collector he had met on a previous trip. He needed an update on the Messiah. But now a red-bearded, squinty-eyed round man sat in Levi's booth, with a guard on either side. A new tax collector.

"Peace to you," Titius said.

"Peace to you as well," the tax collector replied. "What can I do to serve a nobleman of Rome?"

"I am Portius Festus, formerly of Alexandria," Titius said. "There used to be another man here. Levi. Curly hair, russet robe."

The squinty accountant knit his eyebrows together. "If you owe him something, forget it. He's gone off with that new Messiah."

"What do you mean?"

"Strangest thing. I'm here talking with Matthew Levi about expanding our booth, and this Yeshua ben Yuseph from Nazareth walks up to us with his fishermen and says, 'Come, follow me.'"

This didn't sound right. "So…?"

"So Levi goes. Leaves everything!"

Titius scratched behind his ear. "Is this Messiah against paying taxes?"

"Not at all. He even pays the voluntary ones. When some of the religious leaders and tax collectors came up from Jerusalem asking about the temple tax, Yeshua sent Simon out fishing—with a hook and line, if you can imagine! Simon came back with a fish, and in its mouth… a shekel! Yeshua told him to pay their tax with it."

"Where do I find this Messiah?"

"Walk into town and follow the crowd," the red-bearded man said. "You can't miss him."

Titius turned to leave.

"One warning," the tax collector called.

"What's that?"

"Watch your neck." He slashed his throat with his finger. "With the zealots around, there aren't too many Romans walking the streets. You might be safer in Tiberias."

Chapter Thirteen

Titius heeded the warning, returned to the forest, and changed into his Grecian olive merchant clothes. He descended the hill and, after re-entering the town, came upon a familiar fruit merchant.

"May the peace of Aphrodite rest on you," said Titius to him in Greek. "I am Stephanus from Corinth."

"Shalom," the vendor answered. "I am Zechariah from Damascus."

"I seek sustenance and information."

"The price for either will please you."

"A shekel's worth of dates to begin."

The merchant scooped several handfuls of dates into a bag and laid it on his cart. "What would you like to know?"

"Who in this town knows everyone and everything?"

The man pointed toward the inn. "Hiram, the innkeeper."

Titius paid his shekel and made his farewell.

Men lounged outside the inn drinking, laughing, and making ribald comments at passersby. Two men mocked Titius's short white tunic and joked in Hebrew that he had a woman's knees. He brushed past them into the building.

Inside, he found Hiram conversing with three others at a table. Titius ordered fish soup and waited until the three men left. Then he asked Hiram for information.

An hour into the innkeeper's dissertation, Titius had heard everything about Galilee anyone would want to know: how the land could be travelled north to south in one day or east to west in one day and every step was fertile for olives.

Hiram told him the whole history of the immoral Samaritans to the south, the Phoenicians north and west, plus the people of Gaulanitis and the Decapolis across the Jordan River to the east.

There were over two hundred villages in Galilee and every one of them produced olive oil. There was no end of possibilities for a wise merchant. And this innkeeper just happened to have a cousin who knew the man who could make the right deal for just the right price.

Titius knew a con when he heard one. He paid for his meal and left.

Afterward he went to the beach and skipped a few stones. Suddenly, a fisherman appeared beside him. The man had strong shoulders under his rich red tunic; he worked hard. His blue-banded head covering showed high status. His face was Hebrew, but his beard had been cropped short.

"Peace be upon you," the fisherman said. He had the same accent and vocal inflection as Cleopas.

Titius bent down and selected three more smooth stones. "And to you."

"I am Isaac of Magdala."

"I am Porpherus of Corinth," Titius said, having forgotten which name he had used just a short time ago. He skipped another stone.

"Are you here for the Messiah?" Isaac asked.

"Isn't everyone?"

"He's in that fishing boat." Isaac pointed at a vessel several lengths from shore. It was large enough for twelve men or a few hundred fish. "Walk with me."

Titius kept pace with Isaac as the man increased his pace over the rocky shore. Titius's ankle turned at one point, but he ignored the pain and pushed on.

"Are we going to hear the Messiah?"

"Two hundred boats on this lake and the Messiah chooses Simon's," Isaac said. He indicated the dozens of low-sided craft bobbing just offshore. Men were casting their nets and pulling them back in, over and over.

The boat carrying Yeshua was crowded with men, but no one in it cast nets. Yeshua stood in its bow, facing the beach. People were crowding onto the shore, straining to hear.

"You have a boat?" Titius asked.

"Of course," Isaac said, "I'm a fisherman. Even my cousin Mary is there, with the crowd, listening to Yeshua's every word. He cast seven demons out of her."

Cleopas screeched in his head; Titius put his hands against his ears.

"I assure you," Isaac said. "She is well."

"How is your cousin now? Without the demons, I mean?"

"It's a whole new world for her. But I can't get her to help me pickle fish anymore. She's enamored with the Messiah and wants to spend all she's earned on him."

"It must make you mad at this Messiah," said Titius.

"No, praise the Almighty. I found a new girl, Abigail. Says she learned to pickle fish in Rome. Finding her was a miracle."

"Abigail?" Titius asked.

"Yes," Isaac replied. "She says her family used to live here when she was young. She doesn't want to talk about what happened there, but she seems happy to be back."

"Is she married?"

Isaac squinted at Titius. "None of my business. I haven't heard her speak of a husband. All I care is that she does the work."

"Maybe I'll come see what kind of pickled fish you have."

"Good, Porpherus," said Isaac. "Now, I need to hear this Messiah for myself."

Titius tried to listen, but Cleopas spoke louder and louder in his head. He had to move away from the crowd to deal with the pain.

"Did you hear?" Cleopas said. *"This Messiah bewitches women! Steals them from their homes!"*

"What?" Titius asked. "Isaac has found Abigail. We need to get to her."

"This woman isn't who you thought she was when she was young," Cleopas said. *"She's been gone for years. She may be married, or ruined by other men. Let her go."*

"I have to know!"

Titius looked back at Yeshua's boat, which was slowly headed toward the shore. People began to go back into town, the crowd so thick at times that Titius couldn't move. He finally gave up and sat on a log while he waited for the beach to clear.

When there was enough space to move around again, he noticed that Yeshua's boat had actually changed direction and headed away from shore.

"Forget about him," Cleopas said. *"You're not really looking for him anyway, are you?"*

"I need to find Abigail," Titius agreed.

He decided that by mid-afternoon, he'd change disguises and go on to Magdala. But first he needed to find out where Isaac prepared his fish.

As Titius rose to go, a great yelling sounded from the fishing boat on the lake.

"James, John!" someone was shouting. Titius recognized it as Simon's voice. "Bring your boat! There's too many! Hurry, we're sinking! Hurry!"

The water around the boat was lit by silver flashes. Titius moved to the edge of the lake to get a better look.

Before long, a second fishing boat had joined it. When the two boats were side by side, the men began pulling up their nets, bringing in load after load of fish. The filled boats settled so low in the water that it seemed they might indeed sink. Dozens of men from the beach, shouting their amazement, waded out to help.

Yeshua stepped off and waded ashore soon after, laughing with the others. He looked to heaven. "Praise be to the Almighty who gives us the bounty of the sea."

Titius stepped toward him, but Cleopas screamed, *"Run!"*

A woman, her smile radiating like sunshine, twirled and danced, surefooted and carefree, along the beach toward Titius. Her cream-colored robe fluttered in the breeze like butterfly wings. Her midnight-dark hair floated over her shoulders.

Five other women walked serenely in her wake, chatting. They stopped to look back at the fishermen hauling the last of their netted fish ashore.

"Yeshua is Lord," sang the dancing woman. "Yeshua is Mighty, Yeshua is Messiah, our hope and our life."

"Mary," called another woman to her. "Your cousin Isaac was looking for you."

She stopped dancing. "I hope he doesn't expect me back in Magdala. I'm done with pickled fish. I follow the fisher of men."

They all laughed.

Titius stepped in the women's direction. "Mary?"

"Do I know you?" she asked. "Do you follow Yeshua?"

"I spoke to your cousin Isaac about your business in Magdala. I think I know the woman working for him, Abigail."

Mary smiled. "I haven't met her. I've been with Yeshua since he freed me."

"Freed you?"

"Yes! The voices are gone, my mind is clear. My spirit sees the Almighty as he is."

"Leave! Run! Don't listen to her."

Titius's stomach churned. His mind fought as a blind man gropes in a maze. Claustrophobic darkness surrounded his soul. His heart raced. His knees weakened.

"Does the Messiah help everyone?" he asked.

"No, but he helped me and I'm free." She stared into his eyes and he looked away. "This peace is worth everything you have."

With that, she danced away, the other women following.

Titius looked back up the beach to where he'd last seen Yeshua, but all he saw were fishermen filling basket after basket with fish.

Chapter Fourteen

Over the next two days Titius walked the shoreline, skipped stones, argued with Cleopas, and made discreet inquiries about the Messiah around Capernaum. Titius recorded them for Sestus.

"His magic breaks my boredom."

"The place is much quieter when he's away."

"He's good for business."

"I wish he'd get on with ousting the Romans."

Many people loved him.

"He healed my friend."

"He raised my daughter."

"He touched me."

"He held my baby."

"He speaks peace to my soul."

But no matter how much time passed, Titius couldn't stop thinking about Magdala and the possibility of finding Abigail there. He had to get back to Sepphoris, but he decided to at least stop by Isaac's shop along the way. If Abigail happened to be there, Sestus would just have to wait.

He stopped by the tanner's shop to pick up his leopard's hide. It hadn't been perfectly cured yet, but he had no more time to wait. He paid two drachma and claimed his prize.

He worked his way south around the lake, keeping to the lake road. Hundreds of others were on the move after the events at Capernaum and Titius fell into step with a group of peasants.

"Peace to you," he said to them.

"Peace to you as well," one of the peasants replied, sweat pouring down his fleshy cheeks.

"I am Porpherus of Corinth."

"You look as Greek as my grandmother," said the spokesman. "I'm Assander of Magdala, and these are my brothers and uncles."

"I hear Magdala is a great city."

Assander grunted. "It was greater before Antipas decided to steal all our fish processing. Now the best workers go to him."

Soon Titius saw the earthen towers near Magdala ahead, along the shore of the lake. The main road seemed to head straight through the town, but he decided to ask Assander for directions.

"If you want to get to Sepphoris, turn inland when you get to the towers."

Titius thanked him. "Do you know a fisherman named Isaac?"

"There are many Isaacs in this land."

"This Isaac had a cousin, Mary, who used to work for him. She follows the Messiah now."

Assander laughed. "The Messiah? You mean Yeshua, the carpenter from Nazareth?" The rest of his brothers and uncles joined his mocking laughter. "Everyone begs him for bread and freedom. I say get back to work. Earn your own bread."

"I'm more interested in Isaac and his business."

"Yes, we know this man. He has a business near ours. He also has a beautiful new helper." Assander pointed toward a thick-nosed man with a generous belly. "Elkanah, my brother, wants to marry her."

"Is this woman's name Abigail?" Titius asked.

"Who cares?" Elkanah called over, his belly bouncing. "She'll give me beautiful children!"

"Rumor is she's a Roman whore," a tall boney man said.

"You just want her for yourself," Assander declared.

Elkanah turned serious. "I know a zealot who'll slit your throat if you touch her before I do."

Titius restrained himself and stayed silent.

Nearby, a group of older boys began to hurl stones at the peasants' donkeys. One donkey brayed in protest and skittered sideways, almost dumping its load.

Elkanah reached under a blanket and pulled out an Arab scimitar.

"I will cut off your heads and serve them to your mothers!" he yelled at the boys. When he stepped toward them, waving his sword, the boys turned and fled, screaming.

Their journey continued toward Magdala without further incident, Elkanah describing to everyone what he'd do to any boy who disrespected men such as himself.

Assander turned to Titius as they neared the cliffs of Mount Arbel which rose around the town.

"Porpherus of Corinth, see there?" Assanger grabbed Titius and pointed at a large establishment next to the road. "There, where the Arbel stream empties into the lake, is the Isaac you seek. On behalf of my brother, though, keep your mind on fish and olives and forget the Roman beauty doing the work."

The other men laughed as they walked off down the road, leaving Titius behind.

Titius sauntered along the stream and found a shallow crossing. The town was busy, and nobody asked him his business.

He set himself on a tree stump near Isaac's shop and watched as fishermen prepared for night work with torches and nets. Oxcarts were filled with crates of pickled, dried, and preserved fish for transport.

"Forget this woman," Cleopas whispered. *"You heard the men. She's probably been a Roman whore. Let someone else have her."*

She's not an old carpet I can give away, Titius thought. *Love has its price.*

"You know nothing about love."

Titius marched to the main entrance of Isaac's shop and pushed his way in. Smoky olive oil lamps hung from the ceiling, casting a flickering light over the crowded room. Many voices yelled over each other in the market. Two men keeping accounts stood behind a table as two others weighed fish. Still others raced to retrieve the orders of waiting customers.

One of the accountants nodded to Titius as he entered.

"I need to see Isaac and Abigail!" Titius shouted above the noise.

Zeus, Hermes, whatever gods there might be, he prayed silently, *bring her to me.*

"Isaac is on his way to Jerusalem," the accountant said. "Abigail is in Sepphoris."

Titius's heart pounded at the disappointment of having missed her. Was this a cruel game of the gods? But at least she had gone exactly where he needed to go next. If he started back now and rested along the way, he could enter the market gates of Sepphoris at first light.

As Titius passed out of the shadows sheltering the town, the sun slid out of sight. At first he welcomed the fresh sounds of the night—crickets, frogs, and bush babies. Then a leopard's snarl unsettled him. With one hand, he felt in his pack for the skin of the previous leopard who'd attacked him, which he'd gotten cured.

He also grabbed his dagger. Carrying only small weapons was a hazard of some of his disguises.

Titius turned in the road, looking for movement in the trees around him. There was no snarl, no footfall, no breathing.

No fear.

"You were safe in a tree last time," Cleopas noted. *"Now you're in his territory."*

"If he gets me he gets you," Titius whispered to himself. "Don't distract me. I need to keep my senses."

"If you had your senses, you'd have stopped chasing this woman. I told you your weakness for women would destroy you."

The hairs on his neck stood up like a cat's. He felt it in his flesh: something, somewhere, was hunting him. It was closing in on his left, tracking him, waiting. He moved to the far side of the road as the moon slid up, a mere sliver in the night. Clouds covered most of the stars.

At a bend in the road, the presence seemed to fade briefly, but then it reappeared on his right. He crossed the road again.

Titius reached an oak tree and flung a rope from his pack over a low branch. He wrapped the rope around his wrist and pulled himself up. A demonic snarl pierced the darkness and he felt fire pierce the calf muscles of his trailing leg. He'd been bitten! He kicked back, but the cat slipped past his foot and sank its claws into his back and stomach, attempting to use its weight to pull him to the ground. In desperation, Titius kicked out again and sent the leopard flying.

The cat was up the trunk in a moment, but Titius kicked it a third time, this time with both feet. It landed on its paws and began to circle the tree.

Blood flowed down his torso and he knew the cat could smell it. Would it wait for him to bleed out or attempt another attack? He tied off the wounded leg, then wrapped a strip of linen around his midriff to staunch the flow of blood. He wrapped his leg as best he could—and waited.

The cat circled and snarled.

Titius took out his leopard skin and hung it from the branch. He braced himself, set his dagger, and yelled as loudly as he could. The noise angered the cat and it made several jumps up the trunk. Twice, Titius was sure his dagger cut into its paw.

An hour into the standoff, he heard human voices and saw torches coming down the road.

"Help!" he called. "Help!"

He repeated the call for help in Greek, then Latin, then Hebrew, then Aramaic, then Arab.

"Where are you?" responded an Aramaic voice. "What's wrong?"

"I'm in a tree," Titius yelled. "There's a leopard here."

The torches moved quickly toward him and the leopard ran into the darkness. Six bearded faces looked up at him.

"The cat seems to be gone," one of them said.

"There's a lot of blood here," said another.

"It's mostly mine," Titius said. "But I think I got him a couple of times with my dagger."

"Please, let us help you down."

Titius lowered his pack and they caught it.

Their leader started laughing. "What's this? A leopard skin? You have one and now you're using yourself as bait to get another?" The others laughed, too

"I needed to get to Sepphoris," Titius declared, lowering himself and preparing to jump down.

"You're out of your mind to be walking alone at night," said the leader. "You're not even dressed for hunting." He pulled a wig and tunic from the pack, then held up a bag of coins. "Look! Thank you for contributing to our cause!"

The men began to walk away with the coins, his pack, and the leopard skin.

"Wait! Those are mine!" Titius yelled.

"The gods left you a choice," the leader called back. "Stay here and face the leopard alone, or express your appreciation by rewarding those who rescued you. Our hope was to capture a caravan and relieve them of their treasures."

"There's nothing valuable in my pack," Titius pleaded. "You'll only increase Rome's wrath if you rob its citizens."

The leader held his torch up toward Titius. "Are you a Roman citizen?" They broke into laughter. "Hung in a tree like a side of venison? We'll see what Rome does to protect its citizen from the leopard."

And the men left him.

Delirious, suffering from blood loss, and stumbling around a forest in the dark, Titius soon forgot all about the leopard. Eventually he collapsed on a log at the side of the road. He pictured himself back in Rome, sitting with Cleopas as they had discussed his future in the Roman senate.

Cleopas had led the lesson: "You need military and administrative experience."

"How can I get that without getting killed?" Titius had asked.

"Focus on the swordplay instead of that girl."

"But she's more interesting. What'll I do? Beat down Gauls or Germans? Rome has the fittest fighting force in the world. Who'll stop us?"

"Many would love to try."

"I can't be a quaestor or any other Roman magistrate for ten more years." Titius had moaned. "After that, I'll have to get my aedileship, then praetorship, then consulship. It could take half my life!"

Cleopas had pointed to the chart he had prepared. "As soon as you become even the lowest magistrate, you'll gain political and judicial powers. Your word will carry life and death, and you and your class can choose and advise the emperor. When people see your purple-fringed toga, you'll get privilege, position and recognition at the games."

"How gullible are people?" Titius had asked. "Is one man better than another because of what he wears?"

"Do you think one woman is better than another because of what she wears? Look beyond what you see."

"Yes," Titius had said. "One woman is definitely better."

When Titius next sensed light, it felt like an earthquake had seized him. He reached out to steady himself and heard a woman say, "He lives… he moves."

He felt a cool cloth against his forehead, then the caress of a woman's hand.

"Peace, my friend," she said. "Peace."

Warm sun stroked his body and he had no strength to move. Trees blocked the sunlight for a moment and he saw a raven-haired princess smiling down at him. Her ruby nose ring matched the studs in her ears.

"We found you by the road," she said, her voice like a dove. Titius groaned. "Micah says a leopard got you, so we're taking you to Cana. There's a healer there."

Before he could say anything, all went black again.

Titius dreamt of his mother in Rome as she stood beside a sobbing woman and her husband, neighbors of theirs. The husband suddenly slapped the woman in the face, and she stumbled back, quiet but in shock. The woman then watched as her newborn son was given to a white-clad priest. Drums and horns drowned out the boy's cries.

The priest walked up to a large stone statue of the god Chemosh. A fire burned in its hollow belly. Its extended arms glowed red hot. The priest held up the child and spoke an incantation before laying the babe on the glowing arms. The arms then fed the child into the god's fiery mouth.

Titius's mother shielded herself from the terror, crushing her own son in her arms. Moments later, they fled.

"We have no god but Caesar," Titius could remember his mother saying. "Caesar takes my father and husband but leaves my son."

Abigail and her sister had tried to calm his mother with incense, jasmine, and rose petals, but nothing helped. Mother had never been the same again. She just paced the garden, mumbling. Father never spoke of the matter and stayed away from home for longer periods of time.

Cleopas had worked hard to distract Titius from what was happening. He lengthened his class hours and planned more trips to the pool and countryside.

Despite all Cleopas taught him about a Creator, Titius vowed to never trust another god. He'd seen many gods worshipped in the temples and arenas. Now their faces haunted him. They reached for his soul.

In the midst of his family's confusion, Cleopas had taunted Titius about his weakness with women, Abigail in particular. Titius had become more belligerent, even throwing his slate at his teacher on one occasion. As the days passed, he refused to leave the house. He skipped lessons, feigning illness.

Father was distant and paid more attention to slave girls than to his wife. To get his father's attention, Titius had chosen to report Cleopas as an informant. He had watched, unflinching, as Cleopas was crucified.

Now Cleopas's gasping face on the cross forced itself into his dreams.

Chapter Fifteen

When the world came back into focus, the raven-haired beauty was wiping his brow.

"Hello, stranger," she said. "I'm Rachel, and my brother is Micah. You're with my family in Cana."

"May the gods bless you," Titius whispered.

"Oh no. We follow Yahweh, the Almighty, the true God, the only God."

"My allegiance is to Caesar."

The woman dipped the cloth into a bowl. "Today is the Sabbath. Micah went to the synagogue, and he says that Yeshua ben Yuseph of Nazareth read the Torah scroll. He spoke of deep things that made the rabbi and the landowners angry. The Pharisees got even angrier when he healed an old woman in the service."

"I know this Yeshua," Titius said.

"I wish Micah had brought him here to heal you. Six days is a long time to have a fever."

As soon as he tried to move, Titius felt the stiffness in his legs. He noticed many scabs and wounds on his leg, along his arm, and across his stomach. He'd been severely wounded.

Rachel spooned broth into his mouth and brought him water. His parched throat protested.

"My mother used to make us chicken broth when we were sick," Rachel said. "My mother died of a fever. I didn't want you to die like she did. It was very painful."

Titius drank in the light of her dark eyes. "Thank you for rescuing me."

"We had to," she said. "Yeshua told a story about a Samaritan stopping to help someone who had been beaten by robbers. Micah says that helping a Greek hurt by a leopard is the same thing. But how did you keep the leopard from killing you?"

"Bandits," Titius said.

She spooned more broth into him. "Bandits?"

Titius swallowed. "Bandits came by while the leopard was attacking. It ran away."

"Did they help you?" Rachel asked, tipping the water to his mouth.

"No. They stole my things and left me."

She stood up and paced the floor. "What? They just left you to die?"

"They left me nothing."

"Well, praise the Almighty we found you. The leopard could have killed you. You could have bled to death! God is so good."

"That's not exactly the way I'd put it."

Rachel knelt beside him and put the cloth back on his forehead. "I don't know your name."

Titius attempted to raise himself up onto his elbows. "I think you're an angel…"

She smiled and pushed him back down. "You're more delirious than I thought."

An hour later Micah arrived, and that was the last Titius saw of Rachel.

"She's gone to my cousin in Capernaum," Micah said. "She needs to know more about the Messiah and less about you. Where can I take you? Your family?"

"I've got no family," Titius said. "If you will, take me to Sepphoris. There are people there who will care for me. I thank you for what you've done."

They went to Sepphoris two days later, with their donkey pulling up to the gates just after noon. The city's noise seemed greater than Titius had ever heard it before.

"Ask for the optio named Jaennus," he urged Micah.

Micah argued with a legionnaire for a few minutes, and then the legionnaire peered over the edge of the cart at Titius.

"I'm Titius Marcus Julianus," he said, "servant to the centurion Sestus Aurelius. Jaennus is the optio."

An hour later, Jaennus himself peered into the cart.

"So the prodigal has returned, Jaennus said. "You let a leopard get you? What was the point of all that training?"

Several legionnaires dragged Titius out and carried him wordlessly into the soldiers' quarters. They left him on a blanket near the entrance.

Soon after, Sestus walked in.

"What kind of guardian are you?" the centurion asked. "Your cross maker is finishing the crosses for the zealots we captured, and you can watch. Then I'll expect your report on the Messiah."

Titius had no intention of watching the crucifixions, but a pair of legionnaires gave him a new robe and walked him to a site overlooking the scene where thousands had gathered. Vultures circled overhead.

Six zealots were being led to the crosses. Titius recognized three of the young men he'd trained across the Jordan. Jeremiah's dark braids had been chopped off; he stumbled forward, bent and broken. Magdiel looked more like a boy than a man. Ethan hobbled silently. The other three were equally subdued.

Sestus presented the six to a magistrate. Then a legionnaire stepped up behind each captive and forced him to his knees, a dagger to his throat.

The youngest openly whimpered when sentenced. His companions turned away, ashamed of his betrayal. Other legionnaires approached the men, carrying crossbeams and tied them to the zealots' outstretched arms. When the beams were secured, the soldiers forced the prisoners to their feet and prodded them on their death march.

When his former trainees were nailed in place, Titius looked away. Their screams joined all the other memories he had tried to bury.

As their screams continued, he steadied himself against a wall and got to his feet. He inched away along the cobblestone path, Cleopas mocking him at every step: *"You could stay and watch me being crucified but you can't watch these children?"*

For a day after that, no one came to see him. For three days, no one brought him food or water; his hunger and thirst raged.

Finally, two legionnaires picked him up and walked him through corridor after corridor. When they at last put him down, Titius recognized the fireplace, the place of incense, and the cushions. This was the assassins' den. Two flagons of wine sat alongside some bread, fruit, and goat cheese. He ate without hesitation and lay down on a cushion to rest.

After some time, the blanket covering the passageway shifted and Marcus stepped in, with Octavian following him. They smiled at him like grinning hyenas.

Marcus set two javelins against the wall near the tunnel entrance.

"We almost got our necks cut because of you," Marcus said. "We made it through two camps of those rebels, but I couldn't get close to Barabbas's sister. Because she thought she was in love with you. She thought someone must have killed you!"

"That Hosea," Octavian snarled, drawing his dagger. "He wouldn't let us out of his sight!" He hurled his blade into the wall above Titius's head. "They interrogated us. We insisted we knew you and that you were a great threat to Rome. How did we not know you'd been imprisoned and cut? How did we not know about your exploits with 'the desert fox' in Libya?"

Octavian stepped up to the table and drained the flagon of wine. Titius struggled to sit upright and moved back against the wall.

Marcus picked up a handful of dates. "Those zealots praised you as a great friend of Barabbas. They vowed revenge on the Romans. Those young zealots were crucified because you made them believe in themselves."

Octavian finished off the second flagon of wine, then wiped his mouth and sighed contentedly. "For that, we thank you. I enjoyed looking into their faces and telling them who you really were. Hearing them scream. It's time to get the rest of those naïve zealots."

"However, we can't thank you for breaking our code." Marcus pulled out his dagger and got down on one knee next to Titius. "Somehow Jaennus found out that Octavian had a contract with Cretius... he found out we were working to keep you from your inheritance. Jaennus tried to ship us back to Rome, but here we are."

"And here *you* are," Octavian said. He retrieved his dagger from the wall above Titius and handed it to Marcus, who swung it back and forth inches from Titius's nose.

Titius watched it for a moment, but it was the eyes he had to watch—and Marcus's eyes were intense. On fire.

"Yes, here we are," Titius said.

Marcus pushed a table toward the exit into the hallway, blocking Titius's escape that way. "You know we can't finish this here."

"Finish what?" Titius asked, kneeling before the fire, his back to them.

"Our honor is at stake," Octavian said. "The zealots think they know who you are, we know who you are, and soon Cretius will know who you are. You won't see it coming, but by next full moon I'll have my sack of gold and you'll finally meet your father again."

Titius stood and walked to the marble bust of Caesar, near the doorway. The emperor's head would be a useless weapon against two professional assassins, but he caressed the carved laurel wreath.

"What do you know of my father?" he asked.

Marcus put on his hungry hyena smile. "It wasn't the Germans who got your father. He was too smart to die in battle. Lord Cretius wanted your estate, and your father was in the way."

The realization hit Titius like an avalanche. "Lies! My father died a hero. Cretius is a worthless thief."

Octavian picked up a javelin and pointed it at Titius. "Let's hope he never hears you say that in one of his torture chambers." He snuffed a nearby lamp wick between his fingers.

The two assassins picked up the remaining lamps, stepped into the passageway that led out to the bakery, and were gone. The embers in the fireplace hardly penetrated the deep shadows.

Exhausted, Titius rested against the wall and slept.

Early the next morning, a servant girl relit the lamp, rekindled the fireplace, and straightened the cushions. When she saw Titius lying in the dark, she screamed and stepped back.

"Peace," Titius said. "Peace. I mean no harm."

She slipped out the door in a hurry. Two legionnaires arrived minutes later with their gladiuses drawn. Titius hadn't moved.

"Peace," he said again. "Peace. I wait for the optio to hear my report."

"Come," the senior soldier said. "The centurion wants you."

Titius tried his best to keep up as each soldier held an elbow and forced him to walk quickly. Once inside Sestus's quarters, he was thrown to the floor and left. Four legionnaires, swords drawn, stood along the wall.

He struggled to his feet and surveyed the room. The floor-to-ceiling Persian carpets belonged in a palace, not a soldier's room. There were marble statues, the best of Rome. Golden incense bowls, silver wine flagons, jade sculptures... Sestus had exquisite taste. A chair covered in a lion skin sat at one end of the room.

"What's this about?" Titius asked.

No legionnaire moved a muscle. Titius stepped toward the chair; every eye moved with him.

Someone knocked on the door softly, twice. The legionnaires drew their swords and hemmed him in. Titius's shoulder and neck muscles tightened with anticipation.

Sestus opened the door and walked purposefully toward the chair. He sat straight-backed and extended his centurion's stick. "Kneel."

Titius knelt, as did the others. Sestus had never ordered him to kneel before.

"It's your choice: die slowly or quickly," Sestus said. "By the sword or by strangulation."

Titius's heartbeat quickened. His palms moistened. His shoulder pain moved to his back. "What are the charges?"

Sestus lowered his stick. "Abandoning your assignment. Defecting to the zealots. Refusing to report to your superior. Murdering a Roman officer."

"Who are the witnesses?" Titius asked.

What was this about?

Sestus waved at a legionnaire, who opened the door. Marcus stood there, dressed in his full black assassin's attire.

A shiver raced up Titius's spine. He rested his knuckles against the cool floor.

"Speak truth or forfeit your tongue," the centurion commanded. "Roman justice is swift."

"From my time with the zealots," Marcus said, "I learned that this man, Titius Marcus Julianus, taught zealot fighters how to beat Roman armies. He sought to marry the sister of Barabbas, the zealots' leader. He didn't return from his assignment in Capernaum but followed his own pleasure. Now his bloodied robe has been discovered by the body of Jaennus, the optio who crucified the zealots that Titius trained."

Titius couldn't believe what he had heard. His gut twisted. Jaennus, his ally, was dead? Who would he turn to now? And what were these charges? Everything Marcus had said was technically true, but the way he described it made for deadly implications.

"The record is clear," Sestus said to a legionnaire who had taken up a stylus and wax tablet. "Is there another witness?"

"Yes," Marcus said. He left and Octavian came in and knelt.

"Speak!" Sestus ordered. "Speak truth or forfeit your tongue."

"From my years training as a thespian assassin with this man, Titius Marcus Julianus, I know he has broken the brotherhood's code. He betrayed those he swore to protect. He has not guarded this garrison's cross maker. Because of this, the cross maker was attacked and nearly killed by zealots. When commanded to stay and watch the executions, he left."

"The record is clear," Sestus announced. "The witness may go. We will read the charges."

The legionnaire stepped forward and read: "Let it be known and let it be clear that Titius Marcus Julianus is charged with the following, requiring his death. He joined forces with the zealots. He abandoned his post. He murdered a Roman officer. He broke the code of brotherhood. He was delinquent in his responsibilities. He refused an order."

Sestus turned to Titius, still kneeling. "How do you answer to these charges deserving your death?"

Titius bowed low, as he'd done in the cave when he had first submitted to the centurion.

"Thank you for letting me speak. I know that such charges usually result in immediate death without defense. First, I know nothing about the death of my dear friend Jaennus. Until this moment I hadn't heard of it. I am willing, before this judgment seat, to give a moment by moment account of my whereabouts to prove I am blameless."

"So you shall," Sestus said.

The recording officer readied himself to write down Titius's words.

"Regarding the code of brotherhood, I have been instructed by the centurion in command of this proceeding that truth spoken to officers does not qualify as breaking the code," Titius said. "I will tell you what I told him before this judgment seat, as long as there are no non-officers in the room."

"This too will be," Sestus said, furrowing his brow.

The recorder finished writing and Sestus nodded for Titius to continue.

"Regarding the charge of abandoning my responsibility for the cross maker, I was reassigned to find out more about the one called Messiah. I was doing my duty when the cross maker was attacked. I am willing to give a full account, before this judgment seat, of where I was and what I learned."

"It will be arranged," Sestus said, nodding again.

"Regarding the charge of training zealots to defeat Romans and betraying my command by seeking to marry Barabbas's sister, I have already reported to Jaennus and my centurion. I deny any act outside my assignment—to infiltrate and gain wisdom on the strengths and plans of the zealots. I can give a fuller report before this judgment seat if that is required."

"So you shall," Sestus said. "Next charge."

"Regarding leaving the execution, I was dragged to the event without my knowledge. I was recovering from a leopard attack and a fever. I have only my ignorance to blame for disregarding a command. This I admit, but I am also willing to give a full account of what happened when I left."

"My judgment will be just," Sestus pronounced.

"Regarding my failure to return directly to this city and instead following another path, which led to being attacked by the leopard, I say that coming from Capernaum to Sepphoris through Magdala is still a somewhat direct route. I was following up on new information, and I'm willing to give a fuller report before this judgment seat."

"So you shall," Sestus said. "Legionnaires, you've protected me well. Send three officers who can take your place, all of whom can record. We'll be here a while."

Titius kept his head bowed low as the soldiers were exchanged.

When Sestus dismissed himself, Titius was left alone—except for Cleopas. *"I would choose the sword. You deserve the cross, but you're a Roman, so they can't do that. Strangulation is too clean. Beheading gives them a mess to clean up."*

Titius put his hands to his own throat. *Hush, spawn of the evil one.*

"What did you call me?"

Titius looked around. Dozens of oil lamps burned overhead, giving off an olive oil scent. The polished marble floor shone. A strange presence lurked at the edges of the room, something that smelled like peace. Inside, Cleopas whimpered.

The door opened and Sestus returned, followed by three other optios who took their places behind tables. Each held a stylus and a long parchment on which to write.

The interrogation for Titius's life began in earnest.

After one hour, Titius's knees and back cried out for mercy. After two hours, his mind begged for relief from having to recall so many details. After three hours, his soul craved release. After four hours of repeated questioning, he prepared his spirit for a quick end.

At last it was over. Sestus rose, called for the optios to bring their parchments, and left.

Chapter Sixteen

Titius's bladder ached as he stared at the door and willed Sestus to return. He shifted from knee to knee. He was preparing to disgrace himself when an elderly slave stepped in and placed a chamber pot in the corner. Titius used it quickly and knelt again in the center of the room.

He heard legionnaires changing shifts as they finished their half-day watch. This happened twice, and still he had heard no word from anyone.

Titius slept on his knees, his forehead to the ground, waiting. His body ached, but he dared not add another crime to his list.

When a third shift of sentries came on duty, he began to wonder.

"He's arranging your execution," Cleopas said. *"It won't be long until you're with us."*

The door opened and the same slave arrived to replace the dirty chamber pot with another. A young girl also stepped in, carrying a tray of food. Titius ate the dates, figs, bread, cheese, yogurt, and apricots. If he was to die, at least he'd die satisfied.

"That's your last meal..."

"Sestus wouldn't waste food on a condemned man, especially one who murdered his optio," Titius murmured. "I rest my soul on Roman justice. This centurion will not come to judgment quickly."

"If you'd run and come back instead of going to Magdala, this judgment may never have happened."

"I had to search for Abigail." Titius thought of her twirling happily in the Roman rose garden.

"Now you never will," Cleopas said.

A legionnaire came in and pulled Titius to his feet, but his legs felt like rubber. He forced himself to move alongside the soldier.

He led Titius through a series of tunnels into a spacious room in the fortress dungeon. Another tray of food sat on a small table, and a fresh chamber pot rested in the corner.

A fortnight of sunrises and sunsets passed without any human interaction except for with the slave who changed his chamber pot and the girl who brought him food. Although they never exchanged a word, near the end of the second week the girl looked him in the eye. He nodded, and she blushed and hurried out.

"Next time I will speak," Titius said to himself. "I will appeal to the great gods. No Roman subject should feel the cruelty of isolation for so long."

Sitting unwashed day after day started to make his skin itch and he wanted to ask the girl for a little water to wash. His beard itched, his back itched, his head, his legs, his feet… everything itched. Pacing became his only daily exercise.

One morning, as a rooster crowed, the door opened and a new legionnaire led him back to Sestus's room. Titius knelt and waited.

Sestus marched in with his guardians and sat.

"Titius Marcus Julianus, stand!" the centurion commanded.

Titius stood, his head bowed.

"Titius Marcus Julianus, I have considered all the evidence given." Sestus took out a scroll and examined it. "It's clear that the zealots still don't know you are with us. Yet there is more to be considered. For now, I sentence you to forty lashes less one for putting yourself in unnecessary danger, which made you unable to guard the cross maker. This sentence will be carried out immediately, after which you will be returned to your quarters until further decisions are made. So it is decided, so let it be done."

As two legionnaires pulled Titius from the room, he didn't know whether to be happy or terrified. The leather lash, with its embedded bits of bone and stone, would rip the skin and flesh from his back. It would be like the leopard attack all over again. His legs felt heavy as his mind fended off images of other floggings he'd witnessed.

But at least he'd be alive.

The soldiers dragged him through a tunnel, and into a courtyard. There, he walked numbly to a post where the soldiers stripped off his robe. Witnesses surrounded him, watching as his wrists were bound.

The lashes began. He screamed loud enough to drown out Cleopas's laughter.

At lash twenty, the fire across his back and sides became so bad that his senses went numb. He forced himself to remember a picnic he'd once gone on with Abigail and her sister. The girls had chased butterflies and birds and splashed in a small waterfall. White clouds had tumbled into different shapes, and they'd all talked about what they saw in the sky. All had been at peace.

Searing pain ripped at his chest and Titius gasped for air. Another bone-tipped strip of leather bit into his rib.

On that picnic, he'd fallen asleep in the sun. Today, under the lash, he longed for the lotion Abigail had applied to him for days after his skin had burned.

He awoke to the sound of a young girl singing as she bathed him. He was stripped down to a loincloth and a coat of bloody wounds. He tried to pretend the girl was Abigail, but her voice was wrong, her touch was wrong, her smell was wrong.

Titius forced himself to dwell on childhood adventures, hunting expeditions, and the awe he'd felt at the victory parades through Rome. When he was alone again, he rolled onto his side and clenched his teeth. Pain was his friend. He was *alive*.

Abigail's face sustained him, but another face had begun to surface in his thoughts. Yeshua ben Yuseph, the people's Messiah, had clearly seen through Titius's disguises yet had never exposed or humiliated him. How had Yeshua done it?

While Titius had been playing an olive merchant, Yeshua had said, "The Almighty looks behind the mask to the actor's heart. Nothing is hidden from his eyes." And very time the man had seen him, he'd nodded knowingly, acknowledging who Titius really was.

The healings, the miracles, the acts of compassion... they all moved like puzzle pieces in his mind. Some miracles could be explained away as fortunate coincidences, but what about the face of the blind man at Bethsaida? The joy on his face had burned itself into Titius's memory.

Who is he? Titius thought. *Who am I?*

As Titius lost track of days, he also lost hope. Eventually his wounds healed and the girl stopped coming around with her life-giving songs. Life's only constant was the changing chamber pot. He stopped pacing the room, and for two days he lay curled in a corner.

One day, a legionnaire opened the door and dropped a clean robe on the floor. Titius forced himself to his feet, pulled the robe over his scabbed and scarred torso, and wobbled down the hall after the quick-stepping soldier.

After many corridors, they climbed some stairs and emerged at the edge of the agora. Titius blinked in the unfiltered sunshine.

"Resume your duties," the legionnaire said. And he left.

Titius collapsed against a wall, but his wounded back recoiled from it. Through blinking eyes, he surveyed the scene. Everything looked normal. The almond trees were blooming. Piles of oranges and lemons dotted the marketplace. Several tables had taken down their canopies and stood open to the sun.

Titius shuffled toward the bakery and discovered someone working there he didn't know. He continued past it toward the fish vendor.

"No," said Cleopas. *"Don't go there."*

Titius stopped and looked at the pickled fish, none longer than his fingers. "Are these from Magdala?" he asked.

The vendor smiled. "The man knows fish. Yes, the best pickled fish in Galilee come from Magdala."

"Are these from Isaac?"

"You know Isaac?" The vendor grabbed a small bag from under his table. "His are the best, but they don't come cheap, my friend. How many would you like? Perhaps, since you're his friend, we can make a deal."

Titius's pulse quickened. "Did Abigail come by?"

"Ah, you know fish and women." The vendor began to scoop fish onto a scale. "She has a face to dazzle a man's heart. But I warn you, many men would kill to have her for their own."

"Do you know when she'll be back?"

The vendor leaned across his table. "My friend, my fish smells better than you—and a wild dog would be better groomed. The beggars look healthier. Don't chase what you can't catch."

"I just need to know when she'll be here," said Titius, surveying the other stalls. He then grabbed the vendor by the wrist. "Where did she go?"

The vendor wrenched his arm away. "I believe I overheard her tell her partner they'd enjoy their new place in Caesarea."

"Her partner? Not Isaac?"

"A young wealthy businessman. She seemed quite happy with him. Now, do you want the fish or not?"

"Typical woman," Cleopas snickered. *"Puts a hook in your heart and then rips it out."*

Titius turned away in a daze and made his way to a nearby fountain. He sat, ignoring the water slowly soaking his robe.

A month after his release, a trumpet sounded near the city's main gate and a cohort of legionnaires in full regalia marched into the square. Sestus stood atop a staircase and read a proclamation.

"Our Roman legion is proud to announce that Emperor Tiberius himself has asked two of our best to represent him in the Best of the Gladiator Games in Rome. Marcus Flavius made it to the second round. Octavian Juventus made it to the fourth. Their memories will be honored. They died honoring their emperor. Long live the emperor!"

The crowd's cheers seemed out of place to Titius. Two thespian assassins had given their lives for the emperor, but they were no heroes. No, they'd betrayed him and tried to destroy him. And now they themselves had been destroyed. While Titius had been in the dungeon, feeling the sting of injustice and death, Marcus and Octavian had faced the real strength of Roman justice.

Sestus stood, fist on his chest, chin square, back straight. There was neither pleasure nor sadness in his expression. Titius knew that if he himself had been the one chosen to die by the centurion, he would have worn this same look. He shuddered.

When the commander and honor guard disappeared into their quarters, Titius realized what this meant: Sestus had believed him. It didn't take away his body's scars, but it healed something deeper inside.

On the Sabbath, he stopped by the synagogue to see if any of Yeshua's followers were there. Dressed as a Jewish carpenter, few paid him any attention.

The attendant took a large scroll from a cabinet and handed it to a visiting rabbi. Titius recognized him right away as the rabbi from Nazareth. The man read a passage Titius didn't understand, then spent an hour warning people about false prophets, seditious leaders, and presumptuous and prideful men. Clearly he was referring to Yeshua ben Yuseph.

If the talk in the service hadn't been obvious enough, the talk among people afterward certainly was.

A burly butcher shook his finger in a scribe's face. "He speaks of Yeshua, doesn't he?"

A weaver said to a tailor, "That Nazarene has made enemies. There've been too many Messiahs. Rome will crush him as it did the others."

A young Pharisee raised his fist. "It's true! I heard it from Rabbi Gamaliel in Jerusalem. All false Messiahs will fail."

Something was changing. Messianic fever had been strong in this land for years, and everyone knew that Rome had destroyed the last three "Messiahs." In the year Antipas's father, Herod the Great, had died, Simon of Perea had led a rebellion that Rome crushed. A few years later, a shepherd named Athronges had raised a rebellion against Herod's son Archelaus. He, too, had been defeated. About the same time, Judas of Gamala had founded the zealots in this area and faced his own destruction.

"But if Yeshua isn't the Messiah, how can he open the eyes of the blind, or heal lepers?" asked an old man, bent and frail. "How did he change water to wine?"

Bodies swirled around the man, every one screaming his own viewpoint. Titius pushed his way out of the synagogue.

After freeing himself, Titius changed and walked through the city, taking in all he could observe. As a blind man he'd gained much information; people let their guard down around him.

Day after day he waited near the fish vendor, until he hardly noticed the smell anymore. There still hadn't been any sign of Abigail, and he'd had no contact with either Sestus or the optio who'd replaced Jaennus. However, he noticed Sestus riding out into zealot territory several times. Rumors among the legionnaires claimed these trips meant significant zealot losses.

Chapter Seventeen

Titius, wrapped in two blankets and an extra tunic, was hiding beside the fish vendor's stall one day when he heard a series of ear-piercing wails. He jumped to his feet and saw that two nearby vendors were embracing and wailing.

"The Baptist!" cried the date vendor. "The Baptist is dead!"

A shudder ran through Titius and he grabbed the herald. "How? Why? Where?"

"Herodias—that Jezebel—tricked Antipas at Machaerus," said the man. "Herod was drunk during his birthday party. Herodias's sleazy daughter seduced him into agreeing to behead the Baptizer. They put his head on a silver platter."

The fish vendor turned to Titius. "What do you think the Messiah will do? The Baptizer is his cousin. Maybe he'll join Barabbas and help us finally get rid of these Romans."

Until that moment, the Messiah had seemed unstoppable. It was rumored he'd fed five thousand men plus their families with only five loaves and two fish and stilled a storm with a single word. Another blind man had been healed. Indeed, he was healing people everywhere.

Titius noticed that the legionnaires on duty in the market grew tense.

"What do you think this Messiah will do?" one said to another.

"If he tries anything, we'll call in the legions and crush him. For now, he's just a distraction. Keeps the people's minds off of their troubles."

But the days went by without rioting or revolt. The soldiers began to relax.

A month after Titius's flogging, Sestus called for him to meet in the assassins' den. This time, Caleb was there, too. None of them said a word about the trial or its aftermath.

Sestus paced as usual. "Titius, you will mentor Caleb in the ways of the assassins' art. He remains my cross maker, but he needs to be more. You must ensure this."

Sestus left, leaving Titius and Caleb alone.

With a flick of his wrist, Titius produced an orange from his tunic and tossed it to Caleb.

"People use language to communicate *and* to conceal," Titius said. "They hide secrets in language they think others won't understand."

Caleb tossed the orange back to Titius. "I already know Hebrew, Greek, Aramaic, and Latin."

"Your Hebrew and Aramaic are fine," Titius replied. "Your Latin needs help. It sounds like pigs rooting for acorns. Greek should sound like an eagle on the thermals; you make it sound like a fox flushing a partridge."

"Most people understand me."

"You must do more than get by." Titius reached behind Caleb's back and produced a gladius. With a quick movement, he made it disappear again. "You must understand what others say accurately, and you must speak so that it sounds natural to any passerby."

Caleb flopped down on a cushion. "The only reason I'm doing this is to avoid the dungeon, to protect my family, and to get my slave Nabonidus back. Why do you put up with Sestus's insane demands?"

"I wanted to become a man," he said.

"And how has serving him helped you become a man?"

Titius sat down, deciding to ignore the question.

"Our art is tenfold," he said. He raised his left hand and counted off. "The five abilities are distraction, disguise, sleight of hand, silence, and quick kills." And then he moved to his right hand. "The five qualities are power, endurance, healing, knowledge, and loyalty."

Caleb held out his hands, fingers splayed. "Left is distraction, disguise, magic, silence, and death. Right is power, endurance, healing, knowledge, and loyalty." He clasped his hands together. "When the two become one, the assassin is unbeatable."

Titius smiled.

"You're creating a monster," Cleopas snarled inside. *"He'll be the one who sends you to me."*

For two weeks, they worked on the ten fundamentals of the assassin's art. Titius then brought in others who were fluent in different languages to work out the finer points of pronunciation. At first Caleb stuttered like a goose trying to clear water, but he improved as the days passed.

Titius spent mornings with his charge, then, as the Greek olive merchant, he roamed the market. One day he stopped by the fish vendor and sampled the pickled fish.

"The finest in Galilee," he declared in flawless Greek. "It could be even better than what we have in Corinth."

"This dealer gets orders from all over the world," the vendor affirmed. "I can get a crate sent to your door, for the right price."

Titius took another nibble. "All the way to Corinth? That's a deal. Any way to work out a deal with the master himself?"

"Maybe… if you can wait three days. That's when I get the next delivery."

Titius looked around. The awnings rippled like a sea in the breeze. "Is this a man I can trust?"

The vendor smiled as he leaned over his fish. "You can trust him, but his representative isn't a man. It's a woman, as smart as she is beautiful. Looking into her eyes, you forget about how much money she's asking for."

"I'll be careful. And I hope my olives will entice her as much as her fish entices me."

"Come mid-morning," said the vendor. "She only stays long enough to do business."

Titius nodded and walked away.

"Don't go back," said Cleopas. *"She'll capture you with her eyes."*

"I always loved her eyes."

"She has a partner now. Live on your memories. Let her go."

Three days later, the day of Titius's appointment with the fish vendor, Sestus met with him and Caleb to review their training regimen. The update was short and Sestus seemed satisfied that they were making good progress.

By the time Titius excused himself, changed, and reached the fish vendor, Abigail was gone.

"She came early this morning," the vendor said, shrugging. "She needed to be in Magdala by nightfall."

"Fool! Shamed by a woman again! When will you learn?"

"It's that wretched centurion," Titius said aloud, forgetting himself for a moment. "Do the two of you conspire against me?"

The vendor stared at him in confusion. "I assure you, sir, I conspire with no one, especially a centurion."

Titius charged into the rush of people moving through the agora. *Wretched spirit, you're going to get me chained up like a zealot demoniac. The whole world will think I'm a lunatic.*

Cleopas laughed again. *"Soon the whole world will know who you really are. Your disguises don't fool any of us who see you for the fraud you are."*

You keep referring to us...

Needing to consider his options, Titius sat with the baker. The baker was a grizzled veteran who'd travelled with many Roman legions.

"Do you know anyone who could help me train a new assassin?" Titius asked him.

"Jason of Thessalonica, the tiler, has proven himself in the arena and on the battlefield, though I'm not sure he will be patient with inexperience."

"Who else?"

"Sosipater of Sparta, the stone mason. He's stronger than three men together. Unmatched in stick fighting, boxing, and sword combat. He could teach your man something if he didn't kill him first."

"Get him for me," Titius said. "Caleb needs him and I could use the workout myself."

Titius met with Sosipater the next day and hired him to lead Caleb's fighting drills. He also sought out Lucius Flavius, a champion in wrestling and the bloody sport of pankration. In pankration, nothing was forbidden except eye-gouging and biting. The mixed martial art was often lethal.

Flavius demonstrated his skill for Titius and Caleb by facing down five strong legionnaires and six slaves, one after another. He unleashed powerful kicks to the heads, elbows to the jaws of others, and brutal blows to ribs and limbs. Blood spattered Flavius's chest, fists, and feet.

"You can go," Titius said to him afterward. "We've seen enough."

The fighter turned without a word and sauntered away past the carnage.

Caleb physically trembled. "I can't do that. I can't destroy people for no reason."

Titius watched as Flavius washed his hands in a fountain. "Pankration follows naturally from close fighting. If you ever lose your weapon, these arts will be essential to your survival. Learn them and pray you'll never have to use them."

The next afternoon, Titius and Caleb set themselves to the task of learning to be ruthless and heartless. They wrestled, punched, and kicked large leather bags filled with sand. Their skin scraped away and blood flowed.

Afterward, still panting from the exertion, Caleb said, "I'm finished with women."

"Why do you say that?" asked Titius.

"What woman would love a man who would destroy someone so easily? She'd live in terror of him. What love could they share?"

"Perhaps we should learn only enough to protect ourselves."

"I don't know about you, but I want a woman who loves me."

Titius wrestled with this. Why become a man everyone looked up to if the woman you loved wouldn't want to have anything to do with you?

Morning rain didn't shorten the line of carts jockeying to get into Sepphoris. However, Titius noticed that the usual cluster of Hebrew carpenters was missing, and when the ram's horn sounded he rightly surmised that another Jewish holiday must be underway.

The legionnaires anchored their sandaled feet against the gatehouse and waved traders and travelers into the city without inspection. On the other hand, the tax collectors didn't miss a soul.

As Titius stretched before a run, Sestus approached him and confided that he was taking Caleb to Jericho and then on to Jerusalem.

"Be outside the Antonia Fortress in Jerusalem in two weeks," the centurion ordered. A legionnaire brought his mount. "But *no one* must know about this. The zealots will be busy this Passover."

Jerusalem was an easy three-day ride from Sepphoris, so Titius calculated that he'd have ten days to himself. He meandered around the market, watching the fish vendor's stall in case Abigail showed up. Dressed as a shepherd, he asked the vendor when the pickled fish would next arrive fresh from Magdala.

"I thought you shepherds swore to live on goat's milk and cheese," the vendor joked. "The supplier will bring more in two days."

Two days later, Titius, playing the olive merchant, set up an observation post near the fish vendor. Under a drizzling rain, carts moved in and out of the market around him.

Within a few hours, a man greeted the vendor familiarly. He was a young man with bushy black eyebrows and a big nose above a scruffy attempt at a beard. Powerful shoulders rippled under his tunic as he unloaded a basket of fish onto a scale.

"The rains are making the roads difficult," the Hebrew newcomer said. "But praise the Almighty for good harvests coming."

The fish vendor then nodded at Titius, who slipped into the vendor's stall.

"Peace to you," Titius said, taking off his blue cape and smoothing a wrinkle on his sleeve. "I am Porpherus of Corinth."

The young Hebrew set his basket on the ground. "Peace to you. I am Emmanuel of Bethlehem."

Titius watched the fish as the vendor poured them out of the scale and into his own basket. "My friend tells me you help bring him the best pickled fish from Magdala."

Emmanuel nodded. "The fish belong to the Almighty. My uncle Isaac knows the secret of pickling. I'm a salesman and sometime escort."

"You escort fish?"

"I escort one who benefits our business. Because she's a woman. I was supposed to teach her the business, but she's already shrewd."

"I trade in olives," said Titius. "I believe we can help each other. Can you take me to this dealer so we can talk?"

Emmanuel shook his head. "She's done so well that we've sent her to Jerusalem to open the markets there, for Passover."

"She has no husband?"

"If I weren't betrothed, I'd be first in line for her hand." He checked the coins the vendor had given him. "She's given her heart to someone for whom she waits. She spurns all who court her."

Titius's heartbeat quickened. "May the new year bring blessing to you and your business."

"May the Almighty give you your heart's desires."

Titius clenched and opened his fists, trying to relax. Cleopas was quick: *"She has given her heart to another. Leave her. She spurns all men."*

He nodded to Emmanuel and the fish vendor. "I'll take my leave and consider my options," he said. "Thank you for your service."

He wandered away among the stalls.

Emmanuel blessed me, Titius thought. *By asking the Almighty to give me my heart's desires.*

"You don't even believe in the Almighty," Cleopas countered.

I'm keeping my options open, he thought back.

The next morning, clouds parting and the sun streaming, Titius borrowed a stallion and began his trek to Jerusalem. He dressed as a Roman noble to avoid questions about where he'd gotten his horse. The roads were full of pilgrims heading for the Passover ritual.

Titius rode slowly, enjoying the beauty around him. Wildflowers bloomed everywhere. Hawks, pelicans, pheasants, ravens, and songbirds dotted the sky as if the sun had freed them from hidden prisons.

Once he'd passed Nazareth, he headed for the village of Nain southwest of Mount Tabor. The barley and flax harvest was underway and people were busy in their fields. Cart after cart of grain clogged the road. Green pastures spread out in all directions like a grassy sea. Titius imagined how much Abigail would have enjoyed this journey.

The main houses in Nain sat above the sepulchral caves, beyond which the ground fell toward the Plain of Esdraelon. He let his steed drink briefly outside the village, then filled his gourd with cool, clear mountain water and walked his horse down Nain's main road. At a small market, he bought dates, figs, and apricots.

Suddenly, an old woman shuffled toward him holding out a small bag that smelled of aging fish.

"Roman! Roman!" she called. "Pickled fish, from Magdala… fresh for you."

"When did you get it?" asked Titius, trying not to turn away in disgust.

"Only a week ago," She smiled. "Still fresh for you."

He tightened his grip on the reins. "Who sold it to you?"

"An angel. As beautiful as Abraham's Sarah."

Who Abraham and Sarah were, he had no clue, but only Abigail could be compared to an angel. He declined the old woman's offer and pressed on.

As he passed through the Jezreel Valley, he noticed that most traffic had veered east, toward the Jordan Valley. It seemed the Passover pilgrims didn't want to defile themselves by crossing Samaritan lands. In the distance, the Carmel Ridge rose to the west and the mountains of Jerusalem rose majestically straight ahead.

He was within a stone's throw of Sabaste when he heard a man shouting: "Hail! The Messiah lives! Praise be to the Almighty! The Messiah lives!"

Titius waited for the excited man, bone-thin and waving a wad of rags, to get closer.

"What are you saying?" Titius asked.

The man jumped up and down. "The Messiah lives! I am one of ten lepers he healed!"

Titius dismounted and approached the man. "There's already someone claiming to be the Messiah in Capernaum. How many Messiahs can there be? One for Galilee, one for Samaria, another for Jerusalem?"

"I know no other but Yeshua of Nazareth. Yeshua of Nazareth healed me. He's my Messiah."

Titius backed his horse away from the ragged man and looked around. A small crowd had begun to gather.

"Yeshua's here? In Sabaste?"

"Herod the Great may have named this city Sebaste, but we still call it Samaria," explained one of the travelers who had been listening in.

"Hush," said Titius. "Was the Jewish Messiah here?"

"He was close by two days ago," said the former leper, scratching new stubble on his chin. "He spoke and we were healed. For the first time in seven years, I can be with my family."

"Why are you here then?"

"They've gone to Passover. They don't know yet that I'm clean. Praise the Almighty!"

Titius sighed. "Why don't you go too?"

"I have to complete the days of purification. Once they're back, we'll celebrate!"

That didn't make sense to Titius. If the man had been healed, he was clean. What a strange religion.

The leper continued up the road and the people made way for him.

"The disease has gone to his head," Cleopas said. *"No man can cure leprosy."*

But perhaps this Yeshua was more than a man.

Titius took some refreshment and booked an inn for the night. This Messiah wasn't going to be a problem for Rome just in Galilee. Titius would have to report this to Sestus.

Chapter Eighteen

The innkeeper sent a maid with fruits, bread, and cheese for breakfast, with a flagon of cheap wine. Titius washed, then dressed again in his Roman nobleman's tunic.

As he walked to the stables, the innkeeper called, "Roman, wait!"

Titius instinctively looked around for a possible ambush. "If what I paid you isn't enough, I can give you more."

"No, you've been generous."

Titius watched the man's hands and eyes. The man betrayed no ulterior motive.

"I want to warn you," the innkeeper continued. "A few days ago, a centurion and his helper came this way. They were ambushed by Barabbas and other Sicarii. You may be in danger, a wealthy Roman on a horse."

"What happened to the centurion?" asked Titius.

The innkeeper smiled. "You care about the centurion but not yourself? Somehow, they survived. I think Barabbas got away, but two of his men did not."

Titius looked toward Jerusalem. By horse, the city—and Abigail—was only half a day away. By foot, though, it would be much longer.

"Will you look after my horse if I decide to walk?" he asked the innkeeper.

The innkeeper nodded. "A good choice."

Titius repacked, leaving behind half of the supplies he'd carried. The pack he brought along with him bulged with tunics, hairpieces, and shoes.

"You know she'll be gone by the time you get there," Cleopas whispered.

In a grotto out of sight of the inn, Titius changed into the guise of a Galilean shepherd, with a full beard and a shepherd's staff.

At the Jordan River, he met high levels of rushing water. He examined the banks on both sides for anyone watching. Seeing no one, he removed his tunic and stepped into the strong currents. He successfully kept his tunic and pack above water. He slipped only once but kept from going under. On the far bank, he dried his body with another robe before redressing.

He heard laughter nearby and quickly stuffed his pack as three families with young children passed by, also heading toward Jerusalem. One father led a donkey carrying his daughter and another walked beside a donkey cart carrying two women, three children, and supplies. A third father walked beside a donkey carrying his wife and young child.

"Peace to you," Titius called. They returned his greetings. "I'm travelling to Jerusalem for Passover. May I join you?"

The man beside the cart spoke up. "I've never seen a shepherd walk this road alone. Not without sheep."

"My brother's in Jerusalem preparing flocks for Passover sacrifices," Titius explained. "He sent word asking me to join him. I began the journey alone, but I've been warned there are zealots and bandits ahead."

"Very well," replied the man. "We could use another man to keep us safe from those zealots and bandits. But we'll go only as far as Jericho tonight, then on to Jerusalem tomorrow."

Along the way, Titius entertained the children with stories of his exploits with lions, bears, leopards, and wild dogs.

"Which one had the biggest teeth?" a child asked.

"That's difficult to know," he said. "I was too busy running to notice."

The child laughed. "You should have used a slingshot. My daddy can kill a wolf across the road with one stone. Shoot your slingshot for us."

"I left my slingshot with another shepherd," Titius lied.

"Don't worry. My daddy will protect you."

Sometimes, with so many different personalities and disguises, it was hard to remember what he'd told people. In this case, the man leading his daughter on a donkey had been listening more closely than Titius had realized.

"So you're from near Cana but you keep your flocks near Sepphoris?" the man asked. "Your accent sounds Greek or Roman."

Titius responded with a laugh. "You have a good ear, my friend. I have a Roman master who's trying to warp my tongue with Latin lessons. And my mother spoke Greek."

This seemed to satisfy the man, and the trip to Jericho passed without further incident.

As the travelers neared Jericho, they saw camel caravans and elegantly robed Arabs. A high tower sprouted above the date palms, and women carrying pots on their heads hauled water from a well near the main gate. Legionnaires stood on duty near a tax collector's booth. Ravens scavenged in the garbage dump.

The families bid Titius farewell and he went on to explore the market. At the fish vendor, he noted that the pickled fish weren't like the ones Abigail had been bringing from Magdala. He ate his supper and settled down for the night among the sea of tents.

As he rested, Titius thought back to his early days with the cross maker. Caleb had worked hard to get away from Sestus back then, but without success. The centurion had maintained a hold on him, as he did on so many. After burying the zealots' bodies in a shallow grave outside Caesarea, Titius had enjoyed playing the blind man and following his charge around the city.

He had tapped his cane right into Caleb one day.

"Old man!" Caleb had called out. "I'm here. Where do you want to go?"

Titius remembered what followed. Caleb had been standing on a log and leaning against a warehouse.

"I am Rome's eyes in this city," Titius had declared. "I saw you take on those zealots. I saw you ready to make a deal with the devil."

Titius had noticed the knife hidden under Caleb's carpenter's apron. He'd tapped Caleb's ankle with his cane and, when the cross maker looked down, Titius had stolen the knife.

"If the devils possess you, old goat, then go prophesy at the shrine of Pan," Caleb had said. "Leave me alone. And return my knife."

Titius had smiled. "You are not as alert as you think, are you? I was sent to keep you alive for Sestus." Titius had then held the knife up—out of Caleb's reach.

"Give me the knife!"

"Take it!"

Caleb had reached for it, but Titius made the knife disappear. Titius then held out an empty hand and Caleb grabbed for him, but after a short scuffle Titius had held the knife at his throat.

"Things are not as they appear, carpenter."

"I hope for your sake that is true. What do I have to do?"

"As part of your training, you will learn to listen to my stick," Titius had said. "It will signal what is happening around you."

He'd held out the knife so Caleb could take it.

Caleb had backed away. "I don't need any more training. I've had enough. These hands have tasted enough death for one lifetime. The Almighty can find other hands to do his work."

Titius had spoken carefully. "This Almighty you speak of, do you believe he fights only for the Jews? Is he someone the Romans will have to conquer like the gods of other nations? Is he someone I will have to contend with in our training?"

"The Almighty cannot be conquered. He is not a god to be betrayed and angered. He claims to be the Creator of all things. His temple is open to the people of all nations, but his followers do not always let others into their place of worship."

"What must we do to silence these zealots who rise against us?" Titius had asked. "Will there be peace if we take their lives, or do we have to take their temple and their land as well?"

The memory was as clear to Titius as though it had happened yesterday. Now he was a day away from the city where the Almighty held sway. Where zealots, religious fanatics, Messiahs, and people from many nations mixed in a tension that Rome barely kept under control.

When he got there, Titius would have to guard a man who made the very crucifixes the people feared. He would then take his vengeance on the Roman noble who'd stolen his estate.

And find the woman he loved.

The shouts and celebration of visitors in the streets delayed his sleep, and early in the morning he was awakened by the sounds of traders getting ready to leave the city. Nonetheless, he lay still until roosters began to crow.

He dressed as a shepherd again and picked up food from the market. As he left, he suddenly noticed three familiar faces: Sarah, Issachar, and Timna from the zealot camps. They walked beside a donkey carrying large baskets of apricots.

Titius circled a potter's stall, a carpet dealer, a wine merchant, and the fish vendor as he worked his way back toward the fruit stalls. He backed toward the apricot dealer, pretending to examine some figs. The canopy helped block him from view.

"What do you mean you can't give us the same price?" he overhead Timna ask the vendor. "This fruit is as good as the last we brought you."

The vendor's voice shook. "A centurion was here two days ago. He said if he finds out my fruit comes from anyone connected with Barabbas, he'll see that I'm crucified."

"He was trying to intimidate you," Issachar said mockingly. "Barabbas almost got that centurion in an ambush. We're trained and ready."

"I need to lay low for a while," the vendor insisted.

"What about the oath you took for the cause?" Timna said.

"They took six of your people from this market and sent them for crucifixion in Jerusalem," the vendor replied. "And several more on their way *to* Jerusalem. That's not how I'm spending Passover."

"Amnon, please," Sarah said to the vendor. "You know we have more people here all the time. The fig dealer, the carpet weaver, the potter… I can send my cousin to assist you. She looks just like me."

A long silence passed. "When can she come?" Amnon asked.

"It will take a little time. I'll send her with the next shipment."

Titius waited until the three zealot travelers moved off before slipping away.

Within an hour, Titius had joined a caravan heading toward Jerusalem. The traders and travelers welcomed him easily. Like them, he wore simple leather sandals, a plain brown tunic, and a shepherd's headscarf.

The heat was intense as they climbed the hills. An old man, already weary from the journey, lay atop several baskets of figs in a cart and covered his head with a shawl. His grandson drove a donkey as boney as the old man.

He fell into step with three young men in a deep discussion. Benomi, Saul, and Crissus were students of a young rabbi named Gamaliel. Most of their talk seemed to center around the finer points of Jewish law, but within a half-hour the discussion turned to the subject of their new Messiah.

"Did you hear what that innkeeper said last night?" Benomi asked. "He claimed Yeshua of Nazareth took seven loaves and a few fish and fed four thousand people in the Decapolis."

"Do you think it's true?" said Crissus. "Or is it just another version of the story where Messiah fed five thousand men with five loaves and two fish near Bethsaida?"

"Two separate miracles," Saul answered. "I checked. The details are different. This Yeshua is reaching out to more than our people."

"Why would he go into the Decapolis?" Titius asked, breaking into the conversation.

Benomi threw a stone into the trees. "Good question. Nothing over there but pagans tripping over themselves to be Greek or Roman or whatever's fashionable these days."

"Don't forget the zealots," Saul added. "Some go there to get away from the Romans."

"He doesn't act like a Messiah should," Benomi said. "He was in Caesarea near that shrine called the Gates of Hades and told his followers that they'd overcome such places of evil someday."

"In Capernaum, he healed a centurion's son," Crissus noted. "And in his own synagogue he told people that God's favor was on outsiders. He said that during Elijah's time, God spared a widow in Sidon and during Elisha's time he healed Namaan the Syrian's leprosy. No wonder his own neighbors tried to kill him."

"Should the Messiah be only for the Jews?" Titius asked.

"You've been in Galilee too long," Benomi said angrily. "Be sure, he'll be in the temple causing more trouble. Last year he turned over tables and chased the moneychangers out of the Court of the Gentiles."

Crissus hesitated. "Didn't he say the temple was meant to be a house of prayer for all nations?"

Titius looked back and noticed that they'd gotten ahead of the rest of the caravan.

"Let's wait," Saul said. "There've been attacks in this next section of road. We shouldn't leave the merchants unprotected. That old man and his grandson aren't going to fight bandits."

Crissus turned to Titius as they waited. "What do you know about the Messiah?"

"I look for truth wherever I find it," Titius said. "I saw him give sight to a blind man in Bethsaida. I saw him fill a fishnet to overflowing. I don't know how and I don't know what it means."

Benomi stamped his feet. "No! No! No! He is possessed by devils. How else could he do such things?"

Saul touched Benomi's shoulder. "Calm, brother. Calm." He pointed toward Jerusalem. "Perhaps if we talk to this Messiah, we can convince him to use his powers against tax collectors and prostitutes. Instead of befriending them, he should teach them more about Moses's law."

Titius fell back to walking with the merchants and their donkey carts while the three students continued on ahead, seemingly unaware that he'd gone.

By the time the group crested the hill that looked down on the temple's glistening white limestone walls, the whole caravan settled into a moment of awed silence.

The old man raised his bony arms and opened his toothless mouth in a sob. His shoulders shook and the young man beside him put his arm around the frail body.

"He thinks this is his last Passover," the young man said to Titius. "He's come every year since Herod the Great began to build this temple. He fears the Romans will destroy everything if the zealots give up."

"What hope do so few have against so many?" Titius asked. "The Romans have unending armies, like the waves of the sea."

"But we have the Messiah!" the young man replied.

A great cheer rose up around Titius.

"Soon we'll sing the Great Hallel at Passover!" Saul shouted. "We'll sacrifice a lamb on the same Mount Moriah where God gave Abraham a ram. Let us sing!"

"Praise the Lord!" the others sang. "Praise, O servants of the Lord, praise the name of the Lord. Let the name of the Lord be praised for evermore…"

Titius didn't remember the words. He went over to the old man's cart and pretended to weep along with the elderly pilgrim.

Benomi, Saul, and Crissus continued their singing chant as they hurried toward the masses gathering at Jerusalem's gates. From the hilltop, it looked like the whole sea of humanity was pouring into a small limestone box.

They hurried down the Mount of Olives into the valley. The donkeys brayed, the camels grunted, the pilgrims wept, and the merchants cursed as their loads shifted and threatened to fall under the thousands of feet converging on Jerusalem. Titius helped the old man's grandson tug his donkey up the paved street toward the Roman fortress tower by the market. There, he left them.

Bread, goat cheese, lamb, and a generous cup of tea satisfied his stomach that night as he rested in the upper loft of a horse stable next to the Damascus Gate. The smell of hay reminded him of a certain night when he was young.

His father had been away at war, his mother busy with her books. There had been no one around except Cleopas, and the Hebrew slave had just begun to teach him to read. During the lesson, Cleopas had excused himself and Titius caught sight of him creeping past the great room where his mother was reading. Titius followed and caught the slave going into the stables, leaving the door open. Smelling horse dung and hay, Titius had crept up to the door and listened to the voices inside. He could hear Cleopas whispering and a woman giggling.

As he'd gone inside the dark stable, a gust of wind had blown the door shut. He'd stumbled and stepped on someone's foot. His own screams joined the other terrible screams in his ear as a hand covered his mouth and pushed him under a pile of hay. At first he'd thought he would suffocate in the dust. He kicked, struggled, and screamed, but no help came.

By the time he'd managed to get out later, he had been shaken to the core. A servant had opened the door and pulled him into the light.

After that, his mother had forbade him from going into the stables alone again.

"There are ghosts and demons in the dark," she had said.

Soon after that, Abigail and her sister had come to keep watch over him.

In those first months, Abigail cried any time she thought no one was around. He often saw her with red, puffy eyes and her sister would make excuses for her.

On his ninth birthday, Titius took a rose from the cook and dropped it into Abigail's lap as she'd sat on the stairs near the garden. She'd picked it up, smelled it, and smiled.

He'd do anything to see that smile one more time.

Chapter Nineteen

Sestus had made it clear that Titius was to go unnoticed in Jerusalem. There were zealots from the Decapolis who knew him; traders and fishermen who could recognize him from Sepphoris, Capernaum, and Bethsaida; and pilgrims from Nazareth, Caesarea, and Cana who might sense something familiar about his face or walk. He needed a disguise no one would notice.

He decided that dressing as one of the city's thousands of slaves would be best. He had to appear credible in the markets as he looked for Abigail, but not tempt others to issue him orders. He would need to buy the linen tunic of a privileged house servant, like the one Cleopas used to wear.

On his second day in Jerusalem, Titius stepped out of the stables into the midday crowd and headed for the markets. The smoke and incense from temple sacrifices floated down the hill and mixed with the smells of spices, sweating bodies, rotting vegetation, and sewage in the cramped streets.

Jerusalem dealt with the huge influx of pilgrims by setting aside several areas for vendors. At his third market, Titius found the stall he desired; a linen awning sheltered it from sunshine or rain. He watched as shoppers pawed through the merchandise, listening as merchants and customers haggled.

A tall Nubian held up four tunics. "Lord Cretius is in residence with Herod. He needs these for his servants."

An Egyptian woman raised an armload of linens. "Lord Cretius needs these for his household."

An elderly Jew raised a single rag. "Lord Cretius needs this for his pig."

Several bystanders erupted in laughter.

Sestus had given Titius plenty of money, so he counted out coins from his tunic pocket. He quickly picked up what he wanted, laid down the money for the merchant, and walked away without a word.

Back in the stable, Titius dressed in a fine knee-length tunic with an embroidered neckline and put on his best sandals. He paid a young woman near the stables to trim his hair and his beard.

He had to find out if there was a way to ambush Cretius. If that coward dared show his face away from his armed escort, he would get his revenge. Cretius must die for what he'd done—especially for raping his mother.

"Your mother is with me," Cleopas said. *"She doesn't need revenge."*

Titius pressed his temples with his thumbs. "For Abigail then."

He turned toward the Fortress Antonia, where Sestus would be stationed. The night before, Titius had written a long account of his recent observations. He gave the parchment to a boy and paid him to deliver it to one of the legionnaires on sentry duty. As the boy made his way toward the fortress, Titius hid himself in a doorway a short distance away.

The guards, dressed in full battle gear with bear-head helmets and sharpened javelins, would have intimidated the bravest zealot. The boy walked tentatively toward the third sentry, the one sitting on his helmet and lounging against the wall. The sentry examined the parchment, then motioned to another soldier and handed it off.

Titius slipped away. The message would be delivered.

He found six fish vendors near the Sheep Gate, all selling fresh, pickled, salted, and dried fish. No one had the Magdala pickled fish he wanted.

Titius ambled through the vendors and picked up eggs, emmer bread with salt, honey, goat's milk, a roasted pigeon, olives, cheese, and grapes. A vendor named Enoch was especially jovial and receptive to his inquiries for special foods. The clean-shaven Hebrew even stocked tilapia and herring. Titius bartered for a blanket and a cloak, then dropped off his purchases at the stable.

He spent the afternoon in the baths, receiving a massage and scrape from a muscular slave. Feeling full and refreshed, he then began to scour the city for Caleb's workshop. He started with the shops closest to the fortress, but those he questioned knew nothing about a new carpenter in the city.

Emerging from a warren of alleys, he saw the beautiful sunset of deep purple, brilliant orange, and red. It seemed the whole city had come to a standstill. Priests and peasants alike stood in awe. Merchants and customers stopped bartering. Donkeys and dogs went silent.

With the sun down, he blended in with the slaves, workers, and pilgrims gathering around fires in streets and alleys. Hovering, he listened to their conversations and moved on.

To further blend in, he picked up a carpet that someone had left by a doorway and carried it on his shoulder, looking as though he was going about his business.

He finally settled at the fifth fire he visited. It took one word from one of the people around the fire to convince him to stop—Barabbas.

And it had been spoken by the old zealot leader Hosea.

He set down the carpet as if to rest, keeping his face hidden from the old man. Hosea faced the fire and five other men huddled around the sparking logs, warming their hands and sharing cups of wine. Skewers of lamb rested on a clay platter. Their laughter rolled easily.

A sixth man stood in the shadows nearby, Titius recognized him to be a sentry. The sentry watched as Titius retied his sandal and examined the carpet's edging.

"Barabbas wants us at the Bethlehem vendors by sunset in two days," Hosea said softly. His next words were too quiet to catch.

When the sentry took a step in Titius's direction, he set the carpet back on his shoulders and walked around the corner into a dark alley. Three men appeared behind him, following, but he slipped quickly around another corner and disappeared up some stairs onto a flat roof. The voices and footsteps below him intensified for a few minutes, but then they faded.

"*You're playing with fire,*" Cleopas warned. "*Remember when you burned down that shed back in Rome? You blamed me for it and I took the whipping. I know it was you.*"

That's what you got for scaring me in the stables, Titius thought. *I knew what you were doing with that maid. I heard her crying to Abigail's sister, Lydia. You forced her.*

"*At least I knew what to do with a woman. If a woman cries around you, you melt like goat's cheese in the sun. A woman needs to learn her place.*"

Titius found himself growing angry. *I have a chance to change things. I can become strong. You can't.*

"*The way you live, you'll be with me before long. If Barabbas doesn't slit your throat, Cretius or one of his assassins will. You can't hide forever.*"

Titius stayed hidden for another hour. He left the carpet, peered over the knee-high wall around the roof's perimeter, and seeing no one went down the stairs and slipped into the diminishing stream of humanity.

He took a circular route back to the stable, but no one seemed to be following him. He was grateful to have a peaceful place to spend the night.

Sleep came easily; not even Cleopas could keep him awake.

The rooster had finished crowing by the time he eased himself out from under his straw comforter and washed up. He put on a clean linen tunic and was soon off to visit the nearby wood market to see if Caleb had set up shop nearby.

There was no sign of the cross maker.

Next, he decided to walk through the Jaffa Gate and visit the upper markets near Herod's palace. The surge of humanity in this area was as thick as at the markets near the Sheep Gate. He passed Herod's three towers at the edge of the palace, but the temple stood above even this, blazing white on the highest plateau of land. He took a moment to look to the left of the temple at the high observation perch of the Antonia Fortress.

"*You can be sure the centurion is up there now,*" Cleopas said. "*Watching you chase a woman instead of that cross maker. You can't fool him for long.*"

The fish vendors were easy to find. One of the stalls did seem to have Isaac's famous pickled fish, and he tasted a few samples until the woman at the stall picked up the weights for her scales.

"Are you going to eat them all now or at least buy a few?" she asked, putting her hand over the basket. "They're the best from Magdala, fresh in yesterday."

A long wisp of hair escaped from her headscarf and lay across her nose, and her brown eyes crossed as she looked at it. She blew gently from an extended lower lip, but the strand of black hair didn't move. She shook her head and finally brushed it aside with her hand.

Titius picked up a handful of fish and placed it on her scale. "The woman who brought them to you, is she returning soon?"

The woman took his coins and added a few more fish to his purchase. "Do I look like a prophet? My husband is usually the one to work the booth." She wrapped the fish in a small rag and handed it to him. "I'm only here while he's at the temple. If you ask me, this pickled fish isn't natural. No person with good taste would feed this to their family."

As he walked away, Titius snacked on the fish. Likely it was an acquired taste.

He wandered by the Hippodrome, where the chariots raced, and sat in the temple's shade. As a Gentile, both a slave and a non-believer, he knew the temple was off-limits to him. Smoke from sacrifices drifted down. He tasted iron, like blood, on the back of his tongue.

During the Passover, everyone's energy and attention was focused on the temple. Perhaps Abigail was in the Court of the Women, saying her prayers. Perhaps she was listening to the Messiah teach. Perhaps Caleb was there, too. What would it be like to belong to a people like this?

"They'd kill you before they let you in."

Titius shuddered. Cleopas was right.

He left the temple and passed the pool of Siloam and the Temple of the Freedmen. As he examined the building, a small girl holding a pair of roses emerged from a nearby garden.

"Peace," he called to her.

"Peace," she replied. "Would you like a flower?"

Titius took it and inhaled. As he did, he recalled images of Abigail in the rose garden. He smiled.

"Where did you find such a beautiful flower?" he asked.

She pointed to a path leading behind the pool. "A beautiful woman gave it to me. In the garden. There are more flowers than you can count."

Titius thanked her and hurried down the path. Who could it be but Abigail?

The garden was almost hidden by a wall and a hedge. When he saw the sea of red roses, though, he stopped. He felt the same awe as when he'd seen that magnificent sunset. He refocused and looked around the garden. A bent woman was using a cane to take painfully slow steps, moving from flower to flower.

"Excuse me!" he called. "Peace to you."

"And the peace of Passover to you as well," she said.

"I'm looking for a woman who gave two roses to a little girl. She has long dark hair, strong shoulders, and a noble walk."

"Why, thank you," said the old woman with a smile. "I gave the roses to the girl. I see she gave you one."

Titius was speechless. Where was Abigail?

The woman tapped her cane on the path. "It seems my beauty isn't enough to sway you. Are you looking for the woman from Galilee who walks these paths every evening?"

"Yes, perhaps, I am," he said. "Every evening, you say?"

"Yes, while she was here."

"What do you mean? Has she gone?"

"In this garden, she used to sing of one she loved. She told me that in another garden, long ago, she gave her heart to someone. It's been many years since she's seen him."

"Did she say where? Who the man was?"

She smiled. "Such noble songs about a nobleman, out of her reach but always on her mind. If you've set your heart on this woman, save your tears. She wasn't singing about a servant like you."

Titius wanted to confess his life to her, but he refrained. "Thank you for the flower, the time, and the story. One day I'd like to meet the beautiful woman who sings in this garden."

"Only last night she got word that a man was looking for her in Magdala. She's gone to see for herself."

"When will she return?"

"Only the Almighty knows," the woman said.

Chapter Twenty

On the third day after meeting the woman in the garden, Titius heard the distinctive sound of Caleb's flute as he strolled by the sheep pool north of the Temple Mount. The music came from a limestone hut where someone had placed three planks of rough cedar and a large burl of olive wood against the wall by the door.

Titius, dressed as a carpenter, walked quickly to the door and peered inside. One side of the room was filled with assorted squared cedar logs. The other side had a small open fire with a pot suspended above it. The far wall held a curtained doorway. The work bench was covered with chisels, adzes, saws, squares, and planes.

As Titius watched, Caleb lowered the flute and polished it with an oily rag.

Eventually, Caleb looked up and saw him. "How long have you been hiding around there?"

Titius walked to the door and pulled aside the curtain to find a straw pallet, a few blankets, and some scattered tunics. "Do you share this room with anyone?" Titius asked.

Caleb laughed. "You know my record with women. If Sestus hasn't told you, the last woman I got close to he made me *crucify*."

"I know what it's like to crucify someone you care about."

Caleb set the flute down. "Would you like a drink? Hot goat's milk with cinnamon and honey? There's some pickled fish on the workbench, and apricots and dates."

Titius accepted the hot drink, shifting it from hand to hand as the clay mug cooled. He sampled the pickled fish and knew it immediately.

"Where did you get this?" he asked, searching Caleb's face.

Caleb raised his eyebrows. "Something wrong with the fish? It isn't poisoned, is it?"

"No. It tastes like the fish you get in Magdala, at a place by a friend named Isaac."

"Small world." Caleb picked up a few of the tiny fish and popped them into his mouth. "A week ago, I met a woman coming into the city. She was looking for a fish vendor to sell her wares to." He crouched down and stirred the spiced milk, then set the pot on the floor. "I took her to the upper market where I knew someone. They bought all she had."

"What did she look like?" Titius asked.

"Do I sense something more than curiosity here?"

"I may know her," Titius replied. He took a flute from the workbench and ran a finger along its holes. "But she's given her heart to another."

Caleb stood looking out the door at passing pilgrims. "Whoever he is has had long enough to claim her. She needs a man who can appreciate her for who she is. A woman like her shouldn't have to wonder if she's truly loved."

"What about these crosses?" Titius asked.

The carpenter turned to his half-finished work. "Sestus crucified six zealots and six bandits the first week we were here. There are a few more condemned in the fortress, waiting for these crosses to be done. In the meantime, Sestus is off chasing Barabbas."

Titius dipped his mug into the steaming pot for more milk. "Do you think he'll ever catch him?"

"If he doesn't, someone will. No one can hide forever."

"You can't hide forever," Cleopas whispered.

"I can try!" Titius said aloud.

Caleb looked at him strangely. "You? Why should you hide?"

"It's the art," he said, covering for his mistake. "A thespian assassin bets his life on his ability to hide."

"You'll need to work on this disguise, though. Your beard's too short and neat. Your shoulders not broad enough, your hands not calloused enough. Come work with me for a few months and you can become the kind of man a woman might look at some day." Caleb put on his cloak. "I need to check the market to see if my angel's come looking for me."

And he walked out.

Titius picked up the flute and blew on it as he'd seen Caleb do. It emitted a shrill squeal.

He spotted a gob of sap seeping from one of the crossbeams on the unfinished crosses. He broke it off and stuffed it into the end of the flute.

So the fish vendor had told him that Abigail had gone back to Magdala. Was it possible that Caleb was the man she had committed herself to? He might be broader, more muscled, and of saner mind than Titius was… but according to the woman in the rose garden, she'd given her heart to someone else long ago. Someone else in a garden. Who could that be but Titius himself?

Four people stopped by asking about carpentry jobs, and Titius told them to come back another day. The last was a well-proportioned priest needing a stronger chair.

"I'm not sure the carpenter on duty here can make what you really need," Titius told him. "Perhaps we need the Messiah's help. I hear he's also a carpenter."

The priest's face reddened as he squinted and shook his jowls. "Don't you know who I am?" he said. "If you follow this so-called Messiah, this Yeshua of Nazareth, we'll destroy you both."

"Perhaps the shop's owner can make you a better deal," Titius said. "You should come back tomorrow."

The priest huffed and chugged out of the shop.

After three weeks shadowing Caleb, the only interesting thing Titius noticed was a young woman named Suzanna stopping by the shop for flute lessons. Sometimes she'd sit and talk and other times she'd dance to Caleb's playing. Suzanna's clear interest in Caleb had Titius dreaming about meeting Abigail.

Every day he went to the market and asked whether the pickled fish dealer from Magdala had come by. By the fourth day, the vendor saw him coming and simply shook his head.

Pentecost attracted a massive influx of pilgrims for the harvest rituals, and the Messiah had recently been in the temple teaching again. However, he had now withdrawn to Caesarea with a small band of followers. An informant told Titius that one of Yeshua's followers had actually proclaimed his master to be the "Son of the living God," the same title Augustus had adopted.

"He can't survive long," Cleopas said. *Rome won't endure competition with Caesar.*

Once again, Titius thought the former slave was right.

He perfected six disguises to add variety to his days: the upper-class slave, the Grecian olive merchant, the shepherd, the carpenter, the blind man, and the corpulent bearded Pharisee.

When Caleb worked, Titius slipped away to probe the city for zealot activity. It didn't take long to find it. Men loyal to Barabbas gathered around fires, tables, bathhouses, and certain vendors to make their clandestine plans.

Once a week Titius hired a messenger to drop off a scroll at the fortress. Twice he had seen Sestus hurry out when a scroll was accepted, but Titius had avoided being seen. Sestus had ordered him to remain unseen and unnoticed— and orders were orders.

Titius could see the results of the intelligence he submitted. Each night legionnaires raided the zealots' secret meetings and more were put in chains to wait for Caleb's crosses. Peace from the power of the cross soon began to spread over Jerusalem. Rebel gatherings and zealot activity in the city halted. The zealot daggermen focused their terror on isolated targets outside the capital, and Roman centurions chased them down.

Sestus was frequently away, leaving Caleb free to wander. Titius was relieved that once Caleb had sorted out the disagreement with that priest, he had received many orders from the High Priest Caiaphas's family, from the nobility, and even from the palace. The cross maker had become a carpenter again and, going by the traffic at his door, a very successful one.

Titius analyzed the fat priest's mannerisms and speech patterns. He learned to mimic his voice, his walk, and his temper. He kept track of which market stalls the priest frequented.

Finally, he decided to test his impersonation at the market.

When Titius stepped among the stalls, the date vendor reacted with the enthusiasm he always did when the priest walked by. So did the young man who roasted goat over a charcoal fire. The woman selling oranges and lemons frowned at him curiously and Titius moved on quickly.

An hour later, Titius went to Caleb's shop and ordered four stools. Caleb hardly stopped working long enough to take the order.

"Bartholomew," the vendor said, "the Almighty must be blessing you with many guests. It'll take a few days, but you'll have your stools. Greet your beautiful daughters for me. May you be blessed one day with a son."

On his way home, Titius considered confessing to Caleb what he'd done—to avoid another angry confrontation between carpenter and priest.

Playing the priest satisfied the actor in him, but no one spoke around a priest—they bowed and murmured or looked away—so he didn't learn anything new for a while. But when sitting near the linen vendor, he found that he was readily ignored. Some of his best information came from servants who gathered there.

An Egyptian slave tested a linen stola. "My master bought two Gauls today to work in our kitchen. One of them used to work for Herod in Sepphoris."

A Greek maid picked out several towels. "My mistress is hosting a great banquet for the governor and his wife."

A Galilean cook picked out two new frocks. "The Romans almost found the zealots hiding in our house last night. I had to stall them!"

Near the end of that day, two broad-chested warriors, swaggering like assassins, stopped at the stall. "We serve Sestus Aurelius, Legate of Judea." They sounded Ephesian, Titius noted. "His personal bodyguard often comes by here. When did you last see him?"

"Do you wish to buy this bodyguard a tunic? I need to know his size."

"He's my size," the shorter of the two said. "You wouldn't recognize him. He'd be dressed like an old blind beggar, a household servant, or a harlot. He answers to the name Titius Marcus Julianus."

The merchant chortled. "Are you saying that a top Roman warrior has a blind beggar or a harlot for a bodyguard? The only people here are the ones who are always here." He pointed toward Titius. "Perhaps that priest will satisfy you."

The larger assassin took a step toward where Titius, well-stuffed into his priest's regalia, rested under a canopy.

"That old drunk?" the assassin said. "That's not who Lord Cretius's looking for. Mounting that head on a pole would likely get our own heads lopped off."

Titius burped and slumped against the wall as the assassins left.

The early autumn rains fell with no sign of Abigail. Plowing was underway in the fields, and soon the Feast of Trumpets, Day of Atonement, and Feast of Tabernacles arrived. Little booths sprang up everywhere around the city as residents moved out of their homes to re-enact their ancestors' wilderness wanderings.

One day, Titius heard word of an uproar in the temple courts. He joined the stream of men entering through the gate to find out what had happened. It turned out that Yeshua had arrived from Galilee without his usual contingent of followers.

"Did you hear Yeshua?" asked a Sadducee to his two fellows. "He says he'll be here only a little longer and then we won't find him anymore."

Another replied, "Not only that, he said that if people believed in him, streams of living water would flow out of them."

"They're calling him a prophet" a third said. "And Messiah, Son of David."

"Yeshua clearly is possessed by demons. People are going mad watching his miracles. Rome won't tolerate it. They'll take the whole city from us if we do nothing."

"I can't believe he got away again. I bent down to pick up a stone to throw at him, and when I looked up he was gone."

"The people seem to love him. They flock to him every day, drinking in his every word."

"The people are ignorant. No prophet comes from Galilee. The Messiah will come from Bethlehem, from David. They know nothing."

One day, Sestus took Caleb on a ride to the fortress of Machaerus where the Baptist had been beheaded. It was meant to be a routine security patrol to check out zealot activity in the area.

Two days later, Titius heard about the ambush.

He dressed up as a doctor and stepped into the tent set up to treat the wounded. Herbs and medications lay in haphazard fashion along a shelf. Amulets, balances, scales and weights, bottles, amphoras, clay jars, glass vials, pestles, and mortars also took up space. He also spotted scoops, spoons, forceps, scalpels, and vials of drugs.

An Ephesian physician, with the healing medallion from the Temple of Diana, hovered over the soldiers, deciding quickly which ones to treat and which ones to leave to the fates. An assistant brought the physician a saw and Titius noticed that another two assistants, an Egyptian and an Ethiopian were pouring a drugged drink down the throat of none other than Caleb.

The Ephesian picked up the saw and laid it beside Caleb's leg. The carpenter shivered as the physician poked, prodded, and poured powders into his wound.

"What shall we do with you?" the doctor mused aloud, picking up the saw again. "Do you pray to a god who can heal you, or do we save everyone the trouble, cut this off, and give your leg to the fire?"

Two legionnaires stopped by and spoke with the physician. Ignoring Caleb's cries of pain, they lifted him onto a stretcher as if he were nothing but a sack of grain.

As Caleb reluctantly lost his battle for consciousness, the doctor lowered the saw onto his leg.

"Wait!" Titius commanded. "I'm the centurion's physician and I know this man. Have your assistants bring him to my quarters and I'll care for him."

The assistants were skeptical when Titius showed them Caleb's bed in the carpenter's shop. They weren't given authority to question, though, and they had others to attend to so they left without more than furrowed eyebrows.

Titius stitched Caleb's deep wound carefully and packed it with sulfur and other medications he had brought from the Egyptian doctor's tent. He wrapped the surgery site carefully and checked it daily.

Three days later, Suzanna stopped by and took over Caleb's care.

After that, news from the fortress was little more than word of occasional skirmishes. Titius decided it was time to return to Capernaum and continue his quest, but he stopped by the rose garden first before leaving.

"Still looking for your angel?" the old woman with the cane asked.

"What may I call you?" Titius asked. "And yes, I'm still looking!"

"Please, call me Elizabeth. But she probably won't be here until the flowers come back."

"That may be a while."

"She told me once she had friends in Bethany."

The next day, he watched Suzanna lean coyly against Caleb's doorway. The sight only increased Titius's hunger for Abigail. Too many years had passed.

The next Sabbath evening, just before the city went quiet for its night of worship, Titius changed into his shepherd's garb and bolted for the gates. He ignored the sentries' glances, then descended into the Kidron Valley and climbed the Mount of Olives. Farmers were travelling home from their fields.

Before dark, he settled himself in Bethany. As Titius slurped up the porridge and cheap wine offered by an innkeeper, he talked with a businessman who stopped by the inn.

"I'm going home to Galilee," Titius told the man. "I've been in Jerusalem for six months and need some room to move."

The businessman smiled. "Name's Lazarus. My sisters and I have a little business. Been pretty good since Yeshua ben Yuseph started staying here."

Titius sat upright. "You mean that new Messiah?"

Lazarus reached for another glass of wine. "That's him. We thought he was going to come and take Jerusalem back from the Romans and give us control again."

"Isn't that what everyone expects of every Messiah?"

"Yes. But this Messiah says he's going to be crucified."

Titius picked up his cup and sipped. "Your priests, rabbis, and teachers of the law may stone him before the Romans get him."

Lazarus raised an eyebrow. "You don't understand this man's power. He opens blind men's eyes. He calms storms and raises the dead to life. He feeds thousands on a handful of loaves and fish."

"This Messiah interests me," he said. "He raises the dead yet claims that he will be killed. Your leaders have talked openly about killing him, yet he persists on tormenting them with his teachings. The people worship him almost as an emperor. You know, the Romans won't tolerate it much longer."

"He's on a mission from the Almighty. But I've had enough talk for now. Too much talk will only bring trouble for Yeshua."

"I intend no trouble," Titius assured him.

Lazarus stood. "I wish you peace."

"I wish you peace as well."

All that night, images battled for control in his dreams. Romans, led by Sestus, chased him down with javelins as he tried to escape his oath. Zealots, led by Barabbas, lunged at him with daggers trying to avenge the lives of dead zealots. Slaves, led by Cleopas, pursued him with hammers and nails, threatening to crucify him. Every time, just as he was grabbed, the Messiah would appear and announce, "Stop!" And the dream would fade.

Titius would drift off, dreaming happily of hundreds of fishes swimming into a net, yet he'd awake sweating and in terror, dreaming he was surrounded by rock-throwing Pharisees and Sadducees.

Chapter Twenty-One

Dust billowed from under Titius's sandals as he walked away from the Jordan. Jericho's high walls appeared through a gap in the date palms. As Titius descended the last slope toward the city, a lone rider galloped up behind him.

"Peace to you, shepherd," called the rider, slowing his mount to a walk. "Have you sold your flock and walked from Jerusalem already?"

"Peace to you," Titius said. "I started early. I need to reach Galilee."

"Not even the bandits are up this early. But I love the early light on Herod's palace." He pointed to it. "Even Antony and Cleopatra did nothing to improve it. Augustus was wise to return it to Herod."

Titius scanned the public buildings and the Hippodrome, clearly Roman additions. Date palms grew everywhere near the numerous oases where camels and caravans loaded, unloaded, and reloaded. Tax collectors, under their overseers' eyes, badgered coins from all who passed.

Two bodyguards stepped in front of Titius and the horseman as they neared the gate. Titius handed over the expected coin for the personal tax. The short man who accepted it held it up to the light and bounced it gently in his hands.

"Feels real enough."

"Zacchaeus, good to see you again," the horseman bellowed. "My friend and I have come from Jerusalem. He's tired. Let him get some rest."

"Elkanah," Zacchaeus replied. "I hope your friend isn't a zealot. The Romans are busy today. Five were taken from the market this morning."

"My friend is neither a zealot nor the son of a zealot," Elkanah said. "If you find a dagger on him, you can charge the tax to me."

The well-dressed enforcer, who stood not even to Titius's chest, motioned to his henchmen and they took Titius's pack and pawed through it. When they nodded to Zacchaeus, the tax collector waved Titius in.

Titius bought himself food and filled his gourd with fresh water. Above, the early winter clouds filtered the harshest sunshine, making for a good traveling day. So before the noon meal, he was on his way to Magdala.

The remains of a wild boar killed by a lion lay a stone's throw from the path. Titius calculated how much daylight he had left. With a predator so close, he decided not to travel after dark. He'd learned his lesson by now.

By mid-afternoon the next day, he'd crossed the Fara River and neared the juncture of the Jabbok and Jordan. At dusk he dropped his mat by a tree and rested against it. The deer wandering toward the river reminded him of the last time he'd rested in this place. Among these very bushes he'd changed his clothes once.

From atop a tall tree, he looked across the land toward the zealot camp where he'd trained the young men. He spotted the hill where he and Jonathan had sat, waiting for the elder's decision.

"You should have stayed and married that zealot woman," Cleopas said.

"If I'd married Phoebe, Barabbas or Sestus would have killed me by now."

"If it's not her, it'll be another woman," Cleopas said. *"Just don't let it be Abigail."*

"Why do you abhor Abigail? Mother sent her away because of Father, not you."

"It wasn't only your father. She was with me in the shed one day… your mother found us."

Titius almost lost hold of the branch he was on. "You wicked, evil, liar! I should have crucified you twice and burned down that shed with you in it!"

Titius remembered several times seeing Abigail and Cleopas exchange glances. Before now, he'd thought her looks were fearful. Now he wasn't so sure.

"Shall I tell you what she's like… as a woman?"

"No, no, no!" Titius yelled. "Get out of my head!"

He reached into his pack and took out a rope.

"You know what you should do with that rope, don't you?"

"I'm going to kill myself!" Titius roared. "Then I can come and get you!"

Titius wrapped the rope around a sturdy lower branch and made a noose. He then looked across at the zealot hill… and slipped the noose around his neck.

I'll never have Abigail or Phoebe, he thought. *My real weakness isn't a woman. It's a slave.*

As the shadows crept deeper into the forest, he slid off the branch and plunged.

Darkness and light twisted together in a whirlpool. He felt swallowed as if in quicksand. Everything in his stomach fought to be free. The world spun, and all the while Cleopas spewed hideous, ghoulish laughter.

When light finally came, someone was shaking Titius's shoulder and pouring water on his face. The panic of drowning seized him for a moment and he sputtered and tried to sit up. Strong arms held him down.

"Peace. Be at rest, shepherd," a familiar man's voice said in Hebrew. "You're safe now."

"The lion is dead," another gruff voice said. "Although it looks like there were other attackers before the beast arrived."

The two men propped Titius up. His neck burned with pain.

Someone held a damp cloth to his head and he saw, hazily, a lion's body less than six strides away. He shook his head to clear his vision and almost screamed from the furious pain. His hand rested on his lap and felt a rope there.

"I'm Issachar, and this is Simon," the first voice said. "Our friend Timna shot the lion with an arrow and then went looking for your attackers."

Titius shuddered. He looked carefully at the closest face and recognized him immediately. These were two of the young zealots he'd trained.

A moment later, he realized that he was still in disguise. They didn't recognize him!

"You're fortunate your attackers didn't tie the rope properly," Simon said. "Your neck will hurt, but it didn't break."

"Will you take me to Barabbas?" Titius asked. It hurt a great deal to talk and his voice was raspy and hoarse. "Let me wash my wounds first."

"What do you mean, shepherd?" Issachar asked. "We don't follow Barabbas."

"You're sold out to Barabbas," Titius said. "I know Phoebe. And Elizabeth. Jonathan, Hosea, all of you."

Simon yanked the rope away from Titius's feeble grasp. "Explain. We're no fools, falling for reckless accusations."

Titius struggled to his feet. "I have no strength to fight. No reason to resist. I'm the one you knew… David. On the other side of the Jordan."

Simon drew his sword. "You don't look or sound like David. David betrayed us."

Titius stood with the cloth over one eye as blood trickled down his face into his dirty beard. "I am at your mercy. Things didn't work out as I'd planned."

"Hush, save your strength." Issachar wiped blood from Titius's ear. "Whoever hit your head and tried to hang you was merciless. The beast must have chased them off just before it turned on you. It is to your fortune that we arrived in time. Where have you been?"

Titius placed the cloth over his other eye. "Story's too long. Let's go now."

"We can't take you," Simon said.

"Why?"

"We don't follow Barabbas anymore," Simon replied.

Issachar broke in. "When we met the Messiah, it changed our perspectives forever." He pointed northeast, toward Gadara. "He cast out a legion of demons. Another time he fed four thousand of us. Even though some of our people had attacked his village, killed carpenters… he fed us."

"It's a trap," Cleopas hissed. *"Leave these lunatics."*

Simon handed Titius a fresh rag. "So we've left Barabbas to follow Yeshua. We felt an urgency that we must not wait until morning. When we crossed the river, we found you. Come with us to see the Messiah."

Simon carried Titius's pack, then helped Issachar support Titius as they started down the trail. They kept moving long after the evening shadows had swallowed the landscape, and before long Timna soon joined them.

"It's David!" Simon called to his friend. "He's not dead!"

"You kept your shooting skills strong," Titius said hoarsely. "It takes special skill to kill a lion like you did."

"I'm pleased to serve again," Timna replied. "Now let me run ahead and find a safe place to make camp."

The young man ran off along the darkened path.

Through the night, Titius tossed and turned on the hard earth they'd cleared for his blanket. The phantom pain of the noose around his neck still choked him, leaving him gagging and sweaty. Cleopas was relentless, predicting destruction and taunting Titius for having walked into a trap.

Timna, Simon, and Issachar all took turns stoking the fire and walking the camp's perimeter.

The first morning birds were a relief. Titius tested his muscles in case he'd have to fight. He'd taught the young freedom fighters well. If there were other zealots nearby, they might have tracked these three and wanted to attack them for deserting the cause.

None of Titius's weapons were in sight, but he was skilled in wrestling, boxing, and pankration. He could even fight like a Spartan, and bite or gouge out an eye to save his own life. He would fight to live, although his wounds left no question that he wouldn't be at his best.

As Simon made breakfast, the sound of dry wood catching flame comforted Titius.

"Come, David," Simon said. "I've prepared our jentaculum to start the day: biscuits, cheese bread, apricots, honey, dates, olives, and bacon."

"You provide well," Titius said. "Most Romans have only a cup of water."

The young zealot nudged the others awake with his foot and waited for them to stir.

"Timna learned from a Roman that every legionnaire has wheat, bacon, fish, a bird, cheese, fruit, vegetables, olive oil, and wine almost every day," said Simon. "So he's fit to fight."

Soon Timna and Issachar gathered around the fire. They warmed their hands and stretched stiff limbs as Simon walked to the Jordan for more water. When he returned, he poured some on a cloth and gave it to Titius to wipe his face. The cloth turned red from blood that had dried on Titius's face and neck.

"David, what do you know about this Messiah?" Issachar asked. "Our brothers in Jerusalem say the authorities are looking for ways to kill him before the Romans take the temple away. He makes trouble there during the feasts."

Titius took a bite of bread and chewed thoughtfully. "His words mesmerize people. His magic confounds religious leaders. His compassion confuses those who want to overthrow Rome. He speaks as if he knows men better then they know themselves."

Simon crouched down to sort out the contents of his pack. "That's what I saw in him as well. We couldn't point to anything he'd done to help the Romans enough to deserve a dagger to his throat."

"People said he healed a centurion's servant from far away, just by speaking," Issachar said. "But how can you prove it enough to cut a man's neck?"

"Hosea sent us to investigate the Messiah over and over," Timna said. "We were supposed to find some reason to encourage him to overthrow Rome, and if he didn't we were supposed to attack him quietly when no one was around. He always had followers close by."

"Except when he prayed," Issachar pointed out. "I saw him alone one night and tried to get close. There was strange power around him as he called to the heavens, though. My hand couldn't grasp my dagger."

Titius thought this improbable, but Issachar was clearly sincere. After Titius's own encounters with Yeshua, it was clear some kind of power rested on the man.

"So now we'll follow him," Simon said. "Maybe he'll destroy the Romans with his words, or his magic. Maybe we'll die trying. But it's better than slithering around trying to figure out what Barabbas wants next."

Titius limped along as they set out on the road. The vision in one eye was blurry and his head hurt in ways he'd never felt before. Even the vicious blows of Sestus or Jaennus during training hadn't hurt like this.

The young men took turns updating him on life in the zealot camps. Sarah had sent her sister to Jericho; the Romans had captured most of the zealots posing as vendors there. Phoebe had been courted by two big men who everyone had suspected were Roman infiltrators. They'd called Barabbas, but the men had left before anyone could expose them. Jonathan was now betrothed to Phoebe's cousin, Tamaris. Hosea was coordinating zealots in Jerusalem along with managing the opening of the trade route Barabbas had established with the Parthians.

Titius heard the words but struggled to absorb the message well enough that he could report it back to Sestus. Black phantoms floated across his field of vision. It felt like a chisel was being hammered into the back of his head.

The four of them continued until Titius had to stop for a rest. His back, neck, and shoulders burned with pain. Titius was grateful when Issachar frequently jogged to the nearby river to soak his rag with fresh water.

"David, where did you go when you left us?" Simon asked.

"I was on a mission."

"Why didn't you take any of us?" Issachar asked. "We would have done anything for you."

"It was time for me to leave."

"I found that blood-stained tunic you left behind," Timna said. "I had to show it to Phoebe. I've never seen a woman weep so loudly."

A moment later, Titius heard the unmistakable pounding of hooves on the road behind them.

"What's that?" Issachar said, turning around.

"Romans!" Timna shouted. "Run!"

The three former zealots dove into the cedar forest, which swallowed them up just as a dozen horsemen thundered into view. Caught with nowhere to go, Titius dropped to his knees and rolled off the road into a shallow ditch, hoping he hadn't been seen.

"Check out that shepherd!" Sestus's voice called out.

A legionnaire dismounted from his horse and stepped off the road toward him. The solider turned him over, moved aside his shepherd's head covering, and ran a rough hand over his face.

"Been beaten badly," the soldier reported. "No recent cut to his throat. He's had some care. Probably abandoned as too weak to walk."

"Bandits!" said Sestus. "Zealots would have cut him deeper. Can he talk?"

"Have you seen three zealots around here?" the legionnaire asked. He repeated the question in Aramaic, Greek, and Hebrew.

Titius feigned unconsciousness but groaned for effect when the soldier shook him.

"Leave him!" Sestus commanded. "We need to get to Sepphoris and then back to Jerusalem. I have empty crosses to fill."

The soldier left Titius and the troop charged down the road again in pursuit of zealots.

Once they were gone, he heard Simon's voice coming from behind a fig tree in view of the road: "Are you still with us?"

Titius rolled over and propped himself on one elbow. "See any Romans?"

Issachar reached Titius first and helped him get to his feet. "Come, quickly, in case they return."

Titius set a hand on the young man's shoulder. "They won't be back. I know that centurion. They're on their way to Sepphoris and Jerusalem."

Timna jogged toward them from further up the road where he'd been scouting. "They're gone," he declared. "Blessings to you, David, for not giving us up."

Taking turns, two of the three put their arms around him and lifted the weight off his legs while the third man carried his pack. In this way, they made good time and reached the towers of Magdala just after the sun reached its zenith.

"I'm grateful for your help," Titius said. "I have a friend who works in the fish market. He pickles fish. I'd like to speak with him."

Timna and Issachar eased out from under his shoulders.

"You're a free man," Timna said. "Do you want us to wait for you here or in Capernaum with the Messiah?"

"I'll only slow you down," Titius said. He needed to look for Abigail without these men tagging along.

"Very well," Simon said. "We'll stop for the noon meal. If your host wants you to stay, we'll press on. Lead on."

Titius had hoped to disguise himself as the olive merchant before meeting Isaac, but it seemed he wouldn't have the chance. With his bloodied appearance, full beard, and zealot friends, though, he'd have to find another ploy.

"I feel weak," Titius said. "Simon, could you go down to the market and ask if the owner's there? My friend's name is Isaac. Tell him his friend Porpherus wants to meet him."

Simon returned before the rest had finished eating. He brought a small bag of pickled fish. "The vendor says Isaac's gone to Jerusalem and the woman's gone to Capernaum to hear the Messiah."

Titius's heartbeat quickened. Abigail was only hours away! He struggled to his feet and took the cane that Timna had fashioned for him during the brief stop.

He nodded to the zealots. "Hurry ahead. I can get there on my own from here."

Simon hoisted Titius's pack. "You didn't abandon us to the Romans. We're not going to abandon you now."

Titius stumbled. "I've trained you too well," he said.

The road to Capernaum grew dense with human traffic: donkey carts, horses, camels, and hundreds upon hundreds of people walking. Titius choked on the dust and wrapped a damp shawl around his face.

The zealots finally stepped off the road and rested on a fallen log near the beach.

"Let's walk along the shore," Issachar suggested. "There'll be no dust and fewer people."

Simon took a few steps down the slope. "We'll have to support David even more down here. This ground is rough."

"We can do it," Timna said encouragingly. "We can still make it before the sun goes down."

As the zealots chatted among themselves, Cleopas started in: *"Fool! It's all going to backfire when they find out the truth."*

"I can handle it," Titius murmured under his breath as a flock of pelicans landed on the lake.

"It's insane to chase after that woman. You should've hung yourself properly. You can't do anything right."

"The Messiah will change the world. The Messiah is the hope for all of us."

"Yes!" Simon shouted, having overhead. He grabbed a stone and hurled it as far as he could into the water. "The Messiah will save us all."

Three fishermen stood near a boat a short distance away, examining a net for holes. One of them turned to Titius and the zealots. "Peace to you, strangers," he called.

Simon put down the two packs he carried and waved both arms above his head. "Peace to you!"

"Where are you travelling?" the fisherman asked.

"To Capernaum, to see the Messiah," Simon called back.

"Come with us. We need help with our nets, and we can take you to Capernaum in exchange."

The three zealots discussed this without talking to Titius.

"We'll come with you," Simon said once they'd come to a decision. "But our friend isn't well."

"He can rest in the back," the fisherman offered. "We have room. We're just fishing for sardines."

Issachar looked into the boat. "David, we're going to put you in the back of the boat like a log. Grit your teeth while we move you."

Titius stiffened as they handed him up to the fishermen, who set him down in the back of the boat with a blanket. They then helped the others on board. Two fishermen jumped off and pushed the boat into shallow water. The fishermen then climbed on board, rowed into deeper water, and hoisted the sails.

The wind was boisterous as they bobbed up and down through choppy water. The fishermen shouted orders to the zealots and between them they kept the ship on course. The first waves of nausea hit Titius not long after. He was soon leaning over the edge of the boat, vomiting as water splashed his face and sloshed into the boat.

The shoreline grew smaller as the wind pushed them into the middle of the sea. Timna pointed at the dark clouds racing toward them, which was followed by frenzied shouts and commands. The men strained and groaned against ropes and sails, focused on keeping the ship on course. They lowered the sail as a sheet of rain joined the wind in churning up the whitecaps.

Titius held on in a white-knuckled death grip as his side of the boat pitched toward the water.

"Get away from the side!" one of the sailors warned him. "Lie down!"

Titius let go as his side of the ship jerked skyward. He flew over the keel and plunged into the deep. He let himself twist, sink, and then rise again. Light and dark spun up, down, and around. His training in the assassins' pool kicked in, and he relaxed as his body was pushed violently down.

"Come to me," Cleopas called. *"You've waited long enough."*

"No, come to me," another voice said. It sounded like Yeshua, but could the one who saw through his disguises see him even here? "Strip and swim."

Titius pulled off his tunic and stroked his way toward the surface. The skills Jaennus had taught him served him well. He bobbed to the surface and waved to the men in the boat, who threw a net out to him. It landed perfectly around his head and he held on as they dragged him like a fish to safety.

Wearing only his sandals, they pulled Titius up and he flopped into the middle of the boat. Someone covered him with a blanket. He stayed there, seasick in the sloshing pool of water, sheltered from the sharp whistling wind. His companions took up oars and began rowing back toward shore.

Titius thought of Caleb's big Persian slave. Was Nabonidus still in the gladiator arena or was he rowing in a warship's galley? Was Caleb still safe without his guardian? What would Sestus say when messages stopped arriving at the fortress? Surely Poseidon would claim his life before darkness swallowed them whole.

He wrapped his arms around his knees and prayed in his spirit to the god of the storm. Amidst the crew's shouts, Titius was thrown helplessly side to side. He locked his arms around his head and curled into a ball. The water crashed over him, around him, under him. Time seemed to stop.

Cleopas raged until Titius wanted to be thrown overboard again. Dry heaves convulsed his body. He hugged his ribs to keep them from breaking.

Suddenly, he heard—and felt—a horrendous grinding. They'd hit land. The boat jerked sideways and Simon plunged over the edge.

Titius tossed off his saturated blanket and pulled himself up to the rail, worried about Simon. But the former zealot had scrambled to his feet on shore less than a javelin's throw away. A manic laugh erupted behind Titius; at first he was sure it had come from Cleopas, but then he saw it was only one of the fishermen, laughing at the wind and shaking his fist at the sea.

Titius didn't wait for anyone to help him over the edge. He lowered himself off the listing, shuddering vessel and dropped into the shallows. He scrambled over the rocks and almost lost a sandal. Then he lay on the shore, watching the fishermen trying to anchor the ship as it bucked like a wild stallion.

Simon, his eyes wide with awe, pulled Titius to his feet.

"Can you imagine? The Messiah calmed a storm just like this one with a single word." Simon handed Titius a sopping tunic. "Come, we have to see him. Capernaum is close."

Simon, Issachar, and Timna formed a wedge ahead of Titius as they pushed through the crowds approaching Capernaum. The gentle breeze was a welcome experience after the storm.

The townspeople pushed their way into sheltered courtyards between homes made of stacked basalt blocks to get their evening meal of soup or porridge. Titius was elbowed into a wall as a large fisherman pushed his way through their group. A few stones and a wad of mud fell from the wall to the ground.

"Where can you find this woman you're looking for?" Simon asked.

Titius shrugged. "It's too late now, and the markets are closed. We can shelter at the inn."

The village inn was comprised of four homes huddled around a covered courtyard. Tradesmen, merchants, and vendors gathered to eat there and get out of the wind. Titius pushed in through a narrow doorway, ignoring the stares and whispers of those huddled around three fires. Clay pots, plates, an olive press, and a few grain mills were arranged neatly along the walls. Several dozen clay lamps flickered.

"Let me get you a dry tunic," Issachar said. He disappeared, and a few moments later he returned with a tunic and a blanket.

Titius accepted it, throwing off his wet clothes and putting on the warm, dry garment. "Thank you."

"You're lucky we're following the Messiah now," Issachar said. "The innkeeper said he'd never give anything to a zealot or a Roman."

Simon carried over four bowls of soup, some bread, and a few sardines. They ate as if they hadn't eaten for days. Even Titius felt his stomach settle as it filled. He then accepted a mat and curled up near a wall, not far from one of the fires. Sleep came quickly.

In the early dawn, Titius slipped away from the inn and walked to the sea. Clouds grazed the heavens, as docile as sheep. Gulls, pelicans, and fish eagles whirled through the breezes over the waking village.

Fishermen were already out on the sea in large numbers, tossing nets and hauling in their catches. A middle-aged woman stood quietly gazing at a group of boats not far from shore.

"Peace to you," Titius said.

"And peace to you," she responded, turning. "I see life hasn't been kind to you recently."

"I'm David... and I hope the Messiah might change that."

"I'm Salome, wife of Zebedee," the woman replied. "If you mean Yeshua ben Yuseph, then yes, he can help you." She looked back at the boats. "I'm his aunt, his mother Mary's sister. He's out there with my sons, James and John."

Titius watched the group of four boats working as a unit to gather their catch. "I heard the Messiah lived in Nazareth."

Salome sighed. "He did. The ungrateful wretches tried to throw him off a cliff. He left and came down here to be with family."

"So he lives here now?"

"I actually can't tell. He's here a few days and then he heads off with my sons to the Decapolis, or Caesarea, or Jerusalem... wherever God wants him to go." She pointed at the four boats. "Fortunately our fishing business is good, and we can help support him. He sleeps wherever he can find a place to lie down. I've never walked so much in my life."

"You're a follower of his?"

"Now that's a good question," she said. "I used to think everyone in this part of Galilee was his disciple. Now Pharisees, zealots, tax collectors, lost women... they all surround him. It's hard to know who's for him and who's out to get him."

Titius nodded as he watched the fishermen haul in their nets and begin rowing to shore. Their shouts and laughter drifted easily across the water.

"Come meet my nephew," Salome said. "The next king of Israel."

Titius followed her along the shore until they neared the men hauling in the boat and transferring their catch into reed baskets. They draped the nets over a rack to inspect them for tears.

The confident composure and measured actions of the Messiah were easy to pick out among the group of fishermen. He was clearly the center of attention and everyone stepped aside to make room for him. Once he stepped off the boat, he strolled, almost dance-like, toward those who rushed to greet him. His smile was constant, his face filled with wonder.

As Salome called out to Yeshua, Cleopas let out a scream. *"Run! He'll destroy us!"*

But no one looked bent on destruction. There was only the confident, peaceful Messiah walking beside his aunt.

The screams in Titius's head tempted him to smash his head on the stony beach, and he pressed his hands against his temples. The noise refused to quiet.

The Messiah walked up to him. "Ah, so the blind has come to see."

Titius remained with his head pointed down. "Please, make it go away."

"The play is over," Yeshua said. "Be at peace. When I set you free, you will be truly free."

Yeshua touched his shoulder and lightning jolted him to the core. His body shuddered, and then he was immersed in an inner silence, a peace that went so deep that he wanted to drown in it. Stillness… emptiness… yet fullness. No voices, no confusion, no guilt, no fear, no shame. Only silence.

His body felt strong and whole.

"I must go to Jerusalem," Yeshua said, pausing only for a moment. "Hurry, while you can. Go there. Your friend will need you soon."

But Abigail was here. His newly converted zealot friends were here. Was this really the time to go back to Jerusalem?

Something powerful inside urged him that it was. And this time, it wasn't Cleopas.

Titius left notes with the fish vendor and the innkeeper, both addressed to Abigail in care of Isaac. He also left a note for Simon, urging him to meet the Messiah quickly.

Then, before the town was awake, he was on the run toward Jerusalem.

Without Cleopas, Titius was left with his own thoughts. The Messiah had told him that his friend would need him soon. Which friend? Caleb? Sestus? He wished it were Abigail.

As he passed Magdala, he heard the sound of pounding hooves behind him and slowed to let the Romans pass. Instead of Romans, though, a squadron of fully armed zealots galloped by. The last horse stopped beside him.

"David?" asked the man on the horse.

Titius looked up and was surprised to see Jonathan.

"David, you're alive!" he shouted. "Climb on! We must hurry."

Titius climbed up behind the young zealot. By the time he was seated, he saw that the rest of the squadron had already moved down the road and were almost out of sight. In a few strides, though, Jonathan's stallion was thundering forward again.

"Where are we going?" Titius shouted.

"Barabbas needs us!" Jonathan yelled back. "That Roman centurion has him trapped. We have to save him."

Chapter Twenty-Two

Titius hung on tight as Jonathan galloped between the caravans and foot traffic near Tiberias. The recent rains kept the dust down, and Titius's mind remained clear and quiet as the horse gained on those ahead of them.

By the time the troop dismounted three hours later, a line of early Passover pilgrims was already lined up at the crossing to ford the Jordan. Titius, wobbly and weary, dropped to his knees at the water's edge and quenched his raging thirst.

The horses' sides heaved as the men walked restlessly back and forth along the bank, waiting for the path to clear. More and more pilgrims were joining the line. Knowing it would take a while, the zealots dug into their saddlebags for dates, apricots, figs, and bread.

Jonathan and an old shepherd approached Titius. Not just any old shepherd, Titius realized. It was Hosea.

"Peace to you, David," Hosea said. "Are you a phantom raised from the dead or just a coward on the run?" He waved his dagger inches from Titius's nose. "Barabbas will be interested to meet the man who broke his sister's heart."

Titius looked into Hosea's fiery eyes. "I was dead in ways I can't explain," he said. "I met the Messiah. I'm here now."

"I'd run you through myself, but we need every warrior we can get. I know you can fight."

"I appreciate your mercy," Titius said.

"It's not mercy. I don't dare deprive Barabbas of the satisfaction of avenging his sister."

When it was their turn, several zealots led their horses to the river's edge and started to cross.

Jonathan handed Titius his share of dried fruit and a chunk of barley loaf. "Eat quickly. We're going now," he said. "We'll change horses in an hour at Aenon."

Titius considered bolting, but the Messiah's words kept him focused: "Hurry to Jerusalem. Your friend will need you soon." It was almost as if Yeshua had arranged the transportation.

The change of horses at Aenon meant another brief break and some of the warriors flopped on the ground in a small grove of oaks. They guzzled water or wine from their gourds and refilled them from a village well. Others walked to the Jordan and dunked their heads in the cool water.

For the rest of the ride, the zealots gave Titius his own horse. Then the zealots rode hard along the road, shouting occasionally to clear travelers from the path ahead. But as they neared another river crossing, the path became glutted with oxcarts, donkey caravans, and families with children. Instead of waiting there, the zealots pulled off the path and galloped across the grasslands.

Suddenly, one of the horses stumbled and threw its rider to the ground. The rest of the group pulled up as pilgrims rushed over to help.

"Stay back!" Hosea shouted to them. "Keep moving!"

"What's wrong?" Titius called to Jonathan.

"Looks like the horse broke his leg," Jonathan replied.

"Keep going," Hosea commanded. "Jonathan, David, ride down to the ravine. Shem will meet you there with fresh horses, and then he'll take you to Barabbas." He walked toward the thrashing horse and pulled out his sword. "We know the centurion still hasn't gotten his reinforcements. Hurry!"

The dust thickened as the landscape dipped lower and lower in elevation. As they rode, they encountered fewer plants and animals and Titius wrapped his headscarf across his face to protect himself from the blistering sun. Sweat drenched his neck and back, and pain pierced his legs and buttocks, but he kept riding toward "the ravine," as Hosea had called it. On the way, Jonathan explained that this was the site where Sestus and Barabbas were about to do battle.

Shem, one of the commanders of Barabbas's militia, led Jonathan and Titius through the ravine along the Jordan. It twisted and turned, but Shem knew every step, even as the shadows fell. They soon reached a large cavern and he hooted like a screech owl. A similar cry echoed from the inner passage.

"Wait," Shem ordered before stepping into the shadows. A minute later, he was back with a torch. He waved them inside. "This way. Barabbas says the Romans will attack at dawn. Their reinforcements have just arrived. So we'll attack tonight."

Titius's stomach twisted as he anticipated the battle. He took three deep breaths, just as Jaennus had taught him, to focus his mind. He had to find a way to warn Sestus.

Titius kept his face covered as they moved into the zealot camp. Dark canopies anchored to the cliff waved gently in the breeze and deflected plumes of smoke from small cookfires. The aroma of roasted meat filled the cave. Voices rumbled softly.

Jonathan walked confidently up to a large warrior. The men around him moved to make space for Jonathan and greeted him with nods.

So this was Barabbas! In the dim light, Barabbas's full curly black beard appeared as large as his entire head. His nose jutted out prominently from the mass of hair as his lips constantly moved in a chewing motion. His thick brass breastplate glistened in the firelight and his rawhide leggings marked him as a man ready for war. His sword rested against his hip as he pointed animatedly at something on his parchment.

The zealot leader huddled with Jonathan, then waved the warriors to one side of the grotto. They dropped their swords and javelins in a pile as they discussed their battle plans.

Jonathan came back to find Titius sitting against the cliff. "Let me handle this," he said. "If Barabbas realizes you're the one who left his sister, it might be a distraction. So just fight and make him glad you're with us."

A dozen men huddled around a fire as Barabbas used a stick to draw a map in the dirt. A light rain fell, muddying the map, but the men nodded and gestured to each other as they worked to understand their roles. Titius moved closer and stood under a tarp so he could see the scratching on the ground. He kept his head bowed whenever he thought Barabbas might be looking in his direction. The man was focused and confident, the young men around him patriotic and energetic.

When the discussion was over, Jonathan gathered his group together. He pointed to their current location on the map, then indicated the Romans' location nearby.

"Listen carefully," Jonathan said. "We'll travel up this cliff and approach from above." He pointed at some of the men. "Half of you will shoot flaming arrows and toss pots of hot oil on the Roman tents." He pointed at Titius and the men beside him. "You men will throw javelins at the sentries and then boulders down on the camp."

"What will the others do?" someone asked.

Jonathan pointed to another part of the map. "The others will ambush from this side, trapping them in the grotto they're hiding in. And we aren't waiting for the morning. We do this now."

The energy was palpable as men dispersed and collected supplies. Each fighter carried gourds of oil, arrows, and a sword.

As an owl hooted above the camp, Jonathan led his silent fighters to the edge of a cliff while others dispersed into the darkness.

Titius had little trouble climbing the cliff. He tucked his sandals into his tunic so he could use his fingers and toes to hold the rock face. A few fighters behind him slipped and slid down; there was considerable noise for the first half of the climb, until they figured out how to stay quiet.

Once they were all huddled atop the cliff, they lowered ropes and hauled up javelins and more jars of oil. Scouts scurried ahead to check for sentries.

They returned a few minutes later, divided the supplies, and passed them up a human chain to their attack position. Looking over the edge of the cliff, Titius could see that most of the Roman troops were inside their tents below. The cliff top was bowl-shaped, with a piece of the bowl broken away. The Roman sentries guarded that entrance, but not the heights above them.

Something wasn't right. It seemed too easy.

Titius waited in a dark dent in the rock, gripping his oil. Could he really pour it down on Sestus? Or should he pour it out on the ground and hope the centurion got away? Would he shoot a legionnaire if Jonathan were being attacked? Would he let the gods decide who lived and who died?

He remembered what Jaennus had told him, the reminder that Titius had given his life to Caesar and Sestus—to the emperor, to Sestus, and to the brotherhood of thespian assassins. Death was the only way to be free of the oath.

So if Sestus died, Titius would be free. But Sestus was the only one who could retrieve Titius's ring from the assassin's death pool…

More zealots crept closer to the precipice and readied their weapons. The camp below appeared to be totally unaware.

The legion's standard-bearer and two bodyguards stood by a tent below him. He gripped the gourd of oil more tightly. Could he pour it on Sestus's tent? Would he remain free if he killed his own commander?

At the owl signal, Jonathan whispered a command and open gourds of oil fell on the Romans, followed by flaming arrows. Titius held his gourd and watched as well-aimed javelins skewered two of the sentries. Soon rocks showered down on the helpless legionnaires emerging from their tents. The horses below whinnied and reared as fire surrounded them. Supply wagons burst into flame.

Warrior cries shattered the night. Romans without breastplates, helmets, or shields stood shoulder to shoulder against a mob who attacked from above, from in front, from the sides.

Adrenaline surged through Titius's veins. The glory of men dying for their cause blinded him to the attack's insanity.

Barabbas and three of his men moved along the edge of the grotto toward Sestus's tent, wearing black and disappearing into the shadows. The chaos in the burning camp distracted everyone's attention from them, but finally Barabbas crawled out of the darkness toward Sestus's bodyguards. The two legionnaires turned to face the intruders and were shot with arrows from above. The first sentry crumpled to his knees as another arrow pierced his neck, felling him. The second sentry yanked an arrow from his lower back and looked up. Barabbas sprang forward and thrust a sword into his side.

Sestus, still strapping on his armor, stepped out of his tent wearing his distinctive horsehair helmet. Titius didn't throw down oil as Barabbas charged, neither did he scream in warning. He didn't throw javelins, either. He just hunched in the darkness and watched.

Roman reinforcements streamed into the fight. The thunder of their hobnailed sandals, banging of swords against shields, and roar of their death chant echoed off the grotto walls and rushed past Titius into the night sky.

Barabbas and his companions speared Sestus repeatedly, and then the rebel leader put a dagger to the centurion's throat. Titius watched the zealot leader struggle to take off Sestus's helmet, but the Roman reinforcements surged toward him. Barabbas was forced to abandon his three companions and slip back into the shadows. Titius tracked him as he climbed the cliff face and reached the precipice.

The battle was brief. Dozens of zealots died, but many others ran away, leaving the Romans standing around their dead commander. Only then did Titius throw his gourd of oil down into the fire consuming Sestus's tent.

Several legionnaires began climbing the cliff, but Titius and the zealots had already slipped back down the ropes on the other side. Ten feet from the ground, Titius jumped and landed amid rocks. He tumbled through the mud, ignoring the pain, and then ran through the bushes to where he'd hidden his horse. This was cutting it close.

If the Messiah had sent him to help Sestus, he'd failed. If the Messiah had sent him to help Barabbas, he'd failed.

Titius mounted his horse and galloped away. He glanced back to see archers drawing their bows while the sound of swords clashing split the night.

Barabbas had killed a leading Roman centurion. Rome's rage would be strong, and they wouldn't rest until Barabbas hung on a cross. Then the Romans would kill and capture as many attackers as they could. Caleb would soon be needed again.

More than forty zealots rendezvoused near Aenon, but Barabbas wasn't among them. Titius was warming his hands by a fire when Jonathan joined him.

"I can't believe what a captured legionnaire just told us." Jonathan kicked a stray coal back into the flames. "He said we defeated them only because the centurion and the rest in the grotto were sick with dysentery. He said the other soldiers were elsewhere so they wouldn't get sick."

A flock of Egyptian geese flapped furiously overhead, flying south to the sea.

"That sounds reasonable," Titius said. "I've never seen Romans fight so poorly."

"Don't let Barabbas hear you say that. He's waited a long time for this day. We lost a lot of good men."

Some of the zealots changed into clothing that made them look like pilgrims. Others were repacking their bags and loading their horses. Weapons were packed into an oxcart's false bottom, then covered with bricks and a tarp.

A zealot rider galloped into camp and everyone tensed.

"Barabbas is coming soon," the rider shouted. "We've just heard that the Messiah raised a man named Lazarus from the dead! If we can get him on our side, every one of our warriors will be invincible. The kingdom will soon be ours."

When the rider had gone, Titius turned to Jonathan. "Soon the Romans will come, without mercy. We should scatter and hide for a while. I'll go to Caesarea."

"Is that what you did last time?"

"I did what I had to do," Titius said. "Can you watch my horse for a moment while I, um, use the bushes?"

Jonathan led the horse to a small copse of trees. "Hosea said to wait here until Barabbas and the others arrived."

While Jonathan brushed the horse's neck, Titius slipped away. He ran hard toward the river and dove in fully dressed. He stayed under, swimming and drifting with the current. He'd take a quick breath, then dive back under, swimming hard to get as far as possible without being noticed.

He had a bruising experience in the shallow rapids, avoiding boulders. The water, icy from winter runoff, chilled him to the bone. And he could only hope the water was too fast and cold for crocodiles.

After a long drift down the river, Titius looked for a good place to get out near Jericho. He swam ashore and listened to the sounds of a leopard snarling, frogs croaking, and crickets chirping. A hippopotamus's loud snort rose from the far riverbank. One thing he didn't hear was the sound of horses coming after him.

He slipped back into the river and rode it until the first light of dawn tinged the horizon. Here, the road to Jericho appeared around a bend in the river. Titius slipped into a grove to wring out his tunic and change clothes behind some bushes.

From the road, he heard voices. A large merchant caravan, accompanied by Passover pilgrims from Galilee, was chanting and arguing. Titius waited until they were out of sight before joining the road.

By the time he'd stepped through Jericho's gates, the noonday sun had dried him off. He had left behind his money in his horse's saddlebag, with Jonathan, so he couldn't pay the tax to enter the city. He couldn't beg, either, as that would draw attention to him.

He drank from the town well and waited.

A short man approached him boldly. "Peace to you. I'm Zacchaeus, chief tax collector. My man says you didn't pay your tax at the gate."

Titius looked into the man's dark sparkling eyes and realized they'd met before.

"I've always paid my tax," Titius said, "but this time I have no money. Nothing. I ask for mercy."

Zacchaeus eyed him for a moment and then pointed at a stall against the far wall. "The Almighty demands charity for the poor. Eat your fill there and tell them I sent you."

Titius was shocked. He hadn't encountered charity like this before. In Rome, those with money ruled and those without served.

Titius bowed and backed away from the tax collector.

The vendor by the wall hesitated only a moment when Titius told him Zacchaeus had sent him. He then gave Titius two barley loaves, cheese, figs, salted fish, with a mug of tepid water.

As Titius reclined under a canopy, the sound of hundreds of hobnailed sandals echoed off the Jericho walls. Rome was on the move. Barabbas would soon face Rome's rage.

That afternoon, a camel caravan passed through the gate toward Jerusalem. Its riders wore white headcloths and earth-colored tunics. Titius slipped out with them and jogged along behind as the Arab traders moved quickly, camel bells ringing. The steep ascent was wearying in the hot sun, but Titius kept pace with the beasts.

One of the men dropped out, noticing Titius, and waited for him to catch up.

"Peace to you," he said. "We're Bedu from Perea. The master wishes to understand your business."

Titius nodded. "I only seek protection with your caravan. I'm walking alone to Jerusalem. I mean no harm."

"Consider yourself one of us. I am Shaban."

Titius thought through his catalogue of names for a new identity. He licked his lips and swallowed. "I am Titius, son and senator of Rome."

The Arab chuckled. "The Bedu are people of honor and we speak truth to each other." He pointed at Titius's feet. "No man of power would wear a beggar's sandals."

Titius smiled. "Not unless he had to walk through camel dung."

"We dishonor you. Come, walk with me in front of the camels."

From the caravan's head, Titius could hear men singing to their beasts. He didn't understand the words but understood how well the music calmed those far from home.

"What do you know of the new Messiah?" Shaban asked. "My father told me that when he was young, he met a great caravan who'd seen the star announcing his birth."

"I've met the Messiah," Titius said.

"You've met such a great king?"

"This king wears sandals like mine, a robe like mine." He pointed toward Galilee. "He terrifies Jerusalem's religious leaders, but in Galilee he heals the blind, the lepers, and the demon-possessed. He multiplies bread for the masses, turns water to wine, and fills fishermen's nets with a word."

Shaban rubbed his beard. "Such a powerful man will surely lead his people well. What do the Romans say about him?"

Titius considered his response. "Rome wants peace. They think they can get peace only through the power of the cross."

"So Rome will crucify the Messiah?"

"It's a difficult time for this country," Titius replied.

"I must tell the others."

Shaban jogged back to the other camel drivers and they began a vigorous discussion. Titius walked alone, contemplating the situation. Would Rome truly crucify the Messiah?

When the caravan reached Jerusalem, the sun kissing the horizon, Rome's full power was on display at the city gates. Squads of armed legionnaires searched every pilgrim.

The camel riders turned aside to a caravansary for shelter, and Titius left them, slipping through the Sheep Gate and up to Caleb's carpenter shop. Finding no one there, he stepped inside and curled up on the bench for the night.

If the Romans planned to crucify the Messiah, the cross would probably be made in this room. He could make sure that didn't happen.

In the middle of the night, he awoke to the sudden sensation of a hand grabbing his ankle. He grabbed the attacker's wrist, squeezed, and twisted his foot out of the grip. He put a choke hold on the man who had disturbed him.

A gourd of wine dropped to the floor and splashed on Titius's foot.

"It's me!" the captive howled. "Caleb!"

Titius released him as the carpenter lit a lamp. "Sestus is dead. Barabbas killed him."

"I know," Caleb said. "I was at the fortress and heard the news from the centurion Cato." He cleared his workbench. "How did you find out?"

Titius picked up a few wood shavings to feed the glowing embers in the fire pit. He added more as the flame grew. "Big news travels fast. They say his cohort had the fever and couldn't fight. Barabbas could never have gotten him any other way."

Caleb put two big pieces of cedar in the fire. "All I know is the Romans will have that zealot soon and I'll make a special cross for him." His expression hardened. "I'll have vengeance for my father."

Titius took bread and cheese out of a cupboard. "You knew Yeshua growing up, didn't you?"

"Yeshua loved adventure." Caleb sat on a stool and stirred the fire with a stick. "He loved to laugh. He worked hard. He honored his parents."

"Did you know he'd be the Messiah?"

"Every mother in this land thinks her son will be the Messiah." Caleb joined Titius at the workbench to eat. "Every son wants to make his mother happy."

Titius lifted his bread. "I praise the Almighty. He healed my mind."

Caleb sat up straight. "What are these words, coming from a Roman like you?"

"He healed my mind," Titius said, tearing off more bread.

Caleb shook his head. "Suzanna follows the Messiah. She tells me not to hate Barabbas."

"It sounds like you're getting closer to her."

"That's the problem. I should have been there for Sestus, but I was walking around Jerusalem with a woman."

"I'm your guardian; you're a cross maker." He touched Caleb's wrist in affirmation. "You're not a guardian."

"You trained me to fight, and I almost got Sestus killed. I've been useless here."

Titius thought before he spoke. "I used to believe in fates imposed by the gods. I thought we were at the mercy of their vanity and vengeance." He poured wine into a mug. "Listening to Yeshua, I think the Almighty has other plans. Even you aren't more powerful than the Almighty's designs for us."

Caleb paced to the door and leaned against the frame. "What good am I if I can't help bring peace?"

"I've never seen so many crossbeams in your shop," Titius said, indicating the pile of squared timbers.

Caleb scowled. "Cato told me we'd soon have a message to send these zealots. Sestus always believed the power of the cross would bring peace here. Soon we'll find out if he was right."

Titius slid off the workbench and crouched by the washbasin. "Perhaps one day we'll gain peace without needing the cross."

"I'd love to see that day," Caleb said.

"You need your sleep."

Caleb disappeared into his bedroom and Titius set his empty wine cup near the fireplace. What would a world without the cross be like? How would the powerful bring about peace?

Perhaps he and Abigail would meet again before that great day.

Titius curled up on the workbench and went back to sleep.

At dawn, Titius fed the fire again. When he heard leather sandals approaching the shop door, he hid under the workbench. As he watched, Suzanna entered with a tray and put it on the bench. She stirred the fire, poured some water into a pot, and set the pot to boil.

After a moment, she began to play a haunting melody on Caleb's flute. Caleb soon emerged from his room. The two embraced.

Suzanna tried to keep playing as Caleb squeezed her. She finally spun around, giggling, and backed away.

"You tease me, woman," Caleb said.

"I brought you breakfast," Suzanna replied. "You need your strength. I'll pick up the tray later. There's water boiling for you."

As Titius heard her sandals leave the shop, the aroma of fresh bread and oranges drew him from his hiding place. He split the food in half and ate his share.

"I spent half the night dreaming about Barabbas," Caleb said to him. "My stomach is sick from the thought of his freedom. He killed my father and your centurion. How can you eat?"

"Justice will find its time, my friend."

Caleb threw his food onto the floor. "Just leave me alone!" he yelled, his face red. "My father is dead, your friend Jaennus is dead, and Sestus is dead. The only person who isn't dead is Barabbas. Go find him and I'll make his cross."

Chapter Twenty-Three

The next two days went quickly as Titius kept watch for Abigail at the fish vendor and the rose garden. But the pickled fish tray lay empty, and the old woman, Elizabeth, shook her head whenever she saw Titius standing over her rose bushes.

The upper city was full. All the empire's languages reverberated off the limestone walls as people jostled to and from worship. The Messiah and his followers had found some other place to hide, allowing the priests to appear peaceful and confident as they fulfilled their temple duties.

In the lower city, Titius leaned against a wall near the Damascus Gate, a stone's throw from Caleb's shop. The streets were packed as tightly as pickled sardines, with Passover pilgrims searching for food and shelter.

When a growing rumble began to echo off the walls, Titius stopped to listen. Massive waves of chants and cheers were sweeping like an ocean down from the Mount of Olives into the city.

"Hosanna!"

"Blessed is he who comes in the name of the Lord!"

"Blessed is the coming kingdom of our father David!"

"Hosanna in the highest!"[1]

People all around Titius moved toward the sound. He pressed back against the wall to avoid being trampled. What insanity had possessed the people? Even Herod hadn't been welcomed like this. Surely it couldn't be Caesar himself!

Caleb appeared in the door of his shop, then pushed his way through the crowd. Titius followed the carpenter until they reached the Antonia Fortress.

---

[1] Mark 11:9-10 NIV 1984

Titius then turned back toward the Temple Mount. He'd get a report from Caleb later.

Titius scaled a garden wall and watched as a man who looked like Yeshua rode a donkey into the Kidron Valley and then up toward the gates. A green pathway of palm branches lay strewn around him. Pilgrims had stripped the surrounding trees.

"It's the Messiah!" a man standing on a nearby roof shouted.

This wasn't a good time for the Messiah to be stirring up the people. Someone had to warn him to get back to Galilee.

The shouting poured into the city. Several women danced around the approaching Messiah, and one in particular caught Titius's attention: she held her headscarf stretched between her upraised arms and twirled with an angel's grace. Her long dark hair spun out from her upraised face, which wore an expression of unimaginable joy. A rose was tucked behind her ear.

Color swirled around her as the rose fell, crushed by the donkey's hoof. Several men pushed past the dancers, stepped up to the donkey, and pointed animatedly at the crowd. The man on the donkey simply nodded.

The human river moved uphill and a dozen Pharisees stepped onto the edge of a roof, blocking Titius's view.

"We should have killed him when we had the chance," said one of the Pharisees.

Titius sidestepped to regain his view, but the woman was nowhere to be seen.

He scanned the top of the Antonia Tower and noticed Caleb standing with a Roman centurion. Both men were looking out from the parapet. The centurion was pointing toward the Messiah. Soon the donkey and its rider had disappeared into the mass of humanity.

When Titius got into the street, the crush pushed toward the sheep market. He worked hard to escape and finally got down an alley that led to the Damascus Gate. Thousands were pushing in from there, too, but he forced his way past the tangle of arms and legs, away from the hypnotic chanting and acrid tang of smoke and fresh blood.

He was sure the woman with the rose had been Abigail, but he'd never get close to her if she went into the Courtyard of the Women at the temple. No man, and definitely no foreigner, could enter there. He'd have to wait until the Feast was over. Not a Jew in the world would understand if he approached a woman and tried to convince her to come away and talk.

He navigated through back streets to the carpenter shop, where he discovered two Roman legionnaires waiting outside the door. Sweat streamed down Titius's back.

"Who are you?" one of them asked him.

"Titius Marcus Julianus, former aide to Sestus Aurelius, Legate of Judea, Champion of Rome."

One legionnaire nodded. "He was a good leader." He pointed toward the Antonia Fortress. "You'll be glad to know we've captured his murderer, Barabbas. The Centurion Cato has commanded that crosses be prepared immediately for the zealots."

Titius bowed. "I'm the cross maker's guardian. I'll let him know you need a special cross made immediately."

He stepped past the soldiers into the shop and made himself something to eat. A small bowl of pickled fish made him consider wading through the crowds one more time in search of Abigail, but the crowd was still thick. Caleb would be back soon and he might need some help.

Caleb charged into the shop well after dark. His eyes looked haunted.

"Where've you been?" Caleb said. "They have Barabbas and he's finally going to pay for murdering my father. I need to make a crossbeam that will bring him to his knees."

Titius looked at the pile of crossbeams against the far wall. "You have enough to choose from."

Caleb shook his head. "No, I need a heavier one, as heavy as Sestus. Only an olive beam will do."

"Get some sleep and then decide," Titius said. "The sentries outside will protect you. There are big olive trees in the Garden of Gethsemane."

"Did you see the Messiah's entrance?" Caleb asked.

Titius nodded. "It felt like a new-crowned Caesar coming to claim his throne. But no emperor would display such humility before his people, dressed in common clothes and riding a donkey."

"He isn't acting like the boy I knew in Nazareth, but he isn't acting like a king either. I can't figure him out. Today, in the temple, he threw over the moneychangers' tables, freed the doves, and chased out the sacrificial animals."

"Why?" Titius asked. The Yeshua he'd seen had healed people, and had personally freed him of Cleopas. He cared for people; he didn't deliberately create trouble.

"I didn't see him do it," Caleb said, "but I heard he said the temple was supposed to be a house of prayer for all nations."

"And yet inside the temple you have a sign declaring death to foreigners who try to come near."

"It's our way to protect the temple's purity." Caleb walked to the crossbeams and ran his hands along the top one. "Suzanna's been telling me about this Messiah. He's not as I would've expected. Maybe he can bring us peace despite Rome's terror."

"Was Suzanna one of the women dancing around Yeshua?" Titius poured a cup of wine and handed it to him. "If she was, I might know one of the other women who was with her."

"She was there," Caleb said, accepting the mug.

"When will you see her again?"

When Caleb spoke, he had resolve in his voice. "Not until I finish the cross for Barabbas."

Titius felt trapped in the shop, with sentries outside and a preoccupied cross maker inside. He didn't volunteer any information about the dancers, and Caleb didn't ask.

Titius rose early and stirred the fire into life. In the dawn light, Caleb was stuffing handfuls of parched grain into a fold of cloth. His hands shook and he spilled some wheat on the floor. He picked up a hammer from his workbench and threw it against the wall. It bounced against the ceiling, breaking off the head. The handle fell near the fireplace.

Titius jumped away from the bouncing hammer and stood on a cross beam. "Shalom, my friend."

Caleb turned away without even an apology. He then put on an apron over his carpenter's tunic.

"How will you get the tree back here?" Titius asked, hoping to focus Caleb's mind.

"The Almighty will help me," Caleb said. "If justice isn't dispensed soon, the people will get restless and think Rome is weakening. Peace won't have a chance if we don't work the crosses."

"You sound more Roman than I. Truly you have drunk Rome's poison from Sestus."

Caleb eyed Titius briefly, then grabbed a few tools and set out into the flow of humanity scurrying by the shop toward the markets.

Jews from Egypt, Libya, Mesopotamia, Parthia, Asia, Galilee, and Rome piled into the rose garden like pickled fish in a basket. Titius pushed his way through a gap in the hedge that kept the curious on the cobblestone path among the flowers. Word of mouth had drawn people there, the only place in Jerusalem to get away from the overwhelming smoke of sacrificed lambs.

Titius nudged his way past a huddle of young women looking at a yellow rose bush. The old widow of the garden wasn't with them, nor with the next four groups he saw. He eventually found her near a limestone hut, perched on a stool in a patch of sunshine. Her eyes were closed and a faint smile teased the corners of her mouth.

"Peace to you," he said.

"And peace to you," Elizabeth replied, her wrinkles soaking in the warmth. "Who might you be today?"

Titius was wearing a white tunic, blue sash, and tall sandals. "I am who I always am."

The women's eyelids flickered and her smile widened. "Is this the same man who seeks the queen of roses? Your voice is different. Perhaps my news is meant for different ears."

Titius stepped forward until his shadow fell over her. "Elizabeth, I've waited long enough. I can't play these games."

"Did you find the beauty you sought?"

"I wouldn't be here if I'd found her." He touched her hand. "Has the singer from Galilee come recently?"

The widow smiled as she rocked herself back and forth. "Ah, so this time you come as you are, without hiding. Perhaps this time you'll find her. Now, move out of my sunshine."

Titius stepped back and watched Elizabeth close her eyes and lift her face once more to the sun. She rocked, and he waited. Perhaps she was a prophetess listening to the Almighty. Or perhaps she'd forgotten he was there.

The sound of a screeching hawk made them turn to see a pigeon flying for its life away from the larger bird. The pigeon dove into some shrubbery and the hawk soared back into the heavens, thwarted.

"Two days ago, she was here," Elizabeth finally said. "The woman you're looking for went to Bethany to see the Messiah."

That meant Abigail couldn't have gone far. Titius nodded and left the old woman.

He pushed against the tide of humanity surging into the garden and finally emerged through the hedge behind the pool of Siloam, where he headed past the perfume factories toward the nearest city gate.

Titius followed the road below the city and skirted the huge walls of the upper city. The constant stench of burning trash, human waste, animal carcasses, and criminal corpses in the Valley of Hinnom made him gag. He walked as quickly as he could.

Rounding the corner below the temple, he saw a group of Pharisees huddled together. Titius moved slowly toward them and faded into the shrubbery. None of the black-clad, heavily bearded men looked in his direction. Their voices carried in the wind.

"The whole world is following him. We must kill him before the Romans shut down the temple."

"How? He avoids every trap we lay. He's never alone."

"Is there a woman?"

"No! You see him. He wouldn't fall for such an old trick."

"Perhaps there's a follower we can bribe to betray him?"

"There may be one…"

A wind rustled the leaves, drowning out their words. Soon after, a small caravan of merchants broke up the huddle and Titius blended in with them, going on his way.

The religious leaders seemed to have been talking about Yeshua. How strange that the Messiah so loved by the people could be so hated by their leaders!

The pathway round the wall was crowded with pilgrims, and it soon became apparent there would be no quick way to get to the Mount of Olives.

A squadron of Roman cavalry charged down the road, scattering pilgrims on both sides. A gilded carriage bounced along behind the horsemen as they headed for a main gate near Herod's palace.

Titius cut through the Garden of Gethsemane just in time to see Caleb wrap a golden rag around a tree, claiming it for Caesar. Titius just shook his head and went on his way.

Dark clouds leapfrogged across the hills and charged toward the temple, where the sun stood high and swallows skittered over the graveyard against the towering walls. Wildflowers bent before the strengthening wind.

Ant-sized figures crawled into the warrens of the city that never slept. The religious leaders, in their ceremonial black robes, bowed and accepted sacrifices, pronouncing the Almighty's forgiveness on his people. The priests, he realized, acted out their piety better than he himself had ever acted. Something had changed inside him—he could never pretend like that anymore. These holy men thought no more of killing the Messiah than they thought of killing their lambs.

Once in Bethany, Titius sat at the community well and waited. The village seemed lighter and less windy.

A young girl with a clay jug approached, then hesitated before him.

"Peace to you," Titius said.

"And peace to you," she replied. "Are you here for the festival? You look Roman."

"You are perceptive for your years. Who might you be?"

"I am a servant of Lazarus." The girl bowed her head, almost hiding her midnight-dark bangs and chocolate eyes.

"The one the Messiah raised from death?" Titius asked.

"Yes, the same." She tied a rope to the jug and lowered it. The jug slapped against the water.

"Was he truly dead?"

"Yes, for four days," she said without looking up.

"The Messiah healed me, so I believe."

"Yes, he heals many." She drew the jug up to the rim, untied it, and set it on the rocky lip. "Right now he teaches his followers. Perhaps you can see him tomorrow."

"Do you know if there's a young woman from Galilee among his followers? A singer?"

She glanced quickly at him, then lowered her gaze. "There are many women from Galilee here."

She turned to go, but Titius blocked her path.

"The one I seek wears roses in her hair," he said.

Her eyebrows furrowed for a moment. "I may know someone like that."

"Was she one of the dancers who led the Messiah into Jerusalem?"

"I'm here to serve, not to observe."

"Please, if you see a woman who wears a rose, tell her the nobleman she seeks has come to her from the garden in Rome."

She took a step around him. "I must get this water back. Maybe the one you look for will come get her own water."

Titius watched the young woman walk toward a big limestone house. Two large tents beside it rippled in the breeze. The people huddled in them were preparing to eat their evening meal.

An old man with a cane hobbled up to him. "If you're here to see the Messiah, you'll have to wait until after Passover," he said. "If you're here searching for zealots to betray to the Romans, then leave. Now."

"Peace to you," Titius greeted, his hands open.

"Keep your peace," the old man snarled, waggling his cane. "We have enough trouble."

"I'm waiting for someone I used to know."

A pair of young men joined the old man and reached for Titius's arms. He stepped back, out of their reach, and they grabbed for him again. Titius ducked and put out his foot, tripping one of them. The other charged and Titius flipped him over his hip, flat onto his back.

When he sprang to his feet, all three men held knives and dozens of villagers had formed a hedge around them. The first sprinkles of rain fell, but only a few observers moved away.

Noticing a space in the wall of people, Titius decided he would try to get through. But before he could make a run for it, a broad-chested man closed the opening. The man's face was familiar—

Titius's peripheral vision caught the flash of steel and he stepped sideways to avoid a blade. He moved fast as a cobra, grabbing the wrist, holding it, and elbowing his assailant in the stomach. The knife dropped to the ground.

"Stop!" someone commanded. Titius looked up and realized the voice belonged to the broad-chested man, and then he remember who the man was—Andrew the fisherman, one of the Messiah's followers. "How is this a welcome for our guest?"

"This is no guest," the old man bellowed. "He's a Roman hunting for zealots."

"I came looking for a friend," Titius assured him. "The Messiah healed me and I wanted to share my news."

Suddenly, a woman's loud voice reduced the crowd to silence. "I'm here."

Chapter Twenty-Four

Titius stepped back at the sound of the voice, then almost fell over when he saw Abigail's raven hair, almost hidden by her shawl. Her eyes glistened as she looked at Titius, then glanced down at the ground. Her hands trembled and in her right hand she held a rose.

Titius stared. "I found you," he said, barely able to breathe.

She kept her head bowed. "Is it true Yeshua healed you?"

"I have so much to tell you," Titius said, for a moment forgetting the crowd all around them. "Do you remember the garden in Rome?"

She nodded. "I'll never forget your garden. Wherever I go, I seek the beauty and peace of the rose. But why are you dressed like a servant?"

"It suited my purpose. I'm not the child you knew."

"And I'm not the girl you knew," she replied as a sprinkling of rain fell. "Come inside. I don't remember rain like this in Rome."

The rain soon poured like a waterfall and the villagers scattered. Titius followed Andrew and Abigail toward the tents beside the large house he'd seen earlier.

Titius and Abigail were both drenched by the time they ducked under the white tent. Rain trickled from Abigail's nose and chin. She wiped her cheeks. He saw nothing but her raven curls hiding shyly under her headscarf, her eyes bright and questioning. Titius drank in her face.

"I have looked for you everywhere," he said.

"I've been waiting," She tucked a stray curl back under her shawl. Her eyes examined him. "You look so much like your father. You're so tall, so strong."

Titius shook his head. "Thanks to your Messiah, I'm nothing like my father."

A middle-aged woman interrupted them, bustling into the tent and handing out towels. "Dry yourselves," she said. "Then come and eat. No guest will die of starvation in this house."

"Thank you, Martha," Abigail said. "No one does hospitality like you. I'll be in to help you in a minute."

"Mind your guest, Abigail," Martha replied. "The dishes won't go anywhere."

The woman then nodded at Titius and hurried away.

"I hardly believed this day would come," Titius said. He wiped his face and hung the towel across his shoulders.

"I hardly believe it still," Abigail replied. Raindrops and tears intermingled on her chin.

"You still have the heavens in your eyes!"

"You still have the earth in yours."

Titius was suddenly jostled by Andrew's heavy shoulder.

"Man, stand away from her," the fisherman's boomed in his ear. "Woman, he's a Roman! Consider the Almighty. At least wait until the Messiah comes back and gives his wisdom."

Abigail blushed and backed away. "I need to help Martha with the food. Don't go away."

Titius reached for Abigail, but Andrew's strong grip stopped him. Titius was going to bring an elbow up into Andrew's jaw, but two other men were entering the tent. Titius turned toward them with raised fists and fire in his eyes.

"What is it, Roman?" Andrew asked, holding up his hands. "Will you fight for every woman you see? Come! You and I need to breathe before it gets too hot in here."

Titius darted out into the rain with the towel draped over his head.

In the open doorway to the house next door, he caught sight of Suzanna, Caleb's friend. The woman was watching him closely.

"As soon as the rain stops, the Messiah will be returning from the temple," Andrew called from the tent behind him. "Is Abigail the friend you spoke of? How do you know her?"

Titius turned back toward him. "Are you her father? She's a free woman who deals with her own affairs."

"She's a follower of the Messiah and it's my job to guard her," Andrew said. "She's now my sister and I'm her brother. If you wish to speak to her, you'll have to speak to me first."

He knew he could subdue the fisherman, but Abigail would resent it.

"I understand," Titius said, wiping his face. "Peace to you and to your house."

"And peace to yours," Andrew replied.

To Titius's surprise, Andrew walked out into the rain and gestured for Titius to join him. He pulled on his head covering and kept pace.

"I'm Titius Marcus Julianus, son of Senator Julianus, former owner of Abigail on our estate in Rome," Titius said.

"So you've come to claim your slave?"

"No! I've cared for her since I was young, and we've been separated for many years. I've come to speak to her. To know the desires of her heart."

Andrew ran his hand through his wet hair. "But you're the son of a Roman senator and she's a Jewish slave. How can such things be?"

"The Messiah touched my mind. Now I'm surer than ever of what I seek."

"She's never mentioned you." He stepped around a muddy patch in the road. "Now you've seen her. Go back to Jerusalem and wait until tomorrow. I'll talk with her to see what she wants. Meet me tomorrow at the Sheep Gate and we'll talk."

"I'll stay and speak with the Messiah," Titius said.

"Tomorrow! That's soon enough. Go home and get dry. We have enough people staying with us already."

He hadn't come this far just to be put off, but he realized this was the man he had to impress.

"Before I go," Titius said, "I've heard the religious leaders saying things that could mean harm for the Messiah."

"What have you heard?" Andrew asked.

"The Pharisees are looking for someone to betray him." Titius looked into the fisherman's bearded face. "They want to kill him."

"We know. The people have welcomed Yeshua as their king and the rulers are jealous. There will be trouble. The Messiah has warned us."

"If there's trouble, please keep Abigail away from it," Titius said. "I can take her to a safe place."

"Tomorrow! See me tomorrow."

Andrew turned away and slogged toward the tents.

The torches flickered weakly as a bedraggled Titius limped into the carpenter's shop. Caleb was planing a cedar cross beam and talking to himself.

"You sound like me before the Messiah touched me," Titius said, remembering how Cleopas had plagued him almost every waking moment.

Caleb jumped up and released his plane. "You still live! Were you out chasing a woman and forgetting the job your centurion gave you?"

Titius moved to the firepit and took off his tunic. He threw a chunk of discarded cedar on the flame and draped his soaking garment over a crossbeam. "My duty ended when Sestus died. I'm free."

"So the woman rejected you," Caleb said with a snort.

"I've guarded you over and over. I've fulfilled my oath." He stepped away. "Now we need to work together for the Messiah's sake."

"What do you know of the Messiah? You're a Roman. He's the Jews' Messiah."

"I know what I know."

"Well, the Messiah could be in danger. I've heard rumors."

Titius nodded. "So have I, and that's why we should work together. I can learn more about what's going on, and you can pass that information to the Messiah's followers so they can protect him."

"The people love Yeshua," Caleb said. "What can the Romans do to him?"

"It isn't the Romans I worry about. It's the religious leaders, and they intend to bribe one of Yeshua's followers."

"It won't work. Those men would follow him to their death. And besides, I have to get these crosses done. Maybe after Passover we can make a plan to protect him."

It had been three days since the Messiah had turned Jerusalem into a boiling cauldron of intrigue, and Titius's ears couldn't keep up with the plots and plans. Some wanted to make the Messiah a king and overthrow the Romans. Others wanted to destroy the Messianic pretender.

Titius had slipped out before dawn when the cross maker had been asleep, his head resting on the olive beam he'd designed for Barabbas. Now, as he returned with sardines, oranges, cheese, and olives for breakfast, he heard Suzanna's voice inside.

"Why would the Romans be tense?" she asked. "We have these feasts three times a year without major troubles."

Silence hung like a morning cloud over a lake. Finally, Caleb spoke: "The zealot leaders who murdered my centurion are scheduled for crucifixion in two days. Everyone is tense." Titius heard tools being dumped on the workbench. "Anyway, thanks for the soup. I need to finish this crossbeam."

"I've never seen a crossbeam made of olive wood like that," she said. "The grain looks so beautiful. It's hideous to think about its purpose." She groaned. "Don't you think it'll be too heavy?"

"This one is specially designed," Caleb said. "It will send a message that people won't soon forget. We must show them the terror of the cross."

Titius clutched the food and slipped away again.

On the day of preparation for the Feast of Unleavened Bread, Titius headed to the market. He hoped Abigail might show up, buying what she needed for the Passover meal. But instead of women heading to market, the streets were filled with men moving toward the Sheep Gate, all shoulder to shoulder, tight as stones in a wall. At every intersection, two Roman legionnaires stood on the rooftops, owls peering down on passing rodents.

Titius put on the clothing of a scribe and joined the flow of traffic.

"How will you choose your lamb?" he asked a merchant scuffling beside him.

The man knit his brows and shook his head. Titius asked his question again, this time in Hebrew.

"I will take what I'm given," the merchant said. "Same as always."

Titius nodded. He was like flotsam being tossed toward a beach. Abigail could be anywhere, and he was stuck with guilty men hoping some sheep would wash away their sins.

At the sound of shouting up ahead, the vortex of men pulled Titius up to a blood-stained garment. He realized that it covered a body that had been killed by the large stones now clustered around the head. Screams of rage vibrated off the cobblestones. Passersby spat on the corpse and hurried by.

"Roman spy!" yelled the old man ahead of him. "No non-Jew is welcome in this place."

"There's no lamb for that kind!" the young man beside him shouted. "Imagine, pretending to be a Jew at Passover!"

A shudder convulsed Titius and he was sure it would give him away. No one seemed to notice, fortunately, and he slowly pushed his way out of the river of bodies.

At the Sheep Gate, the momentum slowed as the men offered money and received lambs. Jubilant at their purchases, they shouted for joy, almost drowning out the bleating.

Titius was still pushing out of the crowd when a strong hand grabbed his shoulder. He turned and found himself staring into the eyes of the fisherman, Andrew.

"Come, this way," Andrew shouted. "I've been waiting for you."

"What about your lamb?"

"Others will get mine. We dine with the Messiah for Passover tonight."

Titius looked down at his clothes. "How did you recognize me?"

"I was coming to help that poor man and saw your eyes. I saw fear, not hatred. I knew it was you."

Titius followed Andrew until they reached a small perfume shop.

"We can meet here," Andrew said. "One of the sisters in our group owns the shop."

Inside, the walls were lined with vials and jars. Titius breathed deeply of jasmine, frankincense, and rose petals.

Andrew bowed his head for a moment. "Now, I talked to Abigail. She says she hasn't seen you since she was young. She can't tell me who you are now. So, who are you?"

Titius sat on a stool. "You ask a hard question. I'm not who I seem to be, but I'm not who I used to be."

"Tell me about your family."

"My grandfather was a great Roman general and my father was a senator. Abigail served in my house, a servant to my mother. We were great friends… until one day my mother sent her away."

"Why did you want her sent away?" Andrew sounded harsh.

"I didn't!" Titius stood. "She was my best friend! I believe that my mother saw my father trying to take advantage of Abigail and sent her away for her own protection."

"Who did you marry?"

"I never married."

"Why not?"

"My soul was attached to one woman and I came looking for her." Titius sat again and lowered his head. "I almost found her at Isaac's shop in Magdala. I *almost* found her every place I've been, but I always seemed a step too late. I've never been with another woman."

"You're a Roman, a man of violence," Andrew said. "And you never seem to be the same person twice. How can you be trusted?"

"It's true. I've been working for a centurion, guarding a cross maker. I've done many things I regret. But I'm a different man since I met the Messiah."

"Becoming a different man takes time."

Titius examined Andrew's swarthy face. "You've been with the Messiah for years. Surely you've seen how men are changed with a single touch."

Andrew nodded, then changed the subject back to Abigail. "Why would you force a Jewish slave to marry a man determined to destroy her people?"

Titius winced. "I'd never support anyone who wants to destroy her people. I don't even know if I can ever be a senator myself. A man stole my family estate and I'd have to get it back to qualify…" He trailed off, not sure if any of that mattered. "I'd also have to retrieve the family ring, but I fear it may be forever lost…"

"What would you be willing to do to get your estate back?"

"I don't know," Titius said. "I don't know much anymore. Everything is changing."

At last, Andrew stepped toward Titius and extended his hand. "The truth is, she wants to talk with you."

Chapter Twenty-Five

Abigail, her head bowed, stepped out from behind the shop counter. A scarlet shawl was draped low over her eyes, and all he could see were a few dark curls showing around her temples. She wore a long white stola and leopard-skin belt.

"Abigail, your only master now is Yeshua," Andrew reminded her before she could say a word. "Just tell me and I'll remove this man from your presence."

Abigail raised her eyes slowly and looked at Titius. "Is it true? You've never taken another woman?"

Titius looked away. "Do you think me less of a man for ignoring other opportunities?"

"Not at all," she said, smiling. "It makes you special. Apart from eunuchs, a few slaves, the Messiah, and some of his younger followers, I know no other men who survive without women."

Andrew stretched his arms between them. "Speak the truth," he said. "How is there such intimacy and desire between two people who haven't seen each other for years?"

Titius tore his gaze away from Abigail and glared at Andrew. "I told you, she was my mother's servant and my childhood friend. Her magic captured my heart. Her beauty stole my will."

"Is it true that you never wanted me to go?" Abigail asked.

Titius's mouth dried up like a desert and he struggled to free his tongue. The words came out in a whisper. "I wanted to protect you."

"Why would your mother send me away if not because of you?" Her brows knit as tears filled the corners of her eyes.

Titius wanted to run, but his feet wouldn't move. "She saw you with my father in the garden."

Her face flushed red. Sobs wracked her, and she held herself in a tight embrace. Andrew put a hand on her shoulder.

"Go!" Andrew said to Titius. "Go! And don't come again."

"No!" Abigail straightened up. "Please, let me talk alone with Titius. He needs to know the truth about my life."

Andrew stepped away. "I'll be right outside. Just call and I'll bring down the wrath of the Almighty on this imposter."

Abigail wiped her eyes with her sleeve and smiled feebly. "And I thought the master said that James and John were the sons of thunder…"

Andrew backed out the door without another word.

"I am a sight, weeping like a harlot on her wedding day," she said to Titius. She slumped onto a stool and propped her chin on her fists. "I've spent so many years thinking you loved my sister, that you loved the cook's assistant, that you loved anyone but me."

Titius knelt at her feet.

She looked at him, tears still streaming. "Your father was my master. What could I do?"

He put his hand on her shoulder, but she shook it off.

"You have to believe me," she said. "I never let him have me. My sister gave herself to your father, Cleopas, and the gardener, just to protect me. I've never forgiven myself or let myself get near another man since."

Titius stood. "My mother sent you away to protect you."

"Now I see that." She grabbed her headscarf and threw it across the room. "How could I have known that when I was so young? Everything I knew, everyone I loved, was taken away. I was sent to a place they told me was home. Made to live with others they said were my people."

Titius took a step toward her. "I'm here."

"Yes, you're here. Just when I'd convinced myself you were a dream, that I'd never love again, that I'd be the woman apart."

"I'm sorry," Titius muttered.

"It's not your fault," Abigail said. "The Messiah took my stony heart and melted it before you came back. I thought I would dedicate all my love to him. But now here you are and I'm more confused than ever."

Titius leaned against the counter next to her. "The Messiah healed my mind so I could love again. If I'd found you sooner, I may never have been able to know the joy of watching you dance before the Messiah."

"You saw me dancing?"

He smiled. "Like a butterfly in a garden. A swallow in the wind. A rainbow unleashed."

"It felt like that," she said. "I felt like a little girl in your rose garden again. I could see all of creation in the clouds. I could hear forest songs in the people's celebrations."

Titius picked up a small bowl of frankincense and held it out to her. "I went to your rose garden in Jerusalem."

"Here?" Abigail accepted the bowl, passed it under her nose, and set it on the counter. "Did you meet Elizabeth? Did you talk with her?"

"Yes. She told me about a maid from Magdala who was waiting for her nobleman to come and claim her."

The sun passed its zenith and started its slide toward Passover.

"I told Elizabeth about the nobleman my first time in the garden, to stop her from asking questions," she said. "And as I walked around, I remembered your garden in Rome. I began to believe maybe I truly was waiting for someone. When I met the Messiah, I thought the love I needed was spiritual instead of personal."

"I think I've visited every fish vendor you've ever sold pickled fish to," Titius said, laughing.

Abigail went behind the counter and began to collect her bags. "I have another sack, if you want some." She set a small sack on the counter. "I hear it's an acquired taste. But Uncle Isaac still thinks the Romans will start shipping it all over the empire."

The door opened and Andrew stepped back inside.

"Abigail, we need to go," the fisherman said. "Things must be changing in our favor. I saw Judas talking to some of the priests. Even they're contributing to our cause!"

Titius put his arm in front of Abigail, barring her from following Andrew outside.

"Where are you going?" Titius asked.

"We need to get supplies at the market for the Passover meal," Andrew said. "Titius, I'm sorry, but you can't join us. Abigail can see you again after the holiday."

He picked up Abigail's bags and turned to go.

"But we've only just begun to talk," Titius said to her.

Abigail retrieved her shawl, put it back on, nodded politely, and stepped out the door.

Titius followed them, but they were quickly swallowed up by the crowd. "When will I see you again?" he called.

His only answer was the braying of a donkey—and it was headed straight at him. The animal was pulling its too-heavy cart downhill, and the young boy holding the reins screamed warnings as the cart bounced along the cobblestones. Its load of heavy stone tilted dangerously.

Titius leaped at the donkey's neck, wrapping his arms around it and digging his heels into the ground. This slowed the cart just enough that two other bystanders could grab it and keep it upright until it came to a stop.

The boy thanked him. "The centurion needs these stones right away at Golgotha. You saved my life."

Titius surveyed the load. "Be at peace, and slow down." He examined the donkey's hoof for damage. "Golgotha? Isn't that where the Romans crucify zealots?"

"I just deliver," the boy said. "I don't ask what people do with them."

Titius hurried back to the street where Abigail and Andrew had headed, but they'd disappeared.

On the way back, he stopped by a rabbi's home to inquire about the contents of the marriage contract.

His dreams that night were filled with Abigail driving runaway carts he could do nothing to stop. He woke, shaking and sweaty, before falling back into a peaceful sleep. In another dream, she lay curled up on a marble bench in his family's rose garden in Rome. The light brushed her hair as it flowed over her shoulder. A hawk drifted in descending circles closer and closer to where she lay. She shrank until she was small as a mouse… and then the hawk dove.

"No!"

Titius bolted upright, opened his eyes, and saw a rooster perched on the edge of the roof above him. He hurled a stick at it as it stretched, flapped its wings, and sailed away. In the distance, another rooster crowed. And then another.

He suddenly remembered where he was. The previous night, he'd gone to Caleb's shop only to find it full with the carpenter's Passover guests. As the city celebrated, Titius had climbed onto the roof of a centurion's house and fallen asleep there. As a non-Jew, he had felt unwelcome. He had felt very lonely, and even Cleopas might have been a welcome intrusion.

Titius stretched, then looked down on the streets, which were already filling with slaves and worshippers.

His disguises now seemed pointless, and he wasn't sure how to ignore the training that compelled him to absorb everything going on around him. At last, he put on a scribe's woolen tunic to head out among the religious pilgrims.

As he was about to leave, he took one last look over the roof's edge to locate the fallen rooster. Below, he saw a group of five women rushing toward the city gate. They looked like a group he'd seen with the Messiah—and one of them looked like Suzanna. The women disappeared into a nearby alley.

Feeling unwashed and unclean, he sought out one of the hundred pools and mikvahs around the city. It was no problem to set that aright.

He washed at a fountain with a stable hand and kitchen slave, using a cloth for his face, mouth, hair, feet, and armpits. As he put his sandals back on, he noticed two of Yeshua's close disciples running. Their eyes were frantic with fear.

Then a loud hum took over the streets, like bees gone mad. A legion of hobnailed boots pounded all the way from the Antonia Fortress to the upper city. A swell of people began to move in their wake, away from the temple, toward Herod's palace.

Titius returned to his perch on the roof to see what was happening. A few minutes later, two young men ran up the stairs to watch from the high roof with him.

"What's happening?" Titius asked.

One took off his prayer shawl and turned in amazement. "Where've you been? The priests arrested the Messiah! The Sanhedrin condemned him! They're taking him to Pilate to have him crucified!"

Titius shuddered. Yeshua? Surely not.

"Why would Pilate crucify the Messiah?" he asked. "The whole nation declared him their king just a few days ago."

"They're fighting for the survival of our nation," the other man said. "What will the people do if the Romans crucify both Barabbas and the Messiah?"

Titius raced down the stairs and pushed through the crowds to the carpenter shop. The olive crossbeam and several others were gone. Caleb was nowhere to be seen.

Next, he pushed through the crowds toward the Antonia Fortress. There, legionnaires from Gaul refused to listen as he called for the lead centurion. It didn't help that he was dressed as a scribe, even though he spoke Latin and Aramaic, and his name meant nothing to these men.

He worked hard against the crowds to reach the shop again, where he changed into carpenter's clothes. He wanted to reach Abigail, knowing she would be distressed, but he didn't know where she was. He hurried to the perfume shop, but he found the place locked up.

Shouts reverberated off the limestone city walls.

"Barabbas! Barabbas!" the people shouted over and over. "Crucify him! Crucify him!"

The people had spoken: Barabbas, the head of the Sicarii, was done for. The serpent would be slain; Sestus would be avenged. Even the Jews knew justice.

Titius sat on a wall outside the perfume shop and waited. He wasn't interested in watching Barabbas die. Once Pilate released Yeshua, the city would return to its rhythm and someone would come and tell him how to find Abigail.

As time passed, the population moved as one outside the gates to watch the gruesome executions. The power of the cross would be demonstrated again and Caleb would have his revenge.

Titius watched a sparrow pecking at seeds in the dirt. What would Phoebe think when she heard her brother was dead? How would the zealots respond? Who would rise up to fight for the homeland? As Rome's massive python prepared to squeeze Judea's hero in a death grip, how would Hosea respond?

And where was Abigail?

Chapter Twenty-Six

While everyone else was leaving the city, Titius hiked up the Mount of Olives and kept walking, right past Bethany. On his way, he stopped at the large home where the white tents had been erected. The place was deserted.

As he sat looking over the temple and the city, an unnatural darkness wrapped itself around the sun. A fearsome tremor rocked the hills and Titius had to grab a nearby oak to stay upright. The wind howled as the city's limestone blocks, once a glistening gem welcoming the world, seemed to quiver. Terrified shouts erupted from all quarters.

Behind him, a light shone; in front of him, complete darkness. Sweat soaked his brow and trickled down his back. It looked like the heavens had poured a cask of tar down over the world.

He stood at the brow of the hill, watching and waiting, as the ground stilled. A finger of light lifted a corner of the blanket of darkness and birds sounded again. A rabbit raced past. A baby cried.

The intense quiet felt like a hand on his jugular. He'd heard from Caleb about the plague of darkness on Egypt; that must have been similar to this. Surely the angel of death had come this day to claim a soul. Who hovered around this holy place and what was he doing?

Slowly, Titius started down the hill toward the Garden of Gethsemane on his right. He took half-steps, willing his sandaled feet to find the next step in the darkness. The way had been packed hard by millions of pilgrims and he could easily feel when he strayed from the path.

Halfway down the hill, he stepped on something that moved underfoot. He heard a yelp, the snarl of a dog. The animal bit into his arm right above the wrist and he brought his forearm down on its snout. The dog yelped again and ran away.

Titius crouched, clutching his arm, his senses on high alert. He was in the darkness, as dark as a forest at midnight on a starless night. Evil slithered, prowled, lurked closer and closer.

"Help me, Yeshua!" he called out.

Thunder rumbled across the heavens. Once again, he felt as he had at the bottom of the pool where Jaennus had tested him. Suddenly, he felt something bigger than him pulling him up. Gasping for breath, he hugged his knees. Fire burned in his stomach.

He felt a hand reach down and shake his shoulder, startling him.

"David!" Jonathon called. "David! What are you doing here?"

Titius looked up into the young man's curly dark beard and chocolate eyes. "It was so dark."

"The Almighty has worked his judgment on the Messiah. The authorities will be rounding up his followers. Hurry! The Romans will crucify us all if we don't run."

Titius uncurled and stood. "What are you talking about? It was Barabbas they crucified."

"No!" Jonathan said. "The people chose to have Pilate release Barabbas and crucify Yeshua. He's dead. It's over."

The last dark clouds faded from over the city. "They killed the Messiah?"

"Yes! Now come with me," Jonathan urged, grabbing Titius's arm. "We have to run."

Titius wrenched his arm away. "No! I have to find someone. You go. I'll find you when I can."

Jonathan tried one more time to grab Titius by the sleeve, but Titius resisted. The young man then rushed into the stream of humanity flowing away from the city. Panic, hopelessness, and terror filled the peoples' eyes.

What was happening?

Titius skirted the masses, stumbling over gravestones and small bushes. He ignored the warning shouts from those desperate to get away. He then breached the gate and walked into the tomb-like city.

Hob-nailed sandals began their horrifying rhythm, reverberating off the cobblestones and walls.

"Barabbas is alive and Yeshua is dead," Titius whispered to himself. "Yeshua, if you're dead, how did you help free me?"

The heavens remained silent as the streets began to fill again with everyday worshippers moving toward the temple. Temple guards blocked their entrance, turning them away. Angry shouts echoed up the hill.

As evening shadows fell, Titius pushed his way toward the crucifixion site. A carpenter as fit as Yeshua might last days on a cross, and there were too many questions that needed answering. What did one say to a Messiah dying on a cross?

He rounded a small rise and saw a group of women weeping by the path. As a religious leader hurried by with a sack, the smell of myrrh and aloes filled his nostrils. Vultures circled overhead.

He had to hurry.

The tops of three crosses appeared above the bushes and he hesitated. Three crosses? He hoped they hadn't crucified Yeshua's followers with him. Surely not Andrew and Peter. But when he stepped out into the open, he saw that the crosses were empty.

Titius saw two legionnaires cleaning up the site.

"I'm Titius Marcus Julianus, guardian for our former centurion Sestus Aurelius, legate of Jerusalem," he said as he ran up to him. He panted and raised his right arm. "Where are the men who were crucified today?"

The legionnaires held out the bloody nails and rope still in their hands. "If you wanted to help, you're too late. We've already broken their legs and dumped them in Gehenna to burn with the trash."

"All of them?" Titius asked.

"No," one answered. "Two religious leaders took down the one who said he was the Messiah and put him in a tomb."

"Which cross did the Messiah die on?"

Both pointed to the center cross.

Titius took a step closer and saw that the cross was made of olive wood. Dark stains marred much of the grain's beauty.

"This was the strangest crucifixion," the other soldier said. "I always thought the religious leaders wouldn't defile themselves with the dead, but these men didn't hesitate."

Titius stood by the center cross and looked back toward the city. "Didn't his followers try to stop this?"

The first soldier paused halfway up a crude ladder that he'd leaned against a cross. "The religious leaders just made fun of him. I think they'd have pounded the nails in themselves if we'd let them."

Titius stared up at the cross. "How could this happen?"

"Do you follow him?" the second asked.

"I'm a Roman," Titius said. "Why would you think I'm his follower?"

"Be at peace," the legionnaire replied. "People from many different nations once praised him. No doubt this nation's hope is broken and we can now have peace."

Titius sighed. "The power of the cross…"

"Exactly!" the other legionnaire agreed. "The power of the cross has triumphed again. Rome is supreme."

"Do you know the cross maker?" Titius asked.

"Caleb ben Samson?" responded the first soldier. "Yes. He claimed the nails for the Messiah. He took responsibility. He wept as much as the women."

Titius nodded and marched quickly off. He had to find Caleb right away.

Titius watched helplessly as Abigail stood in a huddle of women, sobbing, her shoulders shaking. The crucified Messiah's followers hid in the shadows close to the tomb of David. Several grieving disciples spun in his direction and then began to move quickly away. Abigail was among them until she looked over her shoulder and noticed Titius. He lifted his palms, imploring her to come to him.

After taking two tentative steps in his direction, he jumped up and ran toward her. They halted a few steps apart and looked into each other's eyes.

"He's gone," she said. "They killed him."

"I know. Have you seen a man named Caleb ben Samson?"

Abigail looked up at an upper room in the building behind her where several of the followers had gone. "The Lord's disciples are taking care of him."

"What are we going to do?"

"We have to hide until the Romans stop looking for us." Abigail looked into his eyes. "You're not going to betray us, are you?"

"How could I betray my own heart?"

"Some of the others say Roman hearts never change, that soon they'll destroy our temple, as they did our Messiah."

Titius touched her cheek and she flinched. "They may be right, but the Messiah has changed my heart. I'm neither Jew nor Roman. I'm someone new."

Abigail touched her own cheek where Titius had touched her. "Come with me! Elizabeth promised to hide some of us at her rose garden."

"We should run to Isaac in Magdala, or to Capernaum, or even across the Jordan. They'll find us here."

"You go if you want. I'll stay with the others. I can't run. Mary, Martha, and Lazarus will need me."

Titius shook his head. "I lost you once and I'm not losing you again. I'll go with you."

"You don't understand. I could never live with myself if you're caught."

"Listen to me. I love you. I always have. I'm not going anywhere without you."

He reached for her, and Abigail pulled away. He caught her wrists and refused to let go.

"You can't love me," she said, hanging her head. "I'm a slave and you're going to be a senator one day. They might stone me, but they'll behead you. I can't lose anyone else."

At last, Titius stepped away from her. "I'm going to the rose garden. If you care at all about me, or about yourself, I'll see you there."

He walked toward the temple, where smoke still rose from the sacrifices. A dove flapped across the courtyard as he stepped around a cart. He noticed that the flowers in a nearby garden were bent over. Next to it, a vendor and customer argued over the price of sandals. Two women sat on stools weaving baskets. A child slept on a blanket near an open door.

"Wait!" Abigail called. "I'm coming! We have to hurry."

They stopped by the market and Titius bought two of the rough tunics that yard servants wore. He then led her through an alley into a shadowed alcove where they could shrug into their new garments. As she changed, Titius turned his back, as if once again guarding the zealot women at the bathing pool.

As the sun slipped toward the hilltops, they reached the rose garden and approached the shack where Elizabeth lived.

"We have a special knock," Abigail whispered. "Wait here."

Seeing no one close by, she rapped three times softly, waited, knocked twice more, waited, and then knocked three more times.

Elizabeth opened the door and ushered them in. Inside, three men sat on carpets, their backs against the far wall. Four women stood near the door, two holding trays of food and drink. Four olive oil lamps hung from the ceiling and cast a flickering light. A clay vessel crammed with roses sat on a table near a side door.

Abigail exchanged hugs with the women.

"This is my friend, Titius," she said, introducing him to the group. "He's new to the faith."

One of the men extended a hand. "I am Thaddeus. It's strange to join a faith whose founder has just died."

Titius nodded in acknowledgement. "I knew Yeshua of Nazareth for two years while he was in Galilee. He healed me. I owe him my life."

"You're welcome to sit and tell us all your experiences with the Messiah," Thaddeus said. "We'll wait here until the city quiets down."

In the evening lamplight, they shared the events of their lives during their separation; memories of Sabbath meditations and their hope in the Messiah gave them both joy and sorrow. Many others gave their own accounts of how Yeshua had changed their lives.

When the Sabbath was over, Titius invited Abigail for a walk in the rose garden. They watched an oxcart meander down the side of the Mount of Olives, past the Garden of Gethsemane, through the Kidron Valley, and up toward the city.

"Ask me the question you dare not ask me," he said.

She looked briefly toward the mountain and then faced him. "Why didn't you marry?"

"My father was arranging a betrothal, but he was killed by the Germans before it was finalized. My mother talked with Lord Cretius about a business arrangement between his family and ours, but she died in childbirth."

Elizabeth emerged from the shack with a tray of fruit. Titius took some dates and Abigail picked up a fig. They stood eating as Elizabeth smiled and went back inside.

Titius touched Abigail's chin. "I suppose that smile means our secret isn't such a secret."

Abigail turned back toward the mountain. "And what secret might that be?"

"I came here looking for you, but Sestus caught me. Now, why didn't you marry?"

Abigail looked into his eyes. She didn't answer his question. "So you've never been with a woman?"

Heat rushed up his neck and into his cheeks. "My mother sent me a few slave girls after you were gone, but I could think of no one else but you."

"Cleopas tried to have his way with me until my sister intervened. When I was sent to Palestine, two sailors had their way with me. I couldn't stop them."

"The past is the past, for both of us."

"I don't blame you if you leave me. I wanted to jump into the sea and end my life, but I didn't have the courage. Isaac and Yeshua gave me hope to keep going." She opened her hands to the heavens. Tears trickled down her cheeks. "I thought I'd never have to think about love again. This is no time for love."

"What we have may not be much right now… but I urge you to think of love one more time."

Abigail followed him to the door of the shack where Elizabeth waited. Abigail sank to her knees and Elizabeth crouched beside her.

"Daughter, the morning will come quickly," the old woman said. "The Almighty will give you strength for your sorrow."

The internal ache wouldn't leave Titius when the lamps went out. He thought of how far he'd come to find his heart's desire. Now the Messiah's death had killed more than hope. He sat with his back against the wall until the fire in every muscle and joint wore him out.

He lay on his side, waiting for the night to end.

Chapter Twenty-Seven

Not long after dawn, Elizabeth nudged Abigail and the two women slipped out into the waking city. Titius propped himself up on one elbow and peeled back his blanket as a rooster crowed in the distance. After several minutes, the women still hadn't come back.

Finally, he crept over the other sleepers and eased open the heavy door. The women were nowhere to be seen.

Dressed as an upper-class house slave, he hurried through the rose garden to an alley facing the Antonia Fortress. Somewhere close by, a group of legionnaires were parading toward him. To keep out of sight, he scampered up a set of stairs onto a roof and lay low as the soldiers marched past. He wasn't sure where he stood with them anymore. Was he Roman? A guardian assassin? A follower of the dead Messiah?

All that mattered was keeping Abigail safe, and now he couldn't find her.

It was early for the market stalls to open, but it made sense that the women would go out to get supplies. By the time Titius had searched the markets, though, panic began to knot his stomach. Everyone knew who Abigail was, but no one had seen her. Strange rumors were floating around: early morning earthquakes, people seeing dead relatives, even a priest admitting that the Holy of Holies had been damaged. From a beggar, Titius learned that Barabbas might be raising an army of zealots to storm the Antonia Fortress before the pilgrims left the city; this had been overheard from a legionnaire. Then three women run by saying that someone had stolen the Messiah's body.

When Titius returned to the rose garden, he used the special knock on the door. Elizabeth opened it.

"What's the news about the Messiah?" she asked. "We hear he's alive."

"What do you mean?" Titius closed the door behind him. "I only heard that someone stole his body."

"Suzanna told Abigail and me that Mary Magdalene saw him alive. The men are mocking her, but they can't find the body. Some say they've seen angels."

"Where's Abigail?"

Elizabeth's eyes sparkled. "She's gone to the tomb to see for herself. If you want to see her, go to the garden of Yosef of Aramathea near Golgotha."

Titius's spirit soared with yearning even while his heart threatened to strangle him with fear. He forced his feet to move toward the skull-like hill outside the city.

An hour later, he found Abigail kneeling at the entrance to an empty tomb. She was running her hands along the edge of a huge stone, the governor's broken wax seal still stuck to it. Tears dripped off her chin and soaked into her blue tunic.

She soon stood, grasping a single rose. But she dropped it when she saw him and approached from across the garden, accepting his embrace and hugging him back.

"He's alive!" she said. "He's alive… Mary saw him. He wants us to meet him in Galilee."

Titius worried they were all delusional. Had Cleopas come back to deceive them all?

He let go of Abigail and together they walked toward the tomb. Cedars seemed to leap straight from the ground behind the sepulcher. He picked up her rose from where she'd discarded it and handed it back. She tucked it behind her ear.

Titius's sandals crunched across the gravel as he stepped into the tomb and saw a folded shroud. He could still smell the frankincense and other burial spices. Sunlight was creeping into the darkness, and he sensed that this place, designed for death, had begun to be transformed into a place for life. For the first time in months, he felt peace.

They went back outside and stood under the blue sky.

"He's alive!" He pulled her close to dance in a crazy circle of joy. "He's alive! If he told us to meet him in Galilee, we have to go to Galilee. He's alive!"

"Come," Abigail urged. "Mary, Martha, and Lazarus will give us provisions for the trip."

Titius looked into her eyes. "We can travel together. But only if you agree to be my wife."

Abigail lowered her head. "You're my master. Whatever you command, I will obey."

"As your master, I free you." He took the rose from behind her ear. "As one who loves you, I beg you: be my wife because you *want* to be my wife."

He held out the rose again.

"But how?" she asked. "No rabbi will join the son of a Roman senator to a former Jewish slave."

"Andrew can be our rabbi," Titius said. "We're both followers of the Messiah. We'll set a new pattern for a world where those differences don't matter. Yeshua will break down those barriers. Will you marry me?"

"If I'm really a free woman, you need to make proper arrangements with Andrew in Bethany."

Titius ran up the hill, not slowing until he reached the Sheep Gate. The flowers were brighter and the raindrops, glistening like jewels, nestled in their broad leaves. A small pup by the road circled and barked with life.

They went to the home of Martha, Mary, and Lazarus, where Lazarus promised to contact Andrew about wedding details. In the meantime, Abigail bought food, clothing, and gifts from the market.

As much as he longed to see Yeshua again, his desire for a union with Abigail was stronger. They'd have their whole lives to be with him. Now was the time to set his life straight.

Titius was almost at the market when he neared four Nubians walking by, carrying a litter with long cedar poles. The golden carrier blocked his path.

"Make way for Lord Cretius!" an Egyptian shouted, standing in front of the litter. "Make way for Lord Cretius!"

The crowds were in no hurry to clear the space, but all thoughts of his wedding tasks evaporated from Titius's mind.

Cretius himself stuck his head through the litter's curtains and surveyed the street, including a group of men debating some topic or another who refused to move.

"Use the whip!" Cretius shouted to the Egyptian. "How dare these peasants stand in the way of the king's counselor? This is the king's litter!"

The golden litter pushed ahead, the Nubians taking one patient step after another. The Egyptian snapped the whip overhead.

In that moment, an idea captured Titius and he raced toward the clothing vendors. He knew one of the vendors who supplied the Roman legions with special orders. Titius found the man, Enoch, napping on his stool with his head on a pile of black cloth. Rather than wake him, Titius decided to just take what he needed and leave money on the table.

He slipped into a stable and changed into his new Roman military attire.

By the time Cretius's litter reached Herod's palace, Titius entered an alley and vaulted over a low wall. He was standing behind a hedge, just a javelin's throw from the palace steps. Those passing on the street hardly looked in his direction. They were used to Romans like him everywhere.

The Nubians set the litter down and stood aside as Cretius clambered out between the curtains and toward the gates of the palace. The sentries stood still as marble.

Once Lord Cretius was out of sight, the Nubians laughed and ambled off together toward the market. The Egyptian threw down his whip and wandered off toward the public baths.

Titius waited for the next shift of sentries to arrive. When the new legionnaires were in place, he walked up to them.

"Where are my litter-bearers?" he demanded in a forceful tone.

One of the guards furrowed his brows. Titius stood nose to nose with him and shouted again: "Where are my litter-bearers? You'd better find me someone to carry this thing or you'll be carrying it yourself."

"Where do you need to go, my lord?"

"The hippodrome. How dare you even ask?"

The legionnaire nodded and marched away toward the market. The three other sentries didn't flinch.

Titius paced back and forth, muttering about incompetent servants, before stepping into the litter and closing the curtains. Not long after, the Nubians jogged back into place, picked up the litter, and began to step quickly. The Egyptian was nowhere in sight.

The litter jostled back and forth. Every once in a while, Titius took quick peeks through the curtains at the crowds parting for the "king's counselor." The people called vulgar names at Lord Cretius, names as foul as sewage.

As the Nubians began the steep descent toward the hippodrome, some angry bystanders threw rocks at the passing entourage. The rocks tore the curtains and

Titius held up his pillows to keep from being hit. They cursed him in many languages.

The litter passed a narrow alley and Titius jumped out between the curtains and ran. He didn't glance back. The mob's angry shouts were enough to keep him running all the way to the stables, where he changed into his servant's tunic and walked casually toward Caleb's shop.

His satisfaction at the trouble he'd created for Cretius lasted only a few minutes. After all, Cretius had raped Titius's mother, stolen Titius's estate, and hired thespian assassins to kill him. Cretius had to die.

Pacing around the shop only increased Titius's hunger for revenge.

Well past noon, Titius stepped out of the shop in his new military clothes and wandered the market. He enjoyed the respect shown to him by the vendors as he picked up dates, figs, and apricots. He considered trying to buy wedding clothes or gifts for Abigail, but he feared it would arouse too much attention. He walked on.

He meandered toward Herod's palace and hid behind the same hedge as before. He waited once more for the sentries' shift change, and when the new group was in place he marched aggressively toward the palace, right past the guards this time.

Two burly centurions at an inner gate held up their shields to block him.

"State your name and purpose," one thundered.

Titius smashed his sword against their shields. "Move aside! General Maxim Julianus has come to settle his accounts with Lord Cretius. I demand his presence immediately."

The shields lowered. "Your message will be sent."

Titius stood firm, sword drawn as a messenger retreated into the palace. A few moments later, he heard a scream of terror from within the halls. Then the messenger returned and spoke something quietly to the centurions on duty.

The two centurions stepped back from the entry. "You may proceed," one of them said.

The hall was shadowy, lit with two silver lamps, and thick smoke hung in the air. The smoke burned his eyes and irritated his nostrils. Heavy purple curtains blocked the outside light and Persian rugs soaked up all sounds.

The hallway narrowed like a funnel as he walked. It felt like a trap.

Sensing a presence to his right, he remembered the leopard on the road from Jericho and ducked to the left. Suddenly, three javelins flew toward the spot where he'd just been standing. One pierced the curtain on the far side of the hall.

Titius seized a javelin from the rug and scrambled further into the darkness beyond the burning lamps. The shadows of two men, barely visible by the flickering light, slipped into the hall. Titius's javelin flew straight into the closest figure's torso.

Amid the screaming, the second shadow disappeared behind the curtains. Titius crept even further into the darkness.

Titius stayed low, moving along the wall. The curtains to his right parted easily and he stepped between them into a room with faint natural light. Pillows and half-full wine flagons were scattered around the place.

The sound of voices drew him toward a door that opened into a small courtyard. Through the door, he saw two maids watering small fig trees. Beyond them, a man cowered behind a low hedge.

Cretius.

Titius stormed into the courtyard, imitating his father as best he could. "Cretius, you pig! How dare you steal my wife and my estate!"

The maids scampered away. He knew he didn't have much time, as the guards would be here quickly.

Cretius stood straight, his hands raised. "They told me you were dead!"

"Do I look dead to you? I was sent to find those who betrayed the empire. Now I come to finish my task!"

Cretius stumbled backward and fell into a pond. He scrambled out of the water. "Guards!" he screamed, racing away.

Two sentries, swords drawn, ran into the courtyard.

"Lord Cretius is a traitor to the emperor," Titius barked at them. He dropped his javelin and drew his sword. "Get him."

The centurions quickstepped around the pond and disappeared in pursuit. Titius waved off a handful of household staff and noblemen who'd come into the courtyard.

"Stay where you are!" he commanded.

Cretius's Egyptian bodyguard, his sword drawn, broke through the small group after a few anxious moments.

"Where is my Lord Cretius?" the bodyguard demanded.

Titius picked up the javelin he'd dropped and held it up to bar the way. "Your lord is a traitor to the emperor! He must pay for his crimes. But first I need to talk with him."

The Egyptian pulled out his whip and snapped it. "I care nothing about that." He waved his sword and stepped toward Titius. "He pays my fees, and if you continue to block my way you'll die by my sword."

Titius braced himself, sword in one hand, javelin in the other. "Today you'll meet your gods if you choose to fight. If gold is all you want, I can satisfy you. If you want mortal combat, neither you nor Cretius will ever see another sunset."

The Egyptian hesitated as they heard the sound of Cretius screaming somewhere in the distance.

The bodyguard charged, snapping his whip and thrusting his sword. The whip wrapped itself around Titius's javelin and yanked the weapon sideways.

The two men parried blows, sword to sword. At last, Titius regained control of the javelin and swung the butt end up under the Egyptian's chin. The warrior staggered back and snapped his whip at Titius's neck. Titius raised his elbow and deflected it. Blood flowed down his arm.

The Egyptian cracked the whip at Titius's ankles, distracting Titius from the sword as it moved steadily closer.

"My battle's not with you!" Titius shouted. "Cretius runs, refuses to fight for himself. Stand down and you'll live."

The Egyptian smiled and brought his whip down again at Titius's ankle. "I never trust a Roman. I didn't survive the arena to be brought down by a jackal like you."

Titius jumped onto a bench and hurled his javelin at the Egyptian's belly. The man tried to deflect it with his sword but was too slow. As the blade sank into him, he stood as though transfixed.

Titius raised his foot and pushed the blade deeper. In the manner of gladiators, the Egyptian fell to his knees and bared his neck for Titius's fatal blow.

Instead Titius left him and ran after Cretius. As he reached the stairs to the next garden, a legionnaire met him.

"General, Lord Cretius chose to fall on his own sword. He is no more."

Titius growled. Revenge had been snatched from his hand. His stolen estate was now a victor's wreath abandoned on the track. His mother's death had gone unavenged.

"Your wish, my lord?" the legionnaire asked.

Birds and butterflies flitted back and forth around him. The fountains gurgled. The city's smells and noises belonged to another world.

"Speak of my presence to no one," Titius said. "Lord Cretius chose to end his own life. Report his death at his own hand to his masters."

Titius knelt by the pool and washed the blood from his arms. He waved at a servant girl, who brought him a towel. He soaked the cloth and wrapped it around his arm. The bandage quickly turned red.

He walked past the still form of the Egyptian and tread deliberately back through the palace. The staff bowed politely or prostrated themselves as he passed.

Memories of his father's public adoration after a victory filled Titius's mind. That same life of power and prestige could now be his.

As he stepped out onto the busy Jerusalem streets, people's attitude toward him changed. They regarded him angrily. An old man spit in his direction. A bony dog ripped at a dead rat near a garbage pile while its master raised angry fists.

Four legionnaires appeared at his side.

"Where is the rest of your legion, General?" one of the soldiers asked. "Should we march you back to the fortress?"

As a small crowd shouted obscenities at him, he looked across the valley toward the Mount of Olives and Bethany, where Abigail waited for her wedding.

Chapter Twenty-Eight

Halfway to the Antonia Fortress, Titius and his escort walked through a market where a small riot had broken out near the fish vendor's stall. Titius turned to the legionnaires with him. "All of you, break up that mob."

The four lifted their shields, drew their swords, and marched toward the group. Titius backed into a nearby alley and once again donned the carpenter's clothes he'd hidden there. He knew the rioters would dissipate like morning mist, and the legionnaires would eventually return to their posts.

As Titius walked, he processed his combat with the Egyptian and his failed efforts to interrogate Cretius. Now he'd never know everything that had happened between Cretius and his mother. He clenched and unclenched his hands, still stained with blood.

The streets were full of pilgrims loaded with supplies for their journeys home after Passover, each carrying the news of the Messiah's death. Not all would know about the resurrection being proclaimed by his followers.

As he watched the pilgrims, he realized he'd never bought the food and supplies for the wedding. He doubled back to the market, where he found two of the four legionnaires still patrolling the entrance, keeping a keen eye on the people as they went about their business.

Titius kept his gaze lowered and wandered to the fish stall.

"Enoch, what's the news?" he asked.

Enoch scooped several handfuls of dried fish into a pouch and made a great show of weighing them carefully. "Barabbas has gone to Jericho. The zealots are staying quiet after the latest crucifixions, and the fishermen are returning to Galilee. Yeshua called them to meet him there."

Titius knew "fishermen" was a codeword for the followers of Yeshua. He pointed to the tilapia, and Enoch bent down to get him his order.

"I'm getting married," Titius said.

Enoch stood up. "Did you say married? Praise the Almighty!" He added an extra two tilapia to the bag. "Who is it?"

"Abigail, the one who brings you pickled fish from Magdala."

"How can you marry a Jewess?" Enoch glanced toward the two legionnaires and lowered his voice. "Who will perform the union?"

Titius noticed one of the legionnaires moving in his direction. "I'm not sure yet, but the fish is for the wedding!"

"Then this is your wedding gift. Take it. May the Almighty bless you!"

Titius slipped out of the market and hurried through back alleys and narrow streets. He stopped by the rabbi's home again to pick up the finished marriage contract. Before midday, he slipped out the Sheep Gate, walked down the valley, and climbed the Mount of Olives toward Bethany.

When Titius crested the hill, he saw Abigail sitting by the well. He set down his load a javelin's throw away from her. He opened his arms to her and she ran toward him.

"You've come," she said, burying her head in his chest. "I thought you may have changed your mind. Andrew's given his blessing. He'll meet us this evening, before he joins the others in Galilee."

"I ask your forgiveness. I had to set some things right."

They gathered up the packages and turned toward the house that belonged to Mary, Martha, and Lazarus.

"Is the wedding canopy, ready?" Titius asked. "I've never been to a wedding like this before."

"Come and see!" Abigail answered, giving a twirl. "I know I'm not supposed to see you before the ceremony, but I begged to be allowed to make sure you were safe. I must go get ready!"

"I brought the ketubah, the marriage contract." Titius held out a scroll. "Who do I give it to?"

Abigail ran her hand along his bearded cheek. "You give it to Lazarus."

She took two of the bags and walked quickly ahead of him to the house. By the time Titius caught up, Martha had stepped outside to take the rest of his bundles.

"Everything is changing," she said. "There was a time when we had a betrothal ceremony and a proper time of preparation. So many questions I have for the Messiah!"

Andrew appeared from inside and laid his strong hands on Titius's shoulders. "So how will we do what's never been done before?" He pointed toward the chutzpah nestled under the main tent for the wedding. "Will you build a room in your father's house for your bride? Will you take her from us to Rome?"

Titius nodded. "My father's home is now my home. Abigail knows it from her youth. It will be enough for her. Her every wish will be my command."

"Will you keep the faith of our Messiah?" Andrew asked. "Will you raise your children in the truth of Almighty God? Will you nurture your wife in true love and happiness?"

Titius looked into Andrew's eyes. "That is my heart's desire."

He handed the ketubah scroll to the fisherman and watched as Andrew read over the contract, nodding as he read. Nearby, two turtledoves settled on a myrtle tree. They jostled each other for position along a branch and then cocked their heads, as if waiting.

"It's a fine contract," Andrew said. "Generous and gracious. You respect Jewish custom and yet keep some of your own ideas. I will pass this on to Lazarus for official acceptance."

Andrew gave the ketubah to Lazarus and took Titius into a back room to change into his white wedding tunic. Mary carried in a tray of dates, figs, cheese, fish, and bread, but in his nervousness he could do little more than nibble. Even the wine didn't tempt him.

As the evening shadows approached, Titius looked out a window at the preparations. Guests in their finest clothes lingered in front of the house, sampling from trays carried by young women. Two lambs were roasting on a spit over a fire. The aroma filled his nostrils.

When the time arrived, Martha escorted Titius to his place beside the wedding canopy. He was surprised to see a centurion among the guests.

"He calls this a contract?" grumbled an elderly bearded man huddled nearby. "In my day, we knew how to value a woman."

"Surely he can't expect us to give up our traditions," said a portly rabbi. "He should wait, like everyone else has to wait."

Andrew raised his hand for silence. "Titius already has a home for Abigail… and he's been waiting a long time."

Another man stepped up to the huddle. He was middle-aged and dressed in costly garments.

"I have questions," said the middle-aged man.

"Ask the questions," responded the rest of the wedding guests.

"Will you love her all her life?" the man asked Titius. "Will you give her children who make the Messiah proud? Will you live honorably wherever the Almighty may lead you?"

Titius smiled. "I will."

The centurion stepped out of the huddle to speak next. "Hear me, before you let this Roman take a treasure from your nation. I too have a question." He held a small bag high over his head. "I know this man is missing something that identifies him as the heir of the Roman estate he claims. Titius, where is the ring your father gave you?"

Titius's stomach knotted, knowing that the thing was at the bottom of the assassin's pool.

The centurion swung the small bag back and forth. "You can see it on his face, my friends. He knows he's missing his family ring."

Titius made a move to step toward the centurion, but Andrew held him in place. "Wait."

The centurion approached Titius. "My name is Anthony. Your friend Caleb couldn't be here himself, but he left me with a gift for you. Hold out your hand."

Titius held out both hands.

"Did you not swear your loyalty to a centurion named Sestus Aurelius?" Anthony asked.

Titius nodded.

"Did he not take that ring and throw it into a pool where it could not be retrieved?"

Titius nodded, feeling heat race up his neck.

"And wasn't your centurion the only man who could dive to the bottom of that pool?"

Titius looked down.

"And wasn't this centurion killed by Barabbas?"

"Yes," Titius said. "Rome has never had a finer soldier than Sestus Aurelius."

"You speak the truth," Anthony said. "Three months ago, your centurion conquered the pool a second time and left you a gift. He gave it to your friend Caleb, who wanted me to make sure you got it today."

Titius's heart raced as Anthony emptied the small bag into Titius's hand. There, resting on his palm, was the family ring—two rubies set in gold, the family crest of a lion clearly etched around the stones.

Titius's yell vibrated off the walls of Bethany. He let loose a belly laugh, mixed with tears, stalling the wedding ceremony for several minutes.

After Lazarus had given his formal acceptance of the ketubah on behalf of Abigail, several men escorted Titius toward the wedding canopy. There, the village men danced to a rousing psalm.

Titius caught his breath when Abigail, a rose secured to her veil, was escorted in. She was beauty itself. He laughed freely as she and her maidens circled seven times around him.

He accepted the glass of wine from Lazarus and shared it with Abigail. He then took the ring from Andrew and placed it on the first finger of his bride's right hand. Andrew officially read the ketubah and Titius joined him for the signing.

Finally, Titius crushed a wine glass under his heel to confirm his commitment.

Everyone present broke into dancing, dancing, and more dancing! The torches flickered as if in rhythm to the swiftly swirling circles.

Delicacies and wine flowed freely until Andrew and Martha brought Titius and Abigail together under the center of the canopy.

"It's time for you to be husband and wife," Andrew said with a grin. "Some parts of marriage never change. We'll save some of this feast for when you're no longer busy."

Titius reached for Abigail's hand, but before he could grasp it Lazarus came running toward them, shouting loudly.

"Run! The Romans are coming!"

Abigail was about to run when Titius grabbed her elbow and held her. "Stay with me," he said.

"But the Romans are coming!" She tugged to get away. "They killed our Messiah. Now that he's risen, they're coming for us."

Titius walked to a small crate, opened the lid, and lifted out a Roman short sword, a gladius, and a helmet.

"If the others are going to make it to Galilee, we may have to provide a distraction," he said.

The faint sound of hobnailed boots echoed through the night as Abigail and Titius vanished through the doorway into the house.

"We'll need to change quickly." Titius handed her an elegant purple chiton. "Put this on over your white stola."

He turned and began to remove his tunic. They had to ignore feelings of personal embarrassment; the thundering of hobnailed sandals left little choice.

"I hope you remember my mother well," he said. "You need to imitate her, behave like a Roman lady, and stay by my side."

Abigail struggled to pull the white stola on. "I hope you know what you're doing."

Titius laughed. "You make a fine Roman matron." He then picked up his gladius, helmet, and cape and slipped the family ring onto his finger. "I am a general and you are my wife. Put up your hair."

He walked toward the door, then crouched down to tie his sandals. "Prepare the wedding feast for our guests, Abigail. You're about to host your first celebration."

Abigail turned to survey the remaining food, still looking tasty under the torchlight.

"I hope they're too hungry to care what they eat," she remarked.

She flew to her task despite the tight, ornamented stola. She combined half-empty dishes into heaping plates, put out clean cups, filled empty ones, straightened linens, and tossed pillows into corners.

"How does it look?" she asked as she picked up the last of the used dishes.

Titius smiled and put on his helmet. "You're a gift from the Almighty."

With that, he stepped out to meet the arriving army. Dozens of torches announced the arrival of the troops, but Titius stood in the road right in front of them.

Two centurions led the soldiers, and Titius recognized one of them from Herod's palace.

"Halt!" one of the centurions shouted. The column of thirty men stopped as one.

"Centurion!" Titius declared. "I see that you received the message. Your feast awaits."

The centurion reached for his sword, but Titius stepped forward.

"It's a feast to reward you for bringing justice to that charlatan, Lord Cretius," Titius said. "You did get the message at the fortress, didn't you?"

The second centurion stepped up beside the first. "Centurion Flavius Segundus reporting. We have orders to capture two zealots here."

Titius looked around at the deserted street. "Looks like they're gone. In the meantime, my wife has everything prepared. At least take a few minutes to enjoy my hospitality and appreciation. I have the use of this fine home only for the day. Your men are welcome."

He held up his ring, and the centurion looked at it closely.

"The men will wait here while we examine the preparation," the centurion finally said.

Fifteen pairs of legionnaires stood like statues, red capes fluttering as both centurions followed Titius under the canopy's flap and examined the spread. It didn't take long for them to sample the food and swallow several cups of wine. Abigail remained out of sight.

Segundus stuffed a pastry into his mouth. "Where are the servants? And where's this wife of yours?"

Titius clapped his hands twice. "The servants were purified Jews and can't stand in the presence of Romans. My wife is here."

On cue, Abigail stepped out in her Roman attire. Her braided hair, pinned up with sapphires, topped her long white stola, purple chiton, and golden belt. Titius stared at her, transfixed.

Segundus nudged him. "You sure she's your wife? She resembles a goddess."

Abigail stared up at the centurion, a full head taller than she. "My husband, General Julianus, would usually be insulted that you compare me to something as ordinary as a goddess," she said in perfect Latin. She brushed her delicate fingers above her ear. "This trouble with Lord Cretius has distracted him. Please enjoy this poor fare." She pointed to the table. "It seems this city is farther away from Roman delicacies than we realized."

Segundus took off his helmet and tucked it under his arm. "You honor us with your hospitality," he said, smiling at Abigail and nodding to Titius. "But then we must continue with our business."

"The emperor's business must not be delayed," Titius agreed. "Please welcome your men."

When Abigail excused herself to freshen up, the centurions signaled the thirty legionnaires to come in. The men were soon cramming food into their mouths while nodding politely and sharing appreciative grunts.

Within minutes, the platters were cleared and the flasks emptied.

Segundus ordered the men back into formation on the road and returned to Titius. "General Julianus, my men appreciate the feast. We're happy to serve Rome any way we can. But we must obey our orders."

Titius unsheathed his gladius. "For the glory of the Empire and the true emperor!" he shouted.

"For Rome! For Caesar!" the troops thundered.

They marched away, the thunder of their sandals echoing off house and forest alike.

Abigail emerged from the kitchen once the soldiers were gone. "Who is this man I married who's so respected by the oppressors?"

Titius allowed a smirk to cross his firm jaw. "I'm only who I am."

Abigail beheld the table and floor littered with chicken bones, lamb shanks, pits, and peelings. "I wonder what our dinner was like…"

Titius rested his hand low on Abigail's back. "I'm wondering more about what *after* dinner is going to be like."

The bride pulled out her sapphire combs and shook out her hair. She put her arms around Titius and looked longingly into his eyes. "The marriage bed awaits us. We've waited long enough."

Chapter Twenty-Nine

Soon after dawn, Abigail slipped out of the house onto the cobblestone patio. The two turtledoves from the previous evening were still pecking at crumbs scattered on the lawn. Otherwise there were no dirty dishes, no leftover food, and no unfinished wine.

Smiling, she turned back into the house and found that the floors and counters were also clean. Her cheeks warmed in appreciation for their hosts cleaning up the remains of the feast as she and Titius had enjoyed the pleasures of the night.

She unwrapped a neat tray of dates, figs, and cheese that remained on a counter.

"Trust Martha not to be able to leave a mess behind," she said to herself. "It's almost as if she can't help making sure everything is in perfect order."

From the bedroom, Titius called out to her: "Is someone there?"

"No, my love. Only me."

Titius came into the kitchen, belting his tunic. "Who were you talking to?"

Abigail turned. "To myself, to God, to the turtledoves…"

"So where will we go? Will it be Rome or Galilee?"

Abigail snuggled into his chest. "No matter how well I play the part, I'm no Roman wife. And you're no common Galilean, regardless of how well you can pretend. Perhaps God is calling us to a place where we can combine our two worlds."

"Where might that be?" Titius's brushed a tendril of hair from her eyes and cupped her face. "The world is yours and you're my master."

Abigail looked into his eyes. "Why don't we board the first ship from Caesarea and go where it takes us? As long as we're together, we'll learn to be who we're meant to be. The Almighty will always be with us."

Titius rested his forehead against hers. "But what about following the Messiah and sharing his message?"

Abigail hugged him. "The whole world needs to hear about the Messiah. Why can't we be the ones to tell them?"

Other Books In This Series

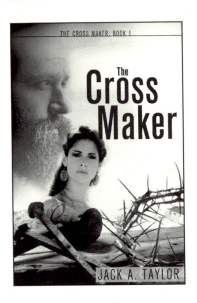

The Cross Maker
ISBN: 978-1-4866-1856-9

First-century Palestine is a hotbed of political, cultural, and religious intrigue. Caleb ben Samson, a carpenter from Nazareth, and Sestus Aurelius, a Roman centurion, both want peace. Can this unlikely partnership accomplish what nothing else has accomplished before? Can they bring about peace through the power of the cross? And what role will Caleb's childhood friend Yeshi play in a land that longs for hope?

In *The Cross Maker*, Jack Taylor weaves a tapestry of creative history, powerful characters, and dynamic dialogue to bring to life a shadowy world. In a land where tragedy is as common as dust, triumph is about to make itself known.

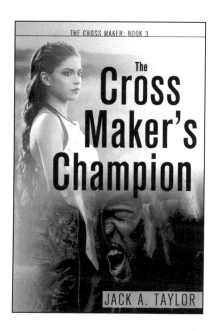

The Cross Maker's Champion
ISBN: 978-1-4866-1860-6

Persian slaves who fight for their lives in gladiator arenas rarely rise to be anyone's champion. But the wounded Nabonidus is soon wooed by two women—a priestess at the Temple of Diana and a humble follower of Yeshua, Daphne. Soon he must learn the truth about himself—is he a missing Persian prince or simply an unwanted orphan?

The arena claims whatever soul may venture there, and Alexander, a silversmith, joins forces with a giant German gladiator, Selsus, to confront the followers of The Way.

Meanwhile, Caleb, Suzanna, Titius, and Abigail fight through their own life-threatening challenges to join the Apostle John and Nabonidus in time. Soon the arena will be packed with chanting patrons. Who will still remain standing when the final blood is spilt?

Jack Taylor weaves his readers through a maze of Ephesian mysticism and terror as Roman and pagan powers combine to destroy the infant movement of The Way before it takes its first steps out of its birthplace.

Other Books by Jack A. Taylor

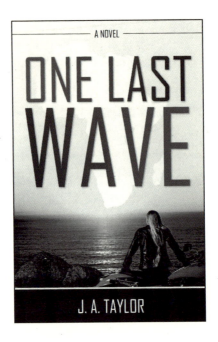

One Last Wave
ISBN: 978-1-7706-9261-9

Katrina [Katie] Joy Delancey has staked her life on keeping the past and future away from her heart. But she is no master of fate or captain of her own journey. *One Last Wave* is a story about being discovered by faith and love no matter where you are, no matter where you've been, and no matter what you think may lie ahead.

No Place to Run
ISBN: 978-1-7706-9786-7

No Place to Run continues the adventures of Katie Delancey, begun in *One Last Wave*. It's a story of rediscovering faith, hope, and love when the maze of life seems to close in around you… about realizing that the whispers of the past can be keys to your future.

Stretching for Home
ISBN: 978-1-4866-0996-3

A blissful love nest amidst a brutal Minnesota winter turns into a fiery ordeal of grief and terror as Katie is caught up in the never-ending pursuit of human traffickers who want to eliminate her from their deadly game. *Stretching for Home* is an education into the heart of missionary kids searching for healing as life tumbles in around them. Their quest for home can be as elusive as a rainbow's pot of gold. Finding old roots and spreading new wings can be a challenge.